Suddenly, lightning bolts began to rain down on the Artifact, from the clear blue sky above. Dozens, hundreds, thousands of bolts of sheer energy smashing into the Artifact and the ground around it.

The plane bucked, twisted, and went dead.

A huge explosion from the Artifact rent the air and—

Reality flickered.

It was as if a veil had been whipped by wind and then split in half. Miller was staring down at the airport—but it was deserted. Weeds grew up through the tarmac and—

Flicker.

Miller was flying over a swamp. Something large lifted its head up to look at him, and then returned to feeding with no interest. With shock, Miller recognized it. It was a brontosaurus. *But that's not—*

Flicker.

A crowd of naked people with bluish skin and feathered crests shaped like Mohawks stared up at him. He stared back, losing altitude now, and—

Flicker.

Lightning smashed at the Artifact.

Another of the huge explosions and Miller was flicked through two dozen realities so rapidly he couldn't even see what they were. For a heartbeat each, he raced through bright light, darkness, tremendous weight, a numbing vacuum where he fought the panic of being unable to breathe; then bright colors, loud noises as if someone were spinning a radio dial through dozens of channels without pausing—

FLICKER!

TIME
BLENDER

MICHAEL DORN

HILARY HEMINGWAY

JEFFRY P. LINDSAY

HarperPrism
A Division of HarperCollinsPublishers

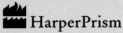 **HarperPrism**

A Division of HarperCollins*Publishers*
10 East 53rd Street, New York, N.Y. 10022-5299

This is a work of fiction. The characters, incidents, and dialogues are products of the author's imagination and are not to be construed as real. Any resemblance to actual events or persons, living or dead, is entirely coincidental.

ISBN: 0-06-105682-0

HarperCollins®, ®, and HarperPrism® are trademarks of HarperCollins*Publishers* Inc.

Cover illustration by Kevin Murphy

First printing: September 1997

Printed in the United States of America

Visit HarperPrism on the World Wide Web at
http://www.harpercollins.com

❖ 10 9 8 7 6 5 4 3 2 1

1

CHAPTER

In the faint predawn light a figure moved on the cliff top. Outlined against the dim glow of the ocean, a man stood, strong but surprisingly graceful. His movements were slow, precise, and smooth.

Breathe in . . . Let the breath find the center . . . Let the movement flow from the breath . . .

Dr. Tony Miller paused in the middle of his morning tai chi. Tall, hard-looking for an academic, black, and handsome, he wore his hair cropped short in the military style he found most convenient.

He stood for a moment in a half-crouch, his arms pushed out to the right, holding the breath and waiting for his mind to clear again.

The images had come back for a moment, but he was ready. He battled them calmly, clearing them with a breath. He was a tenured professor, some might say an unexciting man, but he was not a man who gave up, and never had been. He took another centering breath, pushed the pictures forcefully out of his head, and resumed.

Let the breath fill the chi . . . There is no thought, only the breath, the chi, the movement . . .

Miller had been doing tai chi every morning for three and half years now. He had tried yoga but found it too passive. With work and concentration, the tai chi worked. He could clear his mind, refocus his energy, force the painful images out. He'd had a few bad months without sleep and had tried sleeping pills, herbal therapies, acupuncture, a little of everything. He'd even considered a therapist—but the thought of it made him so uncomfortable he couldn't go through with it.

So he'd hit on this: and the tai chi worked. Every time the images came to him. *The faces . . . The children's faces . . .* A deep, centering breath, a moment of concentration, and the faces were gone. He was sleeping normally again—had been for two and a half years now. He liked to keep his life calm, waking and sleeping. Surprises were not for people with research grants.

And he very definitely had a research grant. His career was on a rising track, and the research he was doing here might at last provide him with academic security beyond tenure. Maybe even a family. Life was good.

Miller slid into a difficult series of movements. Sweat popped out on his forehead.

There is no thought, only the breath . . .

For the next five minutes Miller moved through the exercise, and memory left him alone. The movements flowed perfectly now; his breathing was easy, controlled. He felt the energy flow through him, and for a good five minutes he thought of nothing; nothing at all.

Finally, as he stood in the crane position looking over the ocean, the sun rose out of the water. Miller held his stance for a full minute, just watching the sun, happily aware of its warmth on his face, enjoying the feeling of being ready for work and free from the bad memories for another day.

Miller let out a long breath, slowly straightened—

"It's about time," said a voice behind him.

Miller whirled, dropping by reflex to a combat-ready crouch, hands coming up to fighting position.

Dr. Jay Cook chuckled. "Gotcha," he said. Cook, a short, wiry, and caustic paleobotanist, was Miller's partner on this scholarly expedition. He stood holding two cups of coffee, extending one for Miller to take.

Miller straightened. "I didn't hear you," he said.

Cook snorted. "You're not the only one who's delved into the mysteries of the Far East, Tony," he said. "I can move quietly when I want to, you know. I had a year of *nin-jitsu* training—"

Miller took the coffee cup. "And a year of kung fu, and a year of tai chi. And before that a year of Wado karate, three months of yoga—hell, Jay, you've tried everything. And you've never stuck to any of it long enough to get anything from it."

"Except my marriage," Cook said, making a bitter face. "Just long enough to get a kid. And to get broke." He spit and sat on a rock. "Community property," he said with real bitterness. "I live in a section of town I tell my students to avoid. She lives in Marin. And I still have to pay *her*. Where's the logic of that, Miller? Where's the justice?"

"It's your kid, too," Miller said, sipping his coffee. He liked Cook, appreciated the sharpness of his mind, the man's restless energy. But outside of academia these qualities had not served him well, and Cook's personal life was a disaster. Although Miller hid it well, he had a bit of contempt for Cook's inability to make a marriage work, and his helplessness with, and seeming apathy toward, his son Jerry, who seemed like a pretty good kid.

Part of the contempt, Miller knew, was jealousy. He had put off marriage and kids deliberately, first for military service, then for the tenure track, and now— It was another thought to push away, just for now, but he badly wanted kids someday. And that someday would be soon.

Miller smiled. It *would* be soon. There was no more doubt. This research would put him far enough ahead of the game that he could relax for a while, look around, find somebody truly solid, and make a go of it.

But could he change enough to make it work? Or would he end up like Cook, a poor excuse for an ex-husband and an absentee father? Because so far his work had always come first. And it took him far away for long stretches of time.

They had been here on Runa Puake Island for three and half months. Could he make a marriage work and still make these vital field expeditions? How many ball games or ballet recitals would he have to miss? Kids were damned important, yes—but his work was important, too. Would he be able to find the balance?

Cook never let those doubts into his mind. His passion was all for the work. Everything else was a pointless distraction, something that would interfere with the work if you let it. So he didn't. It was one reason they had been so successful, in their separate careers and together, here on the island. They both drove themselves harder and further than their colleagues.

Miller sipped his coffee. A small, slow smile

worked onto his face. Hell, he was beating himself up for neglecting an imaginary marriage, a child he didn't yet have.

"What's so funny?" Cook demanded.

"Nothing."

"Don't tell me nothing, Tony. We've been nose-to-nose on this goddamned island for thirteen weeks and I've seen you smile exactly *twice*."

"Your jokes are no good," Miller said.

"I don't *tell* jokes. I don't know any, and you wouldn't like them. So what the hell are you smiling at?"

"Berkeley," Miller said. "What would happen to Dean Nagel if the ratio of population to resource reached critical, like it did here?"

"They'd eat him," Cook replied. "And I'd want to watch. Hell, I'd *pay* to watch. You surprise me, Tony. That's actually worth a smile."

"And they'd put up a huge monument to small-minded paper-shufflers on top of his bones," Miller said.

"A giant paper head," Cook said. "Stamped, sealed, and signed in triplicate, stapled to a purchase order. And future generations will wonder why the Berkeleyans worked so hard to bring that precious paper all the way from the library."

"Future generations will wonder what's for lunch," Miller snorted. "And they'll write their names on the paper head."

"Probably so," Cook said, and they sipped quietly for a minute.

Thinking of these things happening on campus was amusing, but here on this island it hadn't been funny at all. There was no real satisfaction in imagining some aboriginal Dean Nagel eaten by his minions.

Because exactly that had happened here, on this once-beautiful island some twelve hundred miles west of Tahiti. The mystery of the wonderful stone heads and the disappearance of the islanders was solved, and it wasn't pretty. Looked at from Miller's distance in time and perspective, it had all been horrifyingly slow and inevitable.

But after three months of careful digging, study, and generating computer models, there was no room for doubt. Miller and Cook now knew where the original inhabitants of the island had gone.

They'd been eaten.

By their neighbors, their friends, their families.

A complex and beautiful paleocivilization had evolved to the point where its enemies were eliminated. Population had grown—and then kept growing, expanding out of control, multiplying out of all reasonable bounds, until the island could no longer support even half as many. And as the population grew, it destroyed more and more of the ecosystem, annihilating all the fish and other food animals, destroying plant life, razing the forests. Until there was nothing left to eat.

Except each other.

A complex clan system had at first controlled and ritualized the cannibalism. But at some point even that control had broken down and it had become eat-your-buddy-before-he-eats-you. End of civilization. End of Runa Puake Island. And soon, end of eat-your-buddy; no more buddies left. A few islanders had probably survived somehow—possibly by taking to their boats and heading blindly out to sea—but that was speculation, perhaps the subject of some future research. There was no life left on Runa Puake, beyond a few straggly strands of grass and a few insects.

And for right now, they had the answers they'd come for. Miller felt a strange mix of triumph at the result of their work, and horror for what they had found. The gnawed skeletons buried under the great stone heads, human teeth marks clearly visible, were deeply disturbing. But Miller had no illusions. He knew what humans were capable of, what he himself had done—

"Back to the salt mines," Cook said, standing and interrupting Miller's unwanted train of thought. "I think I'm on to a pretty good resin residue."

"My God, that's exciting," Miller deadpanned.

"And it is, too," Cook said, ignoring the sarcasm. "My preliminary analysis indicates some highly unusual trace minerals."

"Well, have a nice residue," Miller said, toasting Cook with his coffee mug. "I'll be down in a few minutes."

"See that you are," Cook said. "I'll want another echo scan before too long." He turned and headed off down the hill to their work site.

Miller turned back out to sea, watching the slow roll of the waves and the early morning sun reflecting off the water. He sipped slowly, quietly amused that he had actually come to like the nasty freeze-dried stuff. Four thousand miles from the nearest Starbucks, he didn't have much choice anyway.

He was relaxing. It amazed him, but he could actually feel his shoulder muscles unknot, the perpetual stress draining out of him. After three months here, alone on an uninhabited and nearly uninhabitable island, away from the madness at Berkeley, he felt himself slowly coming back to the controls, in charge of his life again in a way he hadn't felt for years.

No PC-mad pencil-pushers yanking his strings. No undereducated, unmotivated, whining, self-centered, I-deserve-it students pushing at his carefully controlled temper. Whether it lasted, or faded as soon as they got back, it was worth the whole trip just to be himself again for a little while. A man finally back in control.

But of course, just the thought, just thinking he had it beat, was enough to trigger the images. Miller stared out at the ocean, willing his mind to be blank. But the rolling sea changed. The waves became sand dunes. The dark of the water became the night sky—

—and he's racing above the desert under a moonless sky, leading his attack group at low altitude, under the Iraqi radar ceiling. He's once again at the controls of his B–2.

Even at this tremendous speed he can see the damage the war has brought to this precious region, the Cradle of Civilization. The loss of irreplaceable antiquities, sites still unknown, treasures unguessed at, sickens him. But as a soldier he also knows that the only way he can hope to protect any of it is by hitting the enemy, hitting him hard and fast and repeatedly, and ending the war as quickly as possible.

And that's what this night sortie is all about. The plan is to simultaneously hit all the Iraqi control centers, hit with such devastating power and precision that Saddam will have no choice but to surrender.

Miller does not like the choice. But he is a good soldier, and he knows it is the only choice.

"Target coming up. Sixty clicks," he hears the navigator's voice in his ear. The sky around him lights up like the Fourth of July. It seems hard to believe that his

plane has been spotted. But there is a great deal of anti-aircraft activity around them.

And now he is very busy, making all the last minute preparations for dropping his two-thousand-pound laser-guided missile. This is the most sophisticated member of its ancient family. It does not simply fall and blow up. No; it has an in-board computer that will guide it to its target, and a video camera in the nose to relay pictures back to his plane, to confirm that it strikes its target.

And then they are over the target. He releases the missile; the video screen shows it speed true to its mark, Saddam's communications center. And at the last second he sees people in the windows, staring up in horror at the missiles homing in on them, staring and screaming.

Ten years later he can still see those faces.

Children's faces.

Saddam had packed the building with children, whether to protect the building or to sacrifice the children on the altar of world opinion, it was impossible to say.

But Miller could still see the faces. Still feel the horror, still hear the clicking sound as his hand reflexively pulled at the firing switch, trying uselessly to call the missile back.

What kind of man could do that? Sacrifice children like that? Rage blew through him and his hands shook so badly he almost lost control of the aircraft. Had Saddam truly kept this a secret in order to spring it on world press that the U.S. murdered innocent children?

And then the worst questions of all had come.

Had U.S. Intelligence known?

How could they know so much, give him such precise technical data for this raid, and not know about this?

How could they know, or even suspect, and fail to scrub the mission?

How could they not know?

Combat flying was over for Miller that night. It had been his great love, the ultimate adrenaline high. After that night mission over Baghdad, he felt nothing but nausea every time he sat at the controls.

The Air Force could no longer hold him. Instead, he found himself powerfully drawn to history, to protecting the knowledge and relics of history. He became fascinated with the cultures of the past, working quickly and brilliantly through grad school and a doctorate, searching out the answers for how those cultures had survived—and how they died.

And somehow, here he was, ten years later, a tenured professor at a major university, sitting on top of a cliff and trying not to see the faces anymore.

The wounds had scabbed over. They were still there, under the surface, but they were slowly beginning to heal. He buried himself in his work, driving himself relentlessly. If he was tired enough, he wouldn't dream. And the tai chi helped, too. The faces were still there, but not as often, and not as bad. And pretty soon, perhaps they would stop coming.

Shaking the mood off, Miller took a deep breath and raised the coffee cup to his lips.

And paused halfway.

Far out over the ocean, in the shimmer of the early morning sun, something moved. What it was, he couldn't say, but there was something out of place about it, something *wrong*.

Miller stood, shading his eyes and looking hard, trying to make out some detail that would tell him what it was. It appeared to be moving closer. Soon, rising from the bright glare of the water, he could just barely make out a shape.

Miller blinked, rubbed his eyes, looked again. It *was* moving closer. And this time there was no doubt. The shape took on form, and he began to see the terrible expanse of it, and the conviction grew into certainty that he knew what it must be.

Tsunami.

Tidal wave.

Miller turned and raced down the hill.

2

CHAPTER

The path back down to the dig was rough and rocky. But if he was right about what he'd seen moving toward the island, there was no time to take it slowly. Miller sprinted, stumbling several times but catching his balance and running on.

Halfway down he risked a shout. "Cook!" he called. "Cook!" But there was no answer. Miller cursed and kept running. Every second might make all the difference.

"Cook!" he called again as he finally came in sight of the spot they had excavated.

Still no answer; Cook was nowhere in sight.

Miller ran to the pit they'd scratched out in the shadow of one of the great stone heads. He was about to call out again but froze as he stood on the edge of the pit.

Cook lay curled in the bottom of the hole, some eight feet down. Around him lay piles of carefully tagged bones, the skeletal remains of some hundreds of islanders. The spots where they had been discovered were carefully marked in the grid Cook and Miller laid out in the bottom of the excavation.

Cook was lying across the grid, from H–17 to L–29. His coffee cup was beside him, smashed to shards. Several hand tools were scattered around him and the seismograph was tipped over a few feet from his head.

His face, half turned to the side, looked completely lifeless, and Miller was sure he was dead. He had stumbled, fallen into the pit and hit his head, it was obvious.

But even as Miller stared, stunned, Cook twitched. His face muscles jerked violently, his left leg kicked, and his hands opened and closed.

Cook was alive. And they were six hard hours by air from the hospital in Tahiti. In a way, Miller thought, death would have been easier to handle. Since Cook was alive, the choices confronting him were worse. If Cook had a head or neck injury, moving him should be a slow, delicate operation. Any sudden movement could cause permanent damage to brain, nerves, or spinal cord. But Miller knew he had no time for delicacy. And if he didn't move fast, they were both dead.

Miller jumped down into the pit and knelt beside Cook. He picked up his partner's wrist; the pulse was fast, but steady and strong.

Miller swore. He was wasting time. It didn't matter what Cook's pulse was doing. It could be keeping tango time for all the difference it made. If Cook was alive, there was still only one course of action, and it had to be done fast.

Miller bent to pick up his partner—and paused.

He heard a small chittering noise, just barely audible.

At first he thought it must be Cook's teeth, and the

thought of a seizure scared him. He had no time to deal with it, and no real idea of what to do.

He turned Cook's chin with his fingertips. No movement; Cook's jaw was locked tight, his teeth clamped. Miller could even see the jaw muscles, standing out rigidly.

But the chittering continued.

Half turning, Miller looked around him in the dimness of the pit. Spotting the seismograph a few feet away, tipped onto its side, he reached over and set it upright.

The needle was scrabbling across the page. And the chittering sound came each time the tip hit the edge of the chart—which it did with nearly every stroke.

Normally, the needle stayed right in the middle, scratching its small peaks and valleys onto the paper in a steady rhythm. It would take a geologic event of the first magnitude to make the needle hit the edge. An event so cataclysmic, only a few such had ever been recorded.

Something like what was racing toward them right now.

"Oh, shit," Miller breathed.

He quickly turned back to Cook's still body, grabbed it and lifted, throwing the unconscious man over one shoulder. The time for worrying and pondering choices was long past. Now he had to sprint for the plane and hope he made it.

Stumbling up to his feet, Miller adjusted the load. Thank God Cook was a small man. But this was still not going to be easy.

He hurried up the narrow ramp and out of the pit, hitting a running stride with his first few steps. As fast as he could go under the weight of his partner's twitching body, he ran down the path that led to the beach.

It was less than half a mile, a distance Miller could normally make in under three minutes. But with the added weight of Cook, and with the pressure of knowing that every second counted, it seemed to take forever.

Miller stagger-sprinted past the camp where he and Cook had lived for nearly three months. The breakfast coffeepot still sat on the flat rock beside the fire. And Miller's laundry hung from the makeshift clothesline behind the tent.

But there was no time to stop—not even for passports, money—Christ! The research! The hundreds of pages of notes, observations, charts—the dozens of computer disks: It would all be lost, all the thousands of hours of back-breaking, mind-numbing, skinned-knuckle labor that had gone into this project. All gone . . .

In his mind, Miller was howling at the agony of his work's coming destruction. But he didn't slow down, didn't break his stride even for a second. He didn't dare to.

The beach was in sight now. Miller kicked in the afterburner, sprinting now with everything he had. His rented seaplane was pulled up on the beach, and, gasping and panting for air, he got the door opened and flung Cook into the passenger's seat. Then he jumped into the pilot's seat and started the engine. As it warmed up, he belted Cook in, then ran back to unmoor the plane.

As he jumped back in and belted himself in with one hand, he checked the instruments. The engine was still cold, but it would do. It would have to do.

Miller moved the throttle forward. The engine hesitated, then roared. The plane shook, more so than usual. The engine was running very rough. It needed more warm-up time, time he did not have. At least the fuel tanks were topped off, and he had kept up on the routine maintenance.

The little plane lurched down the beach and into the water. A takeoff from the lagoon would be tricky, not that he had any choice. It would be difficult to judge the wind; the waves and the tide would be moving in opposite directions. Add to that a cold engine and full fuel tanks and he knew he'd need more than a little luck.

Miller pushed the engine up to its top speed and headed out.

The sea was an unnatural green, glassy calm as he came out around the headland. The surface of the water seemed slick and greasy, and he could not remember ever seeing anything like it before.

Still, this was no time to question the small breaks. Takeoff would be considerably easier on a calm sea.

Miller throttled back and drifted for a moment, just long enough to gauge the wind. The plane's nose swung slightly. He turned to compensate, heading directly into the stiff breeze and swearing under his breath when he saw where he was headed.

Great, he thought, *directly toward the wave.*

And as he looked down the nose of the plane to the horizon, Miller saw it.

The Great Wave.

Tsunami.

It stretched from horizon to horizon, and it was taller than the spire of the Berkeley Chapel, taller than the U.C. stadium, taller than a fifteen-story building— and it was close. Noticeably closer all the time. It moved with the speed of a Japanese bullet train, and it was headed right at him.

This was going to be a very near thing.

The wind was at least twenty knots, which would help if he could get up to speed before the wave swept him under. And if not—well, at least it would be all over very quickly.

Miller pulled the throttle all the way back. It revved into the red, but that didn't matter. If he didn't make it over the wave, engine wear wasn't going to count for too much.

The engine coughed once, and Miller's heart lurched up into his throat. Then the engine steadied, smoothed out, and roared with all the power it had. The whole plane shook, Miller's hands were vibrating like mad as he pushed the plane to its limit—and beyond.

The wave was bearing down on him now, close enough to hit with a well-thrown baseball. His speed, he knew, was not quite enough, not yet.

"Come on, you bastard," he snarled at the little plane, subconsciously pulling the throttle back still farther, even though it was already hard against its extreme limit.

The wave was close enough to hit with a basketball now. Miller hauled back on the stick; no lift yet, but the plane trembled slightly, wig-wagging from side to side.

And now the wave was so close that he could have hit it with a bowling ball, and still the little plane picked up speed without showing any further sign of lifting off.

Miller leveled the stick, then once more pulled it back with all his concentration and will power. Slowly—too slowly?—the plane twitched, skipped, and the nose began to lift.

And as the enormous, all-powerful tsunami crashed through the space where he'd been just seconds ago, Miller lifted the nose, banked back toward the island,

and grabbed for altitude. It seemed that the wave would snatch at one of the pontoons, dragging them down into that tumbling hell of unimaginable power, but somehow Miller rose above it.

Then, above the wave, he was rising to a comfortable five hundred feet and flying over the island.

As Miller watched, the wave crashed into the stone heads, and they disappeared. They did not teeter, or topple, or crash over. They were simply gone. Swept away by the unbelievable power and fury of the tsunami. So was the camp, the excavation, literally everything on the island. And the island itself, Runa Puake. All gone.

Miller took a ragged breath and blew it out again. That had almost been him down there, a small chip of flotsam smashed under by a wall of water the size of Manhattan.

If he had not seen the wave coming, had not had time—just barely—to get away . . . He shuddered. It didn't do to think about it. After all, he *had* gotten away. But what a remarkable string of coincidences it was that had allowed him to escape. The scientist in him usually reacted suspiciously to such lucky chance, but this time he'd take it. Whether it had been the Hand of God, the Hammer of Thor, or just a lucky roll of the dice, he'd take it.

Miller turned the plane again, and checked his instruments. After some quick figuring, he set his course. He could make Tahiti. It was the closest spot with a major hospital, which he would need if Cook was to have a chance.

He gave a last check to the controls and glanced at Cook. To his astonishment, Cook's eyes were open. He was staring straight ahead, focusing on nothing.

"Jesus," Miller said. "I thought you were dead. How do you feel?"

Cook coughed twice, as if trying to clear his throat, and did not respond. In fact, he didn't even blink.

Miller looked back at the controls. *He's still unconscious*, he thought. But then Cook coughed again, three times, and Miller glanced back at him.

"Cook—" he started, but could think of nothing more to say. Because what was happening to his partner was totally beyond anything he had ever seen or heard of before.

Cook had begun to twitch. His face muscles were jumping, as if each muscle was independent of all the others; almost as if some crazy machine was testing them one at a time.

And then Cook's face began to *flow*.

There was no other way to describe it. Cook's face went through a bewildering range of expressions at a speed that seemed impossible, leaving the impression of a face made of Silly Putty, melting rapidly through a series of mutations. It was like watching somebody channel-surf through dozens of TV stations.

Miller felt his jaw hang open as he watched his partner's face rocket through its changes. The sight was so astonishing, so unnerving, that for a moment Miller forgot where he was. He was brought back to the present when the little plane went into a shallow dive. He quickly put his attention back on the controls and leveled off again.

He glanced back at Cook. The twitching had stopped. The face was Cook now, no question. Miller let out his breath to ask Cook how he felt.

Then Cook screamed.

"Tony! Oh, Jesus God, Tony!" he said, then made a choking sound, and his face flickered once, twice, three times.

A new expression settled into place, an expression of cheerful craftiness. It was Cook, yes—but it was also, ever so subtly, *not* Cook. Not at all.

"Ah," said the voice. "You are—Toe-nee. Yes." The voice, too, was Cook-but-not-Cook. Subtly changed, the sound of it made gooseflesh rise on Miller's back.

Miller could only gape at him for a long moment.

"Toe-*nee*," Cook repeated, as if prompting him to speak.

"What the—Cook, what the hell hap—Are you all right?"

"A-okay," Cook said. "All systems functioning within normal parameters."

"Just stay calm, keep that belt fastened," Miller told him. "You hit your head, Jay. But we'll be at a hospital in a few hours, so just relax. Nothing to worry about."

"No, no," Cook replied with a ghastly smile. "Null set worries, *Toe-nee*."

"Jesus fuck," Miller muttered. "Please, Cook, try to rest, huh?"

Cook frowned. "Reading," he said, and again he stared straight ahead without focus. "Access. Stand by." His mouth opened—and then his face shifted again and he screamed.

"*Ahhhhg*—shit! Oh, God Almighty, they'll kill us all!" he shrieked. "Sweet suffering Jesus—Tony, my God, they won't stop until we're all dead, you have to—" Cook's body lurched against the seat belt as if zapped by an electrical current. He twitched, his face flickered again, and settled back into the screaming Cook.

"Ah!"

"Cook! Take it easy! You hit your head—"

"No, no, goddamn it, Tony, please listen, I can't—"
Cook's body bucked again and he gasped hoarsely with
pain. "War," he panted. "It's war . . . and you're a part of
it now."

"Cook," Miller began, "what the fuck are you—"

But once again the violent spasms shook him, and
this time his face settled into the calm, patient mask of
the Crafty Cook.

"Perhaps I overstate," Cook said. "Real-time hunger.
Food is where?"

And Miller could only stare.

3
CHAPTER

Miller looked at the plane's controls automatically. He was stunned almost into incoherence by Cook's behavior and he needed time to think. But he could not allow the plane to slip out of control again. All his pilot's instincts took over, even as he tried to grasp the implications of the way Cook was acting.

What did it mean? Was Cook totally demented, as a result of a bump on the head when he fell into the excavation pit?

Or was there something else going on inside Cook's head, Miller wondered, something that he could not even guess at?

Like what?

No, it had to be a bump on the head. He didn't know a thing about what head injuries could do to the human brain. He had a working knowledge of first aid, but it didn't include psychology. Cook's bizarre behavior *had* to have been caused by some kind of trauma to the brain.

But how did that explain the face-shifting, the multiple personalities, the strange things he was saying? What the hell was going on in Cook's mind? And would he turn dangerous?

As hard as Miller searched for answers, he could find no explanation. He had never before heard of anyone acting like this. And Cook did not *act* like he was insane—but as if he were taking turns being different people.

Still, he was Cook. He had to be. Who else *could* he be?

It's the head injury, Miller told himself. *There's just no other explanation at all.* And he glanced at Cook to confirm it.

To his relief, Cook was entirely calm, glancing around the interior of the plane with deliberate interest.

Miller sighed, trying to let go of his tension. *At least he's okay now,* he thought. *If he'll just stay okay for a few more hours, I'll have some medical help.*

Cook met his eye, smiled, and nodded at the plane's controls. "Machine speed increase feasible?" he said politely.

Miller blinked. "What do you mean?"

"Ah, ah . . . Velocity of machine in the air relative to a hypothetical calibrating point on the ground below us," Cook said. "Possibility of increase in ratio."

Miller shook his head. Too much was happening, much too fast. He felt as though reality had been yanked out from under him like a cheap, rotting carpet. He decided to pretend Cook's question made sense.

"The airplane will travel slightly faster than this," he said. "But this is the most fuel-efficient speed. It's also a little healthier for the engine not to rev it much higher for a prolonged period of time."

"Yes, I see," Cook said. "Very good, internal combustion, certainly."

"Cook, just relax, okay? We'll be in Tahiti in a few hours."

Nearby—*very* nearby—an enormous crackling bolt of lightning shattered the sky. The plane lurched into the sudden downdraft in its wake.

"Too late," Cook said. "Real-time locus discovered."

Miller struggled with the controls, leveled off. He was distracted by the storm; it had come up out of nowhere. Moments ago he'd had clear skies and unlimited visibility. Now an enormous thunderhead roiled ahead of him, spreading its thick black clouds directly across his path. "What the— What did you say?" he asked Cook.

"Time-space coordinates discovered," Cook said slowly and deliberately, like he was teasing someone stupid.

As if to underline his words, another bolt of lightning crackled close by, and another even closer. The plane lurched and Miller fought to regain level flight.

"Example," Cook said with an uncharacteristic chuckle. "High percentage mission failure. Early return likely."

Miller shook his head; enough was enough. "If you don't shut up and let me get us through this storm, neither one of us will return anywhere, except underwater."

Cook giggled, and Miller almost snapped his own neck as he swiveled to look at his partner. He'd known Cook for three years, and in the last few months on the island had gotten almost as close to him as two heterosexual men could get. And in all that time, he had never heard Cook giggle. The sound was so alien to the man's personality that it made no sense—like hearing the church choir sing "The Beer Barrel Polka" at High Mass.

"I will," Cook said with his bizarre giggle. "I'll be back."

And then, before Miller could do anything but stare, the storm was on them.

Within seconds the small plane was completely absorbed by dark, swirling clouds and they were tossed madly between updrafts and stomach-wrenching drops.

Miller fought for control. But in this case, "control" was an extremely relative idea. He could no more control the plane in this monster storm than Dorothy had controlled her house in the twister that took her to Oz.

The clouds were so dark and thick now that Miller could barely see his hands on the controls. He toggled on the interior lights and snapped his hands back to the stick as they were thrown through a series of moves so violent that Miller feared the plane would break up. Straight down for a thousand feet, then back up again, then from side to side, the storm threw them furiously across the sky. Miller fought to ride it out, but the storm had its way with them. The most he could manage was to minimize the effects, but in the sudden downdrafts, the propeller wouldn't bite and he simply had to hang on and hope they'd make it through.

For a while they did, but Miller knew it couldn't continue indefinitely. Somehow, he had to find a way out of this storm. But it took all his skill merely to keep them in the air, and that would not be enough for long.

Suddenly, they were thrown straight down on one wing. Miller fought the plane back to level just as the ocean came into view, and climbed again. "Shit," he said through tightly clenched teeth. "This is impossible."

"Only in unassisted nature," Cook said calmly.

Miller risked a quick glance at the other man. Cook appeared calm, totally unruffled by their impending death. Miller opened his mouth to speak and the plane was flung straight up. He fought back to level again and glanced back at Cook.

"What's that supposed to mean?" Miller asked him.

Cook regarded him blandly.

"What did you say?" Miller insisted.

"Which time?" Cook said.

"For Christ's sake, Cook," Miller snapped, "you're playing bullshit games with me—you may not have noticed, but we're in actual danger in this impossible storm—"

"Who says impossible?" Cook replied innocently.

"I do, goddamn it! It came out of nowhere, and storms can't do that. And it came up faster than storms can move. Totally impossible—"

He bit off his words as three blasts of very close lightning shook the plane, sending them into a sickening dive that Miller barely pulled out of.

"What if Nature is your friend?" Cook said, in a voice so sweet and reasonable that Miller would have slapped him had he been able to spare a hand long enough.

"Then tell your goddamned friend to calm down," Miller said instead through tightly clenched teeth.

"Not *my* friend," Cook said, with a bizarre giggle again. "Certainly not *mine*, oh no. *Theirs*."

"Glad that's settled," Miller said, guiding the plane's nose around a massive cloud column that shot up from nothing.

"Theirs," Cook repeated. "Entire universe an us and them proposition, Tony. In this case—"

"Them," Miller said. "Not us. I get it."

"Clearly," Cook said. "Superior mentation, Tony. Recognition achieved, yes? Tree-huggers, fertilizer freaks. Pure biotrash."

Miller had begun to feel he was going to lose it. He didn't need the headache Cook was giving him, and he didn't need the distraction right now. "Cook," he said, "could you just shut up for a few minutes? Please?"

"Oh, certainly," Cook replied in an agreeable tone of voice. "But *they* won't."

Three bolts of lightning, each closer than the one before, blistered the air nearby.

"See?" Cook said.

"How about if you ask them real nice?"

Cook giggled. "They won't listen to *me*."

The plane hit a sudden updraft, rocketing upward and trying to flip backward. Miller fought it back to level.

"Whee," Cook said.

Miller had had it. Demented or not, his friend had worn him out. He could not fight the storm and listen to Cook's babble at the same time. "Talk to your friends, not to me," Miller said. "Just leave me alone. Tell them whatever you want, whatever will make them stop."

"Okay," Cook said, and was mercifully quiet for a few moments.

Miller could at last concentrate on flying the plane. He kicked it left into a clear space between two gigantic thunderheads and saw a larger opening ahead. If he could just reach it before—

The engine stalled.

Miller's hands flew across the controls as he tried desperately to restart the motor. But there was nothing; the starter didn't even kick over. Nothing at all.

The plane began to dive.

For five hundred feet, as he watched the altimeter and struggled with the controls, the plane dropped like a rock. He gave up trying to restart the engine and, with both hands on the yoke, yanked it back, attempting to pull the plane out of the dive and into a controlled glide. They might land on the water and die of exposure or thirst instead of crashing and drowning, but there was no quit in Miller. He would keep fighting until he couldn't anymore.

He glanced at the altimeter. He was at six hundred feet and the plane's speed was increasing. He put everything he had into pulling back on the yoke; not just physical strength, but all his willpower, too.

Three hundred feet.

The plane began to respond—slowly at first, then with increasing success. The nose came up, the airspeed began to slow perceptibly . . .

One hundred fifty feet . . . one hundred . . .

With a last surge of power, Miller moved the yoke back, within just a few feet of skimming the waves. Using the speed he'd gained from the dive, he got the plane back up to two hundred feet and leveled off again. He didn't want to go too high, because the storm's thunderheads—

Miller felt his jaw drop. He twisted his head to look one way, then another, searching every corner of the sky.

The storm was gone.

Miller craned his neck, looking in all directions, but there was no mistake. He was gliding through a beautiful clear afternoon in the South Pacific, with no turbulence and no sign of bad weather anywhere.

The storm had vanished. Without a trace. As if it had never been.

"What the . . . ?" he started, and then gave that up, too.

Because the engine started back up.

4

CHAPTER

Miller felt an ache in the right side of his neck. He was sure it had come from whipping his head back and forth between Cook, the impossibly empty sky, and the equally impossible engine. He was not surprised that it had stopped—engines could be finicky, and a problem that might cause a stall was not always apparent—but airplane engines did not spontaneously restart.

Just like monster storms didn't appear and disappear, paleobotanists didn't switch personalities like baseball caps, and . . . ?

Miller shook it off. The storm was gone, and he suspected he would never know what had caused it to boil up, or to evaporate. The doctors in Tahiti would deal with Cook, and there was nothing he could do until they got to the hospital there. But at least he could deal with the engine.

He scanned the horizon. A few degrees to his left a smudge appeared. He banked toward it and in a few

minutes the first details of a South Pacific island began
to stand out.

The cone of a volcano rose from the center. No
smoke came from it; it could have been extinct, or
merely dormant. And soon Miller could see a faint white
line around the edges of the island—white sand beaches
between the blue of the water and green blur of a line of
vegetation. From this distance there was no indication
that the island was inhabited.

He brought the plane up to 2,500 feet, intending to
fly over the island and see if there was a place to land.
Then he could look at the engine. He glanced at the passenger seat. Cook, simply sitting with his hands folded,
looked back at Miller without expression.

"You're awfully quiet," Miller said.

"You requested non-verbal mode," Cook replied.

"Uh-huh. I just didn't expect you to listen to me.
How do you feel?"

"Small," Cook said. "Premiere experience this size."

Miller nodded. It was probably best not to say anything to a remark like that. "I'm going to look for a
place to land on that island," he said. "I want to look at
the engine."

"Primo, Tonee," said Cook. "On-line assistance
available."

"Great," Miller said. "That's a real relief."

The island was much closer now. Miller pushed the
little plane higher, high enough to clear the volcano with
plenty of room to spare.

There was a clearing toward the middle of the island
that might have been natural or man-made—it was
impossible to say from their altitude—but it was too
small for a landing. Fortunately, there was a small lagoon

on the windward side that looked like a good spot to put down, and Miller aimed for that.

They were almost directly over the volcano now. Curious about whether the volcano was really inactive, he flew directly over the cone. A sudden updraft from the cone might indicate heat, which could mean there was still a fire in its guts.

As he approached the opening, Miller leaned toward the window to look. But as the plane passed over the cone, he was jerked back to the controls by something more urgent.

The engine stalled.

"Aw, shit, not again," he said, banking into a steep glide. "Hold on," he said to Cook, "we're going down."

There was no response, and Miller glanced at Cook to make sure he understood.

Cook was scrabbling at the window, trying to see out in the direction of the volcano.

"Hey!" Miller said as Cook fumbled with the door handle. "Leave that alone or you're a pancake!" Cook ignored him. With one hand, Miller grabbed the front of Cook's shirt and yanked him back into place. "Damn it, kill yourself later. We're going down."

Cook stared at him, eyes wide-open and wild-looking. "It's here," he said with stunned excitement. "Real-time herenow, Artifact present!"

Miller returned his attention to the controls. "It's called a volcano, Cook," he said, not even sure whether he was being sarcastic. "It won't hurt you."

But Cook was frowning, ignoring him. "Inside," he said. "Satisfactory explanation. Artifact inside."

Miller shook his head. As long as Cook left the door handle alone, it didn't really matter what he babbled. "I should be able to make that lagoon with no problem," he said. "It's an easy glide. Just sit tight, okay?"

"Certainty required," Cook muttered. "Entirety focused here. *Everything*."

"He's off again," Miller said under his breath. For now, he just had to land the plane; Cook could recite the *Encyclopedia Britannica* for all it mattered.

The wind was with them, which was a piece of luck. Miller was able to glide out to sea and then point the nose at the lagoon. His glide path would take him straight into the wind, and if he handled it just right, they would coast up close to the beach before running out of momentum.

They passed over a coral reef at a height of about twenty-five feet. It lay across the mouth to the lagoon, providing calm water on the inside, another piece of luck. Even as he worked the flaps to bring them down just right, Miller marveled at the clarity of the water. He could see huge clouds of fish clustering across the reef and flowing into the pale blue waters of the lagoon. Trees lined the far edge of the beach; he recognized breadfruit among others.

Paradise, he thought. *At least I picked a great place to be marooned.*

The pontoons touched the calm waters of the lagoon. Twin plumes of spray shot back. Miller eased the yoke back, keeping the nose high, pointing the plane at a clear swath of beach and letting the drag of the water slow them.

They coasted to within fifty yards of the beach and then the plane slowed, stopped, and quietly started to turn with the tide and the current.

"We're here," Miller said.

Immediately Cook began to fumble with his seat belt. "Priority exit," he hissed. "Personal inspection required immediately."

Miller was already opening a locker behind his seat. "Go ahead," he said. "I'll meet you on the beach."

Miller reached into the locker and took out a long coil of nylon mooring line. He would tie one end to the struts and swim the other end in, most likely tying off to a tree. He threw the rope to the floor between the seats and turned, already taking off his shirt for the swim in.

Cook was sitting in the doorway, dangling his feet and looking dubiously at the water.

"I thought you were going to start in," Miller said, pulling his shirt over his head.

Cook looked up at him. "Ah—this, um . . . water . . . ?"

"What about it?"

Cook cocked his head, looked down again, then back at Miller. "It—It— What are protocols of negotiating medium?"

Miller snorted. "I don't know. How did you negotiate it on the varsity swimming team at Princeton?"

Cook just shook his head.

Miller turned away from Cook, folding his shirt and placing it in a plastic bag for the swim ashore. He decided to keep his shorts on. He'd felt a little silly spending so much money on "Expedition Shorts" at Banana Republic, but he depended on them now. He liked the big zippered pockets and the durable fabric. They would take another dunk in saltwater with no problem, and they dried quickly. He dropped a big folding knife into one pocket and some halizone tablets into the other.

He took off his shoes and shoved a pair of cheap

sandals into his back pockets. "Jay, you're a better swimmer than I am, as you like to remind me. So get going. I've got to get the line in before the tide changes." Miller turned away from Cook, pushed open the door on his own side and jumped in.

The water was just a few degrees cooler than body temperature. As it closed over Miller's head he could feel himself relaxing, almost hear the muscles in his neck and shoulders unknotting. He kicked his way to the surface.

"Ahh," he said as he broke the surface of the water. "Jay, you can do what you like, but this water feels great."

Cook eased out the door and onto the pontoon on the far side of the plane. The plane tipped slightly and began to rock. "Safety factor acceptable?" Cook asked. Miller couldn't see his face, but he heard the doubt in his partner's voice.

"It's safe," he said, fastening one end of the mooring line to the plane. "There are no sharks, no moray eels, no giant squids—get in, for God's sake."

But Cook still would not get into the water. Miller sighed and swam around the plane.

Cook stood on the pontoon, one hand riveted to the door frame. He stared down into the lagoon as if afraid that the water might jump up and bite him.

"What is it, Jay?" Miller asked gently, reminding himself that his partner had to be humored for now.

"How does this work?" Cook asked him. "No on-line access."

"How does *what* work, Jay?"

"The, ah, this 'swem' protocol."

Miller stared up at his partner. Cook was a serious

swimmer, had been since high school. Even on Runa Puake he swam every evening. And now for him to say he didn't know how . . .

"You jump in," Miller said. "Then you move your arms and legs. Like this," and he demonstrated a breaststroke.

"Thereby imparting motion," Cook said.

"That's right."

"Theory unconvincing herenow," Cook said.

"Just do it," Miller said wearily.

"Well—" Cook said.

Miller turned toward the beach. He was tired of disaster, tired of humoring Cook, tired of whatever game Cook might be playing. "I have to tie off the plane," he said. "Do whatever you like."

Miller began his slow, powerful stroke, the mooring line shoved through a belt loop on his pants. After a half-dozen strokes he heard a splash behind him. "About time," he muttered, turning to look at Cook.

Cook was gone.

He watched for a moment, treading water. But Cook's head did not break the surface. Miller swam quickly back to the plane and dove under.

The saltwater stung his eyes, but it was clean and clear. He could see Cook, about ten feet down, slowly waving his arms and kicking his legs with an expression of growing panic. As he watched, Cook opened his mouth as if to say something and took in a mouthful of water.

Miller kicked hard and reached Cook, grabbing him by the shirt and pulling upward. Cook's strange and feeble motions were already slowing as the water reached his lungs.

Miller towed his partner up to the surface. The other man sputtered weakly, water dribbling from his mouth.

With an effort, Miller draped Cook across the plane's pontoon. He climbed up, too, and began forcing the water out of Cook's lungs. In just a few moments Cook was kicking and sputtering. Finally he sat up, wheezing and clutching the plane's strut.

"You might have said something," he sputtered.

"Like what?"

"Anything at all regarding the unbreathable nature of the medium," he said indignantly. "About the desirability of maintaining one's head above the surface."

"I'm sorry, Jay," Miller said. "I forgot to say that you can't breath the water."

"A significant omission," Cook said, glaring darkly.

"It won't happen again," Miller said. "Now how do we get you to shore?"

"Suggest you 'swem' in with rope and pull me in," Cook said.

Miller looked at Cook, who appeared righteously indignant. *Maybe I really should have known,* Miller thought. *I really should have told him not to breathe the water.* He shook his head wearily, wondering what was next. "All right, Jay," he finally said. "I'll swem."

CHAPTER

5

Miller looked around him on the beautiful white sand beach. It did, indeed, appear to be paradise of a kind. The air was clean and pure and loaded with the sweet, musky smell of things growing; all kinds of things. Trees, grass, bushes, flowers, fruit trees—the beautiful aroma of life asserting itself.

And in the fringe of vegetation above the beach he could hear insects, birds. A lizard scuttled up a tree branch. A bird dove on it.

If they were stuck here for a while, would that be so bad? Club Med without polyester, without kids throwing sand at each other and yodeling their agony to apathetic parents. It would be just the two of them and their own tropical island, for who knew how long? Miller knew help would come, sooner or later. Maybe a week, when the search planes began to look for survivors of the tsunami.

"Tony Miller!" came the yell from out to sea. "Hello, Tony Miller!"

Cook, of course. Miller turned to see Cook, practically hopping with anxiety, still clinging to his perch on the pontoon of the seaplane. Miller waved to him, which did not seem to be the response Cook wanted.

"Real-time locus instant adjustment!" Cook shouted. "Very important! Cook required on island! Now!"

Miller took a centering breath. *Yup,* he thought as he heaved the rope up to the tree line. *Tropical paradise. Just me and a guy who thinks by committee.*

Miller pulled the plane in and, with very little help from Cook, above the high water line. Cook, after two or three halfhearted tugs on the rope, spent the time impatiently hopping on one foot between the plane and the tree line. Whatever his weird, mad reason, he was very anxious to move into the forest.

"All right, Jay," Miller said, when at last the plane was secured. "Let's go exploring."

Cook led the way eagerly. He flailed at the branches in their way, mumbling, "*Ecck.* Nasty substance. Filthy green biomatter." But after only a few steps they stepped onto a path. Miller stopped to examine it, dropping to one knee.

"Proceed," Cook urged him. "Forward, real-time haste."

Miller shook his head. "This isn't a game trail, Jay," he said. "It was made by people."

"Yes, yes," Cook said, seeming not to care at all. "This way, let's go."

Miller stood. "Jay," he said gently, "it could have been made by people who visit the island occasionally. But if the island is inhabited, I think we need to know who these people are. You know, there used to be an awful lot of cannibalism in these islands."

Cook looked around him anxiously, shifting his weight from foot to foot. "Yes," he said. "Proceed with caution."

Miller moved past him. "I'll take the point," he said.

Leading the way, Miller moved cautiously down the path, leaving all his senses open and keeping Cook ten feet or so behind him. He heard and saw nothing beyond the wildlife; birds calling and insects chittering. Occasionally he could hear Cook behind him, tripping on a root, or smacking at a low branch, muttering things like, "Filty chlorophyll excrement."

With almost no warning Miller came to a clearing. And what he saw there pushed caution all the way out of his head and left him moving slowly out past the clearing's edge, stunned and nearly breathless.

"My God," he said.

"Cannibalism?" Cook whispered with horror.

Miller just shook his head. "My God," he whispered again, moving forward, finding it hard to believe what he saw.

In the middle of the clearing stood a huge stone head, an exact duplicate of the ones on Runa Puake.

Miller stepped to the statue, feeling its power. The people who made this head knew what they were about. It made him feel small and insignificant. He was flesh, this was stone, a god-thing that would long outlive his short span of years.

He ran a hand over the smooth, cool stone. As always, he felt excited instead of humbled by this sensation. It challenged him on a very deep level, and he wanted to stay here with the head and unlock its secrets. Of course, it was impossible to tell without tests; but it appeared to be carved from the same stone as its counterparts on Runa Puake.

The interesting question was this statue's age. Did it come here after the ecodisaster on Runa Puake? Or was this the original, the other, more famous heads, being copies of this one? And how could—

"Miller!" Cook hissed from the edge of the clearing. "Object non-relevant! Proceed!"

Miller didn't even turn, scarcely hearing Cook. He bent as close to the stone as he could, examining the detail. "The carving technique is identical. Might even be the same strokes. If we can compare the quarry marks . . ." he began, and then trickled to a stop, remembering the tsunami. If any of the Runa Puake heads had survived, if they could—

"Miller!"

Cook had put all the urgency he could muster into it, and Miller turned. "What is it, Jay?"

"Let's go! Onward! Temporal factors!"

Miller shook his head. Whatever phase of madness Cook was in now, Miller didn't care for it. But as much as he hated to admit it, and hated to walk away from this wonderful stone head, he knew Cook was right for once. They needed to look over the rest of the island. Because if there were still people here, they were clearly related to the culture of Runa Puake, a civilization that had literally eaten itself to death, on its own human flesh.

"All right," Miller said, running a hand over the surface of the stone a last time. He turned away and moved reluctantly around the head to continue on the path. He got only three steps when surprise jerked him to a stop again.

Fifty yards ahead something metallic showed through the trees.

Miller stood and squinted for details. He got none.

Whatever the thing was, it was large and stood a good twenty feet above the ground. It had a dull sheen to it, like a water tower, so there was no mistaking that it was a fairly sophisticated man-made object of some kind.

Was this island inhabited? Not by neolithic islanders, but by some offbeat modern colony?

But what could keep it far enough off the charts that the stone head was unknown? Was it a leper colony? The private retreat of some billionaire who had stolen a Runa Puake head and moved it here? A secret government outpost—what kind, and what government?

Miller couldn't think of anything that didn't spell trouble one way or another. Whatever the place might be, caution would still be wise.

He dropped carefully back to the edge of the clearing and beckoned. Cook tramped over, making enough noise for a camel train. "What?" Cook said. "What is it? Hostile residents?"

"There's something up ahead," Miller said. "I can't see what it is, but it appears to be metallic, man-made."

"Yes . . . !" Cook breathed.

Miller ignored him. "I want you to stay here while I sneak up and see what it is. Stay hidden and be quiet, all right?"

"Hurry," Cook said.

This time Miller avoided the great stone head in the clearing. Instead, he circled to the right around the perimeter. On the far side he stayed within the vegetation, following the path from about ten feet off to the right.

Moving slowly and carefully, not allowing himself to feel hurry or impatience, he approached the metallic object. He still couldn't see any details, but it began to take on the shape of a monolithic tower of some kind, a giant tombstone, or historic marker, or . . .

. . . or a submarine?

Buried tail first in the ground?

"Impossible," Miller muttered. He moved a little closer.

As he approached, the silhouette began to stand out more clearly. It really was a submarine, buried tail first in the ground, its nose pointing skyward. By its markings, it was Japanese, probably World War II era, and judging by its size, it was one of their small five-man minisubs.

But "mini" was relative, and the size and weight of the thing were still formidable. The labor involved in dragging it this far inland and raising it to a vertical position—it seemed prohibitively difficult for an Oceanic culture, and pointless for a sophisticated modern one.

Miller circled, staying well back in the bush, looking for any sign of human presence and studying the submarine. When he had completed a half-circle without finding anything, he cautiously stepped out of the vegetation at the point closest to the submarine. As he approached he looked for any further clues as to why the thing was planted here.

He found nothing. There were no traces of offerings, neither food nor flowers. There were no signs to indicate that the sub was particularly well-attended. But someone had gone to an immense amount of trouble to bring it here and raise it up. And the reasons someone might do something so difficult and seemingly pointless were few.

A modern eccentric might have done it for aesthetic

reasons, or just to be eccentric. Come see my submarine garden. But then there should be a bench, or a border to the path—a sprinkler head, a cigarette butt, something; some relic of twentieth-century culture. There was nothing. The surrounding underbrush looked wild, natural, the way it would if the island was inhabited by a semiprimitive Oceanic culture.

But if some kind of Oceanic cargo cult had put the submarine here and it was a god-object like the stone head, shouldn't there be some sign of offerings or other votive services? Because an object so unique to isolated islanders, so important that they dragged it a half mile inland and planted it like this . . . No. The only explanation that made sense, didn't make any sense.

Miller stood at the base of the submarine, looking up. The sub just stood there, like a gigantic upraised middle finger aimed at him.

"Incorrect container, not Artifact-related," Cook said with obvious disappointment from two feet behind. Miller spun around, startled and then annoyed that Cook had come up behind him without his knowledge.

"It isn't what?" Miller snapped.

Cook regarded him for a moment, then looked away up the trail. "Forward motion still required," he said. "Urgency, uncertainty, possible hostile action uptime. Geographical context unknown."

"I think I know what's ahead," Miller said. "But I can't imagine what it means if I'm right."

"Download," Cook said urgently. "Share conclusion."

Miller just shook his head. "I'm probably wrong. Drop back and let's go take a look."

Cook stared at him. His jaw opened twice as if he

were going to insist on more, but then he abruptly turned away and moved back into the bushes, back where they had just come from.

Miller moved silently ahead. But only a small part of his brain was keeping watch. The rest was turning over this new problem.

He was beginning to believe that the island really was, or had been, inhabited by some kind of cargo cult. Some aberration of current or weather brought an abnormally high number of things here, crippling them on the way—ships, planes, even the sub. That would account for the weird and violent storm that had driven them down here. And if there were several of these wrecks, the natives would not pay a great deal of attention to any one of them. So the lack of any trace of worship around the sub would make sense.

Multiple wrecks; dueling gods. It was a ridiculous theory. The only thing to be said for it was that it explained all the evidence he had so far. And it was easy to prove. If he were right, there would be other wrecked boats and planes here, perhaps all of them half buried like the Japanese minisub. And this would be one of the most fascinating places on Earth for a cultural anthropologist.

But such a culture would be totally unpredictable, an abomination amid the many Oceanic societies, all similar in many ways. This one would be totally different, and he couldn't begin to guess in what ways. He almost hoped he was wrong.

He'd gone only another fifty yards or so when he saw another dull metallic object sticking up in a small clearing ahead of him. This one brought him to a stop, knocked all the wind out of him, in a way that even a half-buried minisub couldn't.

This wasn't a submarine, or an airplane, or any kind of water- or aircraft he'd ever seen. The lines were all wrong, and the burn marks on the outside showed that this vessel had passed through a heat too intense for plane or boat. The markings on the outside were not in any human alphabet he knew about. And even from the outside he could tell it was too advanced, too sophisticated. The thing was, as far as he knew, impossible.

But there it was. And Miller was reasonably sure what it was, even though it couldn't be.

It was a spacecraft.

It was about thirty feet in diameter, and its lines were amazingly graceful. Aside from the burn marks, the exterior seemed undamaged, even unmarked, as though the metal—if it was metal—could not be damaged.

Miller approached slowly, raising a hand to what looked like a logo of some kind near the hatch—

"Deep Space Command," Cook breathed, again coming up behind Miller, reaching around him to lay his own hand on the logo. "Positive affirmation! Herenow locus confirmed!"

Miller could only stare.

6

CHAPTER

Y**ou know what this is?" Miller finally asked.**

But Cook was already moving around the ship, running his hand across the smooth exterior and babbling in endless excitement. "It's here! *Here!* Identical spacial-temporal context real-time! Found it! The *Artifact*! Just as planned, Artifact location affirmed!"

"Cook—" Miller said, but his partner had disappeared around the far side.

Miller shook his head. For a moment he had been half convinced that Cook knew what he was talking about, that the excitement and talk of "the Artifact" were rooted in something *real*. But that was ridiculous. Cook was nuts from hitting his head. All the babble was a result of disorientation or physically induced psychosis.

Still, a disturbingly consistent pattern had begun to show in Cook's craziness. Did it mean that Cook was settling into a new reality, too far gone to come back, even with professional help? If so, the university, and the academic world in general, would lose a brilliant mind—and he himself would lose a friend.

Miller took a deep breath. There was nothing he could do about it now—except to survive, and to help Cook do the same. At the moment, that meant figuring out whatever threats this island might offer.

He looked again at the spacecraft. The logo on the side, the one Cook had so quickly recognized, was close. He leaned to look at it. "DNA . . . ?" he muttered to himself, frowning. It was, but it wasn't. Something was subtly wrong about it, something obvious, but—

He had it. Truly simple, and he felt stupid for not seeing it at once. It *was* a stylized DNA strand, but it had *three* threads instead of the normal two. Red, blue, and silver. Underneath were what appeared to be four large block letters from an alphabet Miller didn't know. Not Cyrillic, nor anything Oriental. It was almost like looking at ancient Greek; he could almost recognize some of the letters, or what they would someday become, but they were utterly different in this state.

Again he studied the ship. Clearly, it was some kind of advanced experimental vessel that had simply fallen victim to the strange meteorological conditions of the island. From his own Air Force experience he knew there were enough weird Black Projects going on to account for almost anything.

Almost . . . The futuristic design of the hull, yes. But the material of the exterior had a dull, pearly sheen to it unlike any substance he knew. He touched it. His own body temperature was instantly sucked away and he felt a neutral coolness to the surface.

This stuff was impossible. It acted more like one of the new plastics than metal, something like mylar or . . .

He bent to one knee at the base of the craft, where it had been buried. Carefully, he brushed at some moss growing on an outcropping of rock around the ship. He knew beyond question that something like this craft could not be more than ten years old. But if he had to guess without proper instruments for testing geological age, he would have said it had been buried here for something like seven hundred to a thousand years.

That was obviously impossible. The whole thing made absolutely no sense. It was the kind of nonsensical mishmash that simply couldn't be, like the stuff from some cheesy, low-budget Hollywood movie that—

Miller blinked.

Was it possible? The submarine, the preposterous spaceship: Could all this be a movie set? Not a series of naturally occurring paradoxes, but beautifully crafted fakes, made to look like strange and inexplicable wrecks. He knew what miracles the Hollywood technical crews were capable of. He'd been called in himself to the big special effects ranch across the river in Marin County. They'd paid him ten thousand dollars for two days of talking about the Lost Cities of the Sahara. What they showed him while he was there had astonished him; the movie people could do *anything*—or at any rate, create the illusion of doing anything.

"Of course." Miller chuckled. That had to be it. It *must* be a movie set—what else made sense?

He laughed aloud. At first he had actually bought into it, with his solemn theories of a cargo cult and unusual weather patterns. Right. And bare-chested native girls cracking coconuts for him as the whole clan gathered around with their ukuleles.

"Cook," he called, moving around to the far side of

the half-buried spaceship. "Hey, Cook, it's a movie set. It *has* to be." No answer. "Cook—listen to me."

Cook was not listening. He was standing beside what appeared to be the ship's main hatchway. On the frame beside the hatch was a keypad, a clear descendant of the kind Miller used to activate his home security system.

Cook was frantically punching things in with forefinger and thumb; seven digits, a pause, seven more. Each key Cook pressed made a musical *beep*, and at the end of each seven-note sequence the keypad let out a nasal *blaaatt* that Miller clearly recognized: Sorry bud, try again.

"Excrement!" Cook said. "Four standard codes! Emergency mode! System malfunction unlikely!"

"Cook?" Miller said. "What is that?"

"Access authorization," Cook replied, punching in another seven digits, again rewarded with a *blaaatt*.

"Uh, Cook," Miller said gently, not sure it was wise to disturb the madness. "I think it's just a prop. You know, from some movie they shot here?"

Cook didn't look up. "A . . . *moo-vee*," he said.

"Yeah, that's right."

"You mean a series of images captured on—is it magnetic tape?" Seven digits; *blaaatt*.

"It's film, Jay. Video is magnetic tape."

"I see. Very good. Theory more logic-compelling than crash of Deep Space Command shuttle unit."

"Uh—yes, that's right. It does make more sense, Jay."

Cook punched in seven more. "Why do you think that, Tony?" *Blaaatt*.

"Well, that explains everything, doesn't it? The submarine, the futuristic spaceship. I mean, isn't it more likely that they're left over from some lame movie? Instead of, this thing fell from the sky, what, maybe a thousand years ago?"

"Six hundred twenty-eight years," Cook said. "Three months, four days. Two hours, eighteen minutes, thirty-seven seconds." *Blaaatt.*

Miller blinked. Moments like this, when Cook was so damned *certain*, he had to remind himself of his partner's mental condition. "That's very—" he started. Cook looked up at him, a look that was part question and part challenge. Miller retreated. "—very accurate," he concluded.

"But compelling herenow logic absent?"

"Jay, I only said that it makes *more* sense if this were left behind after somebody made a movie here."

"Can you identify the material that the hull is composed of, Tony?" He still didn't look up; just entered his seven digits, heard the *blaaatt*, and entered seven more digits.

"No. I'm sure it's something like mylar. The movie people always get the latest stuff, and—"

"Ability of 'movie people' to create illusion unquestioned? Make the ship look like 628-year crash?" *Blaaatt.*

"Yeah, sure. Of course they could do it, you know that. That's what they do."

"Deep Space Command logo? Fabrication likely, possible, within parameters of technical ability?"

"Jay," Miller said gently, a little alarmed at the course Cook's obsession seemed to be taking. "Somebody made it up. A three-strand DNA? And those block letters are not in the language of anybody who could have sent it up."

"As far as you know."

"There are only a few countries in the world that could do it. I can recognize all those languages, even if I can't read them."

Cook paused and held up the keypad. "This unit operational, Tony," he said.

"That's— I don't know. I guess the battery is still good."

Cook shook his head with pity. "Amazing. Herenow pseudologic part of original briefing, but mission acknowledgment technical only." Miller stared at him; Cook frowned. "Reading . . . Ah. They told me about this, but I didn't believe it until now." He went back to entering numbers. "Your people will believe any— what's the term? Oh, yes. Any 'dumb-shit-crap.' You will believe anything rather than accept evidence that challenges preconceived notions."

"Jay, a spaceship like this just isn't possible—"

"As far as you know," Cook said. *Blaaatt.*

"As far as anybody knows."

"Anybody. I see," Cook said.

"I mean, the scientific mind accepts evidence, not conjecture," Miller said, a little indignantly.

"Good," Cook said. "Very good." Seven more beeps; then the sound of a chime.

The hatch swung open.

"Evidence?" Cook asked, and he turned and went through the hatch and into the spaceship.

7

CHAPTER

For a moment Miller was too stunned to move. Then he followed Cook through the hatch.

The interior was dark. But as Miller hesitated in the hatchway, a strip of luminescence, then two more, striped down the center of the ceiling. The lights did not seem to come from any kind of tube or other source. They just came into being from the smooth gray of the ceiling.

Cook leaned over a control panel, running his hands across the instruments. Some of them lit up as he touched them, emitting a shower of pings and clicks.

"Jay . . . ?" Miller said. "Uh—how did you do that?"

"Do what?"

"The hatch," Miller said. "You knew how to open it."

Still without looking up, Cook shrugged. "Standard emergency access codes," he said. "Well-known. Only thirty-two in existence." There was a loud pneumatic hiss from somewhere below them and Cook turned quickly and disappeared into the bowels of the ship.

"Jay?" Miller called, but Cook was gone. Miller could hear a series of thumps and mumbles below him somewhere, presumably on the deck below this one.

He looked around the cabin. His mind was still numb and he had trouble accepting what he saw. This was supposed to be a movie prop—damn it, it *had* to be a movie prop. No other explanation was reasonable.

Except that it was so real. And it seemed to be functional.

And Cook had made it work.

That was the worst of it, the thought that Cook might know what he was doing. Which meant—what? That the blow to his head had given him special powers that let him understand machines from the stars? That he was in telepathic communication with outer space people from the future? That his body had been taken over by an alien?

No. There was a reasonable explanation. There had to be a reasonable explanation. And he would find it. He would take a cold, objective, scientific look at this thing. If it really was a spaceship—all right. But first he would look at the hard evidence.

Miller took a deep breath and began to examine the control room. Fronting the control panel were three reclining bucket seats. Centered before each seat was a large blank area, perhaps a data screen of some kind. Like the lights in the ceiling, the blank areas looked like they were made of the same material as the surrounding console. But the rest of the panel held what looked like controls, so a large blank space in the middle, logically, should be some kind of viewing screen. Besides, the screens—if that's what they were—were framed by a series of small indentations that might be used to control or adjust the picture. Miller stepped closer.

He could now see that the center chair had a small joystick mounted on the right arm. There was no mistaking it; the pilot in Miller knew it immediately for what it was, what it had to be. This was the command seat, the place from which the craft was flown.

Miller felt himself drawn closer. He reached for the stick, somehow knowing how it would feel under his hand, and—

"Animal reproduction!" Cook snarled as he blasted back up from below. "Gone! Not present! Incorrectly located somewhere else!"

Miller jerked upright. Cook appeared extremely agitated, more so than at any time since the tsunami. "Calm down, Jay," he said, trying to soothe with his voice the way he would a nervous dog or horse. "What's missing?"

Cook practically hopped with frustration. "It!" he said. "Quintessential object! Entire objective of presence in specific locus!" And seeing the look of blank patience on Miller's face, he added, "The Artifact!"

"All right, Jay. If it's missing, we can find it. It has to be somewhere on this island, doesn't it?"

"Perhaps," Cook said, visibly calming a little. "Required environment very specific, but—"

"We'll find it, Jay," Miller repeated, trying to calm Cook further. "Let's just think it through, okay?"

Cook looked at Miller for a long moment. Something behind his eyes glittered. Then he laughed. "Very good," he said. "That one marks me."

"Maybe if we get a better picture of what this vessel is, we can figure out what happened to your, uh, artifact," Miller said.

"Standard System Shuttle," Cook said. "Irrelevant to quest for Artifact."

"Maybe so," Miller said. "But it's extremely interesting. I'd like to study—"

"Nothing worth labor-intensive study," Cook said. "Merely carried Artifact. Vessel. Nothing more. Exit craft now." He turned and went out the hatch.

"Cook—" It was no good. Cook was already outside. Miller bit down and took a deep breath. He wanted very badly to explore this ship. But he had to follow; Cook was clearly in no shape to wander around an unknown, and possibly hostile, island. And in any case, this ship, or prop, or whatever it was, wouldn't go anywhere in the next few hours. He could come back if the island proved safe. And if it wasn't safe, this thing was irrelevant, no matter how interesting.

Miller followed Cook out the hatch.

Cook was already striding purposefully up the path, about to disappear around a bend in the trail, when Miller climbed out of the spaceship. Miller hissed through his teeth with frustration and hurried after him.

"Jay," he said, catching up and putting a hand on Cook's shoulder. "Do you remember that we were going to be careful? Scout out the island in case there are hostile inhabitants?"

"Speed now most important," Cook said, shaking off Miller's hand and continuing without slowing down. "Artifact location unbearably urgent."

Miller gritted his teeth and followed. This whole thing was spiraling wildly out of control, and Miller, if he'd ever really had it in his grasp, could feel it slipping far away from him.

"Jay," he said, trying desperately to hold on to his temper. "Can we talk just a little bit about your artifact?"

Cook was silent for a long moment. He appeared to be considering Miller's request. Finally, he said, "You can't understand." Not *won't* or *might not*; *can't understand*, as if he were a Kalihari bushman asking how television worked.

"What does that mean, I *can't* understand? Damn it, are you forgetting that I'm the one who calibrated all the instruments on Runa Puake? You couldn't even read the seismograph until I—"

"Artifact is different," Cook said, and he surged ahead up the path as if that settled everything.

Miller closed his eyes for a few seconds, totally overcome by frustration, bottled-up rage, and anxiety about his friend rattling around loose on what still might turn out to be a dangerous island. He took two tai chi centering breaths and forced his mind and body to relax. Then he opened his eyes, feeling a little better, and broke into a trot, following Cook.

Miller quickly caught up. "Jay," he said, with what he thought of as admirable calmness, "I would appreciate it if you would tell me what you think this *artifact* of yours is. And while you're at it, why don't you explain why it's so important that we're not being cautious anymore."

Cook glanced at him without breaking stride, then looked away.

"Jay," Miller said again, "I need to know."

"Follow," Cook said. "Support. Instruction nonessential."

Miller snapped. All his carefully cultivated control evaporated instantly, and before either one of them knew what was happening, Miller had grabbed Cook, thrown him facedown to the ground, and sat on his back, holding Cook's arms behind him.

"All right, Jay," Miller said. "Then I have to assume that the bang on your head has made you dangerous, to yourself and to me. I'm going to take you back to that movie-prop spaceship and tie you up while I explore the island."

Cook bucked violently. It was so sudden and so explosive that Miller was almost thrown off. It was as if Cook had released all his adrenaline at once, in a super-human effort. But Miller was bigger, stronger, and in a commanding position. He held on, and just as suddenly as Cook had begun struggling, he stopped.

"Tony," he said, in a calm and reasonable voice, "please explain errant behavior."

"Of course, Jay," Miller replied, just as reasonably. "You are acting in an irrational manner. It is not consistent with your normal behavior, and it does not match your behavior pattern as I have come to know it. I have to assume that you are suffering from a mental disorder brought on by hitting your head on a rock back on Runa Puake."

Cook was silent for a minute. "Cranial area intact and unimpaired," he said at last.

"It doesn't matter," Miller said. "Your behavior is still untenable. I have been humoring you because I thought that was the right thing to do. But you're endangering our lives now, Jay. I'm sorry. I have to tie you up." And he stood, swung Cook across his shoulders, and started back down the trail toward the spaceship.

About halfway to the ship, Cook spoke. "Return

horizontal orientation," he said. "Artifact explanation imminent."

Miller turned his head to look into Cook's face, which was hanging off his left shoulder. Cook's eyes were calm, rational, and his face was relaxed. If Cook got violent or tried to run, Miller knew he could handle him. It was probably worth a chance, if only to get Cook to realize that he was not thinking in a lucid manner.

"All right," Miller said. He put Cook down on the ground beside the path and stood above him, arms folded. "Tell me."

Cook sat and looked up at Miller. "Sit down, Tony," he said. Miller did. Cook studied him, as if trying to figure out where to start and how much to tell him.

"Quit stalling," Miller said.

"Yes," Cook said. He looked around. "Artifact . . . is . . . Omnipresent Everything," he said.

"That's a little vague, Jay."

"Necessary," Cook said.

"Tell me what makes it so important," Miller said.

Cook frowned. "Searching," he said, and his eyes glazed over.

"Jay . . . ?" Miller prompted after a moment.

"Ah . . ." Cook said at last. "Contemporary knowledge of 'Chaos Theory.'"

"Yes. I think I've heard of it," Miller said dryly.

"Description of fundamental force, like gravity," Cook said. "All-pervasive random nature of time and space."

"I wouldn't put it quite in the same class with gravity," Miller said.

Cook nodded. "Result of Artifact," he said. And he

looked pleased with himself, as if he had explained everything perfectly.

"Go on," Miller urged him.

Cook frowned. "Artifact regulates. Suppresses."

"Suppresses gravity?"

"*Chaos*," Cook snapped, flushing slightly. "Balances chaos of time-space into consistent linear pattern."

Miller sighed. It was obvious that Cook had grabbed hold of a truly Big Notion and was far gone into insanity, no matter how reasonable he could sound at times. Maybe if he could get Cook to explain the whole thing, it would be easier to keep him calm and under control. "It sounds like a very useful object," Miller said. "Who made it?"

"Unknown," Cook replied.

"What is it doing on this island?" Miller asked.

"Artifact was removed from its position to prevent exploitation and/or destruction by others. Unfortunate accident induced by effects of unshielded Artifact caused shuttle to crash here."

"Jay," Miller said softly, "can't you see a small problem here? The Artifact, lying here on this island, caused the ship carrying the Artifact to crash?"

Cook shrugged. "Exactly. Proof. Proximity to Artifact results in just such anomalies. Unavoidable."

Miller opened his mouth to speak, to point out how foolish Cook's argument sounded; but he didn't speak. Jay's reasoning was consistent with what Miller knew of schizophrenia, where every contradiction became further "proof" that *they* were out to get you. The fact that it didn't make sense proved that it was true.

There was no point in arguing. The important thing was to use Cook's theory to keep him reasonable.

"All right, Jay," Miller said at last. "But something as powerful and important as your Artifact will be guarded. So we need to approach it very carefully."

"Agreed," Cook said, and in less than a minute they were walking up the trail again, Miller moving cautiously out in front and Cook trailing dutifully behind.

Miller was now prepared for more surprises. Or so he thought. After half a mile of quiet, unmarked by anything more dramatic than a breadfruit tree, the path suddenly widened out and opened into a large clearing.

In the clearing was a village. There were perhaps two dozen buildings, ranging from small huts to a grand lodge hall that could hold a hundred people. It had a chimney on each end, and a small puff of smoke curled lazily from the near one.

And every single building in the village was built from pieces of recovered wreckage. One hut was a section of fuselage from a DC–3. Another looked to be made from a chunk of motor yacht. A large building at the far end was made from the hull of a clipper ship. Others were knocked together from several different kinds of wreckage, making a kind of weird domestic collage. The wreckage seemed to be from every period of human history.

"Incredible," he breathed. Calling this a cargo cult was like calling the Holocaust inconvenient. "Just incredible."

Cook arrived beside him. "Circle around to right," he urged.

Miller ignored his comment. "Look at this place, Jay. It's unbelievable! How is it possible that no one has ever heard of it?"

Cook gave him a pitying look. "Possibly because all ships and aircraft that come here crash," he said.

Miller just shook his head and looked at the amazing village.

And as he watched, he saw movement out of the corner of his eye. He swiveled his head. A person trudged up from the stream with a bucket of water. He stared and almost forgot to stay low and out of sight.

Because this person was the most beautiful woman he had ever seen, and she was almost entirely naked.

8

CHAPTER

Wrapped around the woman's slim, swaying hips was what looked like a piece of brocaded silk. Other than that, she wore nothing but long black hair, perfect breasts, an even tan, and a smile.

Miller was not the type of man to leer or ogle. He was a tenured professor at U.C. Berkeley, the Granddaddy of all Politically Correct institutions, and he would never have made it that far if he had a construction worker's attitude toward women.

But this woman was so perfect, so beautiful, and so wonderfully unclothed, that for a minute all he could do was watch, with his jaw hanging and his mouth dry.

It was Cook who brought him back to earth.

"Correct theory, Tony," he said softly. "Inhabited by scavengers. Safety now in question. Suggested action?"

Miller snapped his eyes reluctantly off the woman and onto Cook. "I suggest we find out if these people are actually hostile," he said.

Cook looked alarmed. "Confrontation inadvisable,"

he said urgently. "Location of artifact primary urgency. Possibility of rescue—"

"We're not going to be rescued, Jay. Just as you say, everything that comes near this island crashes. We've got to find out what makes that happen and figure a way to neutralize it. Then we can get the plane working again and get out of here. But we can't do a thing on an inhabited island if we're trying to hide from the natives. So," he said, turning back to the woman, "we have to find out how friendly they are."

"Hormones dictating action!" Cook hissed. "Irrational state of rut causing impolitic decision!"

Cook grabbed his arm, but Miller pried off his fingers. "I understand what you're saying," he told Cook, "but I'm not being influenced by that woman's looks. The fact is, Jay, we can't get off the island, and we can't avoid these people. Confrontation of some kind is inevitable. It will go better if it starts from us." And without waiting for Cook's objection, Miller stepped into the clearing.

"Ask her about the Artifact," Cook hissed at him before crouching back down behind a bush.

The woman's back was to Miller. She had continued toward one of the huts—constructed from a beautifully rebuilt 1930s luxury yacht made of teak and mahogany—and carried her water pail inside.

Miller followed, unconsciously straightening his clothing, and arrived at the doorway to the hut only a few moments after the woman had gone in.

He knocked on the door frame, built from a mahogany side rail. "Hello?"

There was no sound for a moment. Then he heard splashing, the thump of the bucket, and the woman came out. She had obviously been washing with the water she'd brought in, because even the small swatch of silk brocade was gone now. She came to the door totally naked and looked out at Miller with a warm smile and the totally unselfconscious attitude of many Polynesians. She raised one hand to the door frame, placed another on her hip and said, *"Aku-ahao,"* as nearly as Miller could make out.

Once again he felt his mouth dry up, and his tongue stuck to the roof. He tried hard not to stare, but it must have been obvious to the woman that he found her attractive. She gave a low, musical laugh and beckoned him into her house.

Miller followed. The inside was simple, but many items were displayed that had clearly been gleaned from various wrecks without a clue as to what they were intended to be. A teak toilet seat, for example, hung over the door on the inside. It was beautifully carved with god-faces and what looked like runes, similar to the ones found on Runa Puake.

As they entered the main area Miller glanced up. The ceiling was made of sheets of overlapping metal from airplane fuselages. He could even make out a few letters and numbers: "Lock" with a star superimposed, and then a separate chunk, probably a tail piece, that read, "NR" and under it, partly cut off, a "6020."

The woman led him in to a cooking fire in the center of the house. Around it, a scattering of pillows from several eras lay on the packed earth floor. She beckoned Miller to sit on one.

The next few minutes went by quickly. It may have been much longer, but to Miller it seemed only moments. The woman did not appear surprised to see him, almost as if he were expected. But of course, they must get visitors frequently here, he realized. Where had they gone? Had they been absorbed into the culture, or . . . what?

As sinister as his speculation was, the professor in Miller quickly took over. How much had the ship-wrecked of all ages contaminated this culture? Would the Polynesian traditions of hospitality be in effect here? What would this strange and wonderful hybrid culture find valuable?

But these questions would have to wait. He could not concentrate at all in this woman's presence. She sat very close to him, behaving with all the dignity and pro-priety of a matron lady in a corset, in spite of the fact that her bare breasts were continually brushing against his arm. He tried to put that out of his mind and listen to what she said.

Miller spoke or understood several of the Polynesian dialects, but not the one the woman spoke. Yet her words seemed oddly familiar to him, until, at last, it occurred to him that her speech contained more of the Polynesian root words than any other dialect he knew. It was as if she was speaking the original tongue, the one all others in the region were based upon—which was just possible, assuming that these people had been isolated for a few hundred years.

Concentrating intently, Miller managed to piece together the vaguest outline of what the woman was try-ing to tell him.

Her name was Yuki. "Tony," he said, pointing to his chest. She repeated it, "Toay-neeah," and laughed. He thought it was the most wonderful laugh he'd ever heard. He smiled, and she smiled back, reaching a fin-gertip up to touch his lips.

The touch of her hand felt like a jolt of electricity, and his head was swimming. The fresh, clean smell of her was intoxicating. Miller had always thought it was total nonsense when poets and the writers of popular songs said things like that, but now it was happening, to him. What was going on? Of course, he was not in love with her, not after seeing her for the first time only a few minutes ago—but it was a powerful attraction, beyond anything he'd ever felt before.

Yuki was speaking again. Miller dragged his concentration back to what she was saying. *Something* or other was *forbidden* or *dangerous*—or was it just "on the mountain"? The words were so close—and what was *it*, anyway? She didn't seem terribly worried about whatever it was. Because it would happen to him? Or because he had done something and deserved it? Again, he could not quite make out anything exact, just a vague sense of the direction the words were going in, but nothing specific when they got there. Still, the voice and the words were so beautiful, he didn't mind. He was willing to spend as much time as he could on this problem.

Yuki stopped speaking suddenly and looked up to the door of the hut. The smile was frozen on her face and she stopped moving, even her eyelashes, like a deer caught in headlights. Miller turned.

A man stood in the door. Striped pants billowed around his legs and a bright yellow sash hung about his waist in the style of some eighteenth century buccaneers, and on his head he wore a Japanese Army helmet, adorned with what Miller recognized as two beautiful *kapkap*s—ceremonial ornaments carved from pearl shell. He wore no shirt, and his chest muscles were impressive.

Framed by mahogany railing pieces, the man looked as hard and dark as the wood. His face was carved with deep lines from anger.

Behind him, Miller could see a crowd of perhaps a dozen people, with possibly more beyond them that he could not see.

The man spoke to Yuki. The words that had sounded like pure liquid music coming from her sounded harsh and rough from him. He pointed to Yuki and to Miller back and forth several times; Miller got the sense from the words that he was not pleased to find them alone together—but he didn't need to understand the dialect to figure that one out. The man's face gave it away.

And apparently Yuki's answer—part reasonable explanation and part injured innocence—did nothing to improve the Pirate's mood. He took two huge steps across the room and glared down at Yuki. Then he turned to Miller and grabbed the front of his shirt. He easily pulled Miller to his feet, and stood nose-to-nose with him for a moment, just glaring.

Tony Miller was not an easy man to push around. He had size, strength, and training, and when he needed it, he had the combat temperament. A tough childhood and hard military service had seen to that.

But this wasn't some drunken redneck picking a fight, or some Type A screamer cutting him off in traffic. Miller knew that in the blink of an eye he could easily have the Pirate helpless on the ground. But if he did anything to hurt this man, he was jeopardizing his life and whatever future he might have on this island. There were other islanders with him; they were filing in now, circling the two men and Yuki.

So instead, Miller simply placed his hands on the Pirate's where they gripped his shirtfront, and pried the other man's fingers open, gently pushing the hands away. Then he stepped back and gave a small bow.

The two men simply stared at each other for a long minute. The Pirate seemed to be working himself up to some kind of move when a commotion began outside the hut. Pirate turned away from Miller and followed the others outside, pointing to Yuki and Miller to stay put.

Miller glanced at Yuki. She smiled at him, apparently unworried, and looked out the front door. Miller looked, too. He could hear voices chattering and children shouting, and in a moment two men appeared in the doorway, dragging Cook between them.

Pirate stuck his head back inside and motioned, saying something to Yuki at the same time. It was clear he wanted them both outside. Yuki stood up in one graceful motion and held out her hand to Miller. He took it, and they went outside the hut together.

Well over a hundred people were gathered in the open area at the center of the village. There was a great deal of talk, but very little of it seemed to be serious. Instead, the people milled around, talking with each other and looking at Miller and Cook. They did not seem terribly interested in or surprised at the strangers; instead, they seemed to be waiting for something to happen that would involve the two newcomers.

Cook leaned over to speak to him. "Relevant phrase occurs," he said. "'I told you so.'"

"We'll get out of this," Miller told him, with a confidence he almost felt. "These people are too isolated to be warlike, and there's plenty of food here, so there's no need for either ritual or practical cannibalism."

"Need?" Cook said. "Look at the children, Tony."

Tony looked. The children darted in and out of the crowd, dodging around the legs of the tolerant adults. They seemed happy and healthy. "What about them?" he asked.

"Signs of closed gene pool," Cook said.

"It's a small population," Miller said. "No new bloodlines."

Cook nodded. "How many water-air-spacecraft have landed on island?"

Miller shrugged. "Hundreds."

"Where are signs of interbreeding with survivors?" Cook asked.

Miller looked at Cook. His point was clear: If these people had not eaten or sacrificed the survivors of the hundreds of ships and planes that had crashed on this island, there should be some small genetic sign, like a child with blue eyes, or reddish hair. Instead, the kids looked enough alike to be siblings. And there were fewer of them than there should have been for a population this size. Was there a high rate of infant mortality, or was it something more sinister, like a large number of defectives from inbreeding, all killed at birth?

It was not a comforting thought. Miller knew the double edge of Polynesian culture better than most. It could be seductive, warm and welcoming, and simultaneously cruel and deadly. He'd noted that Pirate had not hit Yuki, and she seemed not to fear that he would; she was not property, not second-class for being female. But Pirate had also showed no hesitation in confronting him. And it was clear that he and Cook were not being invited to hang out and party.

"I still don't see any indication that these people are

hostile—" Miller began. But before he could say more, the crowd fell silent. Miller looked up.

Walking toward them was an old woman. Not a bent and withered crone, but a large woman, authoritative and even majestic in the way she moved. Her white hair was pulled back and held in place by a comb made of human finger bones, and she was dressed almost entirely in red feathers. She carried a staff made from what seemed to be the machine gun from a World War II era bomber turret, topped with the eyepiece from a periscope. A dozen strings of human ears, some of them ancient, hung from the staff. Around her waist was a red sash hung with other dried bits of flesh—and with a horrible lurch of insight, Miller recognized them as human male genitalia.

"I think I see some of those hostile signs now," Miller whispered to Cook.

The woman, clearly the chief or high priestess, stopped in front of them. She looked long and hard at Cook, then at Miller. She was almost big enough to look him in the eye, and Miller found that he unconsciously came to attention, as if he was being inspected by a commanding general.

The big woman nodded approvingly. *"Bakadoa,"* she said, inclining her head to Miller. He felt his pulse quicken. He knew the word, or a word close enough that he was sure they had originally been the same. *Matatoa,* in other dialects, was a member of the professional warrior caste. They were universally feared and respected. This dialect changed a few consonants, but it had to be the same word. The chief clearly thought Miller was a member of the warrior caste. Would he be welcomed as such? Could his protection extend over Cook?

The whole crowd looked at him with friendly approval, now that their chief had proclaimed him a warrior. Miller felt better. Even if there were some ritual challenge, he was confident in his fighting ability.

"What just happened?" Cook asked him.

"They think I'm a *matatoa*, a member of the warrior caste," Miller explained. "That probably means they won't hurt us."

"Certainty?" Cook asked doubtfully.

"Just relax now, Jay," Miller reassured him. "We're going to be okay."

9

CHAPTER

There were no windows in this hut. It was, in fact, not so much a hut as a cell. A faint light came in from a poorly built roof. In one corner someone had scrabbled a shallow pit out of the sandy soil. The unbelievably foul odor rising from the pit was a big clue to what it had been used for in the past.

Miller had paced the perimeter of the room two dozen times, looking for some small weakness he could exploit to get out. It was habit and training more than any real belief that he might escape. Even if he got out of the cell, there was no place to run to on this small island, and no hope of rescue. He played with the idea of paddling away in a small boat. After all, that's how Polynesian culture had spread, people in small boats going from island to island.

But it was no more than a daydream right now. He had not seen any small boats on the island, had no idea where they might be or even if they existed in the weird cultural omelet of this island. If there was a strong bond between this culture and the one they had left behind on Runa Puake, as the stone statue indicated, there would be no boats. Besides, he couldn't leave Cook, and the idea of spending a few weeks in a small boat with Cook in his present state set Miller's teeth on edge.

And in any case, he had found no conceivable way out of the cell. It was built from a section of DC–3 fuselage turned on end and roofed over with pieces of what looked like the wings. There were two small windows, but they were more than half buried, and too small to crawl through anyway. The ceiling was nearly twenty feet up, impossible to reach, as far as he could tell. So after a while Miller gave it up—just for now, he reminded himself—and sat down with his back against the smooth metal wall.

Cook had been sitting since they'd been thrown into the cell, apparently brooding, occasionally muttering his strange pidgin of computer terms and chopped sentences. Now, suddenly, he opened his eyes and looked at Miller. "Resolved," he said. "Situation assessment, Tony?"

"Interesting culture here," Miller said.

Cook nodded. "Possibility of Artifact presence high, based on behavior."

Miller let that go. "I think I can almost understand the dialect," he said. "It's very close to root Polynesian speech, but with a few interesting consonant transpositions. But there are some real departures from standard Polynesian behavior."

"Logical," Cook said.

"For instance, Yuki," Miller said, trying to figure it out by talking. As long as they were stuck here, it made a very interesting field study. "She welcomed me with no fear, with real friendliness." He paused as he remembered the feel of her skin, the touch of her bare breast against his arm. He took a ragged breath and made himself go on. "And yet there were hints of monogamy in her interaction with that Pirate guy. We see the common clues of a matriarchal order—the Chief's a woman, the Pirate didn't lay a hand on Yuki, and so on. But where are the boats? Polynesian culture is maritime. There have to be boats. Except that Easter Island didn't have them, and Runa Puake didn't have them, because it was connected to Easter. But they had more atypical behavior toward women, and this place seems to conform to the Polynesian norm. Some really unusual anomalies."

Cook nodded. "Simple explanation," he said. "Unconscious *uber*culture implanted. Like cell graft."

Miller stared at him. "What in the hell does that mean?" he asked.

Cook held out a hollowed fist. "Base culture," he said. He shoved the pointer finger of his other hand into the fist and wiggled it. "Implanted nucleus. Different DNA. Appearance similar, behavior different."

Miller frowned. "You mean, the influence of all the crash survivors has—"

"No," Cook said, cutting him off. "Influence unconscious, overwhelming. Not survivors. *Implants*."

Miller shook his head, once again forcibly reminded that Cook was still demented. "All right, Jay," he said.

But Cook wasn't finished. "Important information," he said. "Circumstance now requires full briefing realtime. Artifact recovery in jeopardy. Continuity of timespace line accordingly threatened."

"All right, Jay," Miller repeated. The answer seemed to inflame Cook.

"*Not* all right," he said. "Actual emergency now exists herenow. Sum-total human condition perilized."

"Jay . . ." Miller said gently.

"Active coercion to GECO cause required," Cook went on. He stood up. "Revelation of major importance, Tony."

"What revelation is that, Jay?" Miller asked.

Cook held up a finger. "First," he said, "I am not Jay Cook."

Miller tried to stay calm. He knew that head traumas often produced disassociative behavior. "All right, that's okay," he said. "Who are you? And what do you want me to call you?"

Cook pushed that away. "Irrelevant. Minor. Other items of critical importance."

"Like what?" Miller asked.

Cook locked eyes with him. All hints of playfulness dropped away. Miller thought he had never seen Jay look so deadly serious. "First," he said, "most important, the Artifact."

"What about it?"

"This," said Cook, or whoever he was. He raised a finger and pointed. "The Artifact is—"

The door burst open.

The Pirate stood in the doorway, glaring at Miller, daring him to try something, anything. When Miller did not, he nodded and said something over his shoulder. Immediately a swarm of men flooded into the room, surrounding Miller and Cook and hustling them out into the space in the center of the village.

The whole village was gathered. Miller and Cook

were pushed and dragged into the center of the crowd, where the Chief waited, flanked by five other elders. There were three women and two men, all wearing red feathers and dried human body parts; like the Chief's outfit, but not nearly so grand.

The guards pushed them, and Cook stumbled to his hands and knees. Pirate and his group laughed. But Miller, figuring something like that might happen, had been ready, and simply took a step forward. He turned and smiled and shook his head at Pirate.

Pirate stepped forward, scowling, and Miller stepped toward the other man obligingly. Again they stood face-to-face.

This time conflict was halted by the Chief. She gave a hard, short bark of laughter and said one word. Pirate stiffened and stepped back. Miller turned to see the Chief smiling at him. *"Bakadoa,"* she said again, nodding. The other dignitaries with her nodded, too.

Miller gambled. He'd thought this out earlier, when the Chief had first used the word and he had pieced together it's meaning, *warrior*, from what he knew of the many Polynesian dialects.

He stepped forward and faced the Chief squarely. *"Bakadoa,"* he said, thumping his chest and then holding up his fists to show her he was ready to fight. He moved his fist toward her and turned it over, opening his hand, trying to indicate that the fist was for her; he would fight for her, be her *bakadoa*.

The Chief clapped him on the shoulder and turned her back on him, talking to the other dignitaries. Miller thought he could understand the word for *fight* or *struggle*, and something indicating approval of his fighting qualities. But again, it was nearly impossible to get any exact meaning, and he still had trouble following the shifted consonants when this dialect was spoken at normal speed.

Still, he felt hope for the first time since they'd been thrown in the DC–3 cell. "I told them I'm a professional warrior," he told Cook in a low voice. "They may give me a ritual challenge of some kind. If I can win, they might let us go."

Cook, brushing the dust off himself, shook his head. "Illogical flaw. *They* would not permit escape."

"Well, whoever *they* are, they don't have the final say here. *They* do," Miller said, nodding to the group around the Chief. They were opening a package made of broad, pliable leaves and extracting two red silk scarves. "Unless I miss my guess, we're going to put on those scarves and be put to some kind of test."

"Rigged game," Cook said. But he did not have a chance to explain.

The Chief turned back around and beckoned them forward. They stepped in front of her. One of the old men in the Chief's group blew a horn, made of what looked like a piece of exhaust pipe from an airplane engine. Two of the other Elders began to chant, the villagers in general responding with a kind of chorus.

The Chief stepped forward and looked down at Cook. She frowned; he frowned back. The Chief shrugged and, raising her voice to be heard over the chant, tied the scarf around Cook's forehead as she shouted out a short phrase; it sounded almost like *begin*, and then something about *Ku*. Did it mean Tu, the Polynesian war god to whom human sacrifices were made? Impossible to tell—and in any case the Chief was now tying the scarf around his forehead, repeating the phrase.

Miller had no idea what they were in for. He was sure

that the chanting and the horn-blowing meant that his guess was right and it would be some kind of ritual challenge. But there was no way to know what the challenge would be. It could be combat, or it could be trying to swim tied to a shark. It didn't matter. He had to believe they had a chance, no matter how slim. There was no point in thinking anything else. And if there was even the tiniest chance, he would make it. He would survive.

The Chief raised her hands and the people all fell silent. *"Kala valata boway Ku!"* she shouted. The whole village shouted back and began to move. The Chief looked at Miller and beckoned. He followed, Cook trailing behind him.

The Chief and the Elders led the way, with Miller and Cook right behind, followed by Pirate and his group, who were most likely the *bakadoa* of the village. The rest of the people traipsed behind, singing, shouting, the children laughing and running in and out of the crowd.

The procession wound its way down a well-traveled path through the underbrush. There were some trees, but it was mostly bush and long grass, and it was quite easy to see ahead of them. And when the path took a long slow curve to the left, it was easier still to see what was ahead. Miller felt his heart slam against his rib cage. He knew what it meant; it always meant the same thing in every Oceanic culture he had ever studied.

If they were truly going there, then the fighting chance he'd been counting on was gone, and his death was as certain as if he were about to be stood up in front of a firing squad.

They were headed for the volcano.

And Miller was now sure that they were going to be thrown in.

10

CHAPTER

At the sight of their destination, Miller stopped dead. But something bumped him hard between the shoulders and he turned.

The Pirate stood behind him, looking at him with mean satisfaction. He spoke softly to Miller, just a sentence. Something to do with coming together or meeting, and then the name again, Ku, the great god who gets the sacrifices.

"I don't know what Yuki sees in you," Miller said, smiling. "You're a stupid, mean-spirited bag of ugly. Yuki is too good for you." Pirate's face darkened at the mention of Yuki, and Miller turned back around and kept walking.

It was a small point on an easy target, but he had scored it gladly and he felt a little better. If he had to die, he would die fighting, and he would not give Pirate any enjoyment of it if he could help it.

Still, he didn't particularly want to die. He was just getting the hang of living. He yearned for another shot at his life back in Berkeley. His suburban house, ten-year-old BMW, and full class-load of graduate students aching for answers to preposterous questions. If he could just start all over again, he'd get married. He'd never be stuck here, about to be sacrificed to Ku, if only he had a wife and kids to keep him home. Kids—what a great thought. Could a colicky baby be worse than being thrown into a volcano?

Miller didn't have much time to think about the volcano. A tugging came at his arm. He turned to see Cook anxiously trying to get his attention. "Imperative revelations," Cook said.

"We're about to be thrown into a volcano, Cook," Miller said. "Is it more important than that?"

"Yes," Cook said.

"Well, this ought to be impressive."

"Entirely. Destruction of space-time paradigm," Cook said impatiently. "Come on-line, Miller." He pointed to the volcano's cone. "Absence of smoke. Absence of eruption sign over several hundred years. Old growth forest," he said with a shudder as they passed a huge old tree.

Miller looked; it was true. When they had flown over the cone, there had been no updraft, no glow from inside, no recently formed lava spills around the rim, no sign of any volcanic activity. Just the sudden failure of the engine, which certainly didn't have to be connected to the volcano.

"All right," Miller agreed. "The volcano is probably extinct. But we know these people have been on this island for almost a thousand years. They may throw us in anyway, out of respect for an ancient ritual. We'll be just as dead, Cook."

Cook nodded. "Possible. But irrelevant."

"Not to me," Miller said. "To me, my death is extremely relevant. Maybe *ultimately* relevant."

"End result of struggle for Artifact more so. *Universal* relevance. No remaining future, past, present. But with action, improvement of life for all. Ours to decide. You, me. Action therefore imperative. Herenow real-time."

"I guess you're right, Jay," Miller said, and turned his attention back to the volcano. It was a little sad that Cook was going to his death still unhinged, but if it helped the man deal with his fate, he was not going to straighten him out.

Cook grabbed his arm again. "Attention required. High probability exists of exposure to Artifact herenow."

"I'm sorry, Jay, but we're facing an unpleasant death here, and I'm finding it difficult to stay focused on your Artifact."

Cook slapped him. It was not a terribly hard slap, but it got Miller's attention. "You must not die," Cook said.

"I don't see how to avoid it," Miller said wearily. "Do you?"

"Unclear," Cook said. "Engage cortical synapse in primitive action sequence leading to solution. Basis of Miller selection for mission."

Miller closed his eyes. Well, if you had to go, why not go making light conversation about the end of the world with a maniac? "What does that mean, Miller was *selected*? Who selected me, and why?"

"We did," Cook said. "High probability of Miller success."

"Success at what?"

Cook looked to the guards. They were chatting, enjoying themselves. He turned back to Miller. "Mission background," Cook said. "Speed required."

"Go ahead," Miller said.

"Future composed of two groups, Bodhis and GECOs. Tree-huggers and progress. Valid input?"

"Okay, I get it," Miller said. "We have the same thing, environmentalists fighting lumber companies, construction companies, chemical companies—"

"Future struggle evolved to full-scale war. Struggle for total domination by manipulation of time-space. Control deadlocked, system in balance. No winner. Time-space manipulation allows response before attacks."

"Uh-huh, very clever. So if these tree-huggers make a move, the progressives manipulate time and stop it ahead of time."

"Balance," Cook agreed. "Until discovery of Artifact. Balance in ultimate peril."

They were much closer now to the volcano. Miller could see that the path wound around to the side. Did it go all the way to the top? "Why ultimate peril, Jay?"

"Study of Artifact reveals basic truth."

"That's good," Miller said. "Truth is good."

Cook ignored him. "Time-space is fiction. Linear order of events fragile, unnecessary. A fiction created and maintained by Artifact."

Miller shook his head. "Then who created the Artifact, and when?"

"Unclear. Irrelevant. Possession of Artifact actual point, Tony. Possession equals control."

"Control of time-space?"

"And control of ability to destroy logical sequence and linear connection of universal all-time herenow. Control Artifact, control time-space. Destroy Artifact—" Cook shuddered. "Result unclear. Probable destruction of time-space."

"That's an interesting theory, Dr. Cook." He turned away again. They were about halfway up the side of the cone now, and the path seemed to be leveling off as it wound around to the far side of the volcano.

"Tony Miller," Cook said, and there was real urgency in his voice for the first time. "Belief now imperative. Crisis point approaching."

Miller was not really listening. He had noticed that his body felt heavier. Interesting. Was it a cellular-level response to the threat of death? Reluctance of life to allow itself to be destroyed? "Do you feel heavier all of a sudden?"

"Necessary result of exposure to Artifact," Cook said. "Physical laws affected. Gravity bends."

"I thought you said time and space—is it gravity, too?"

"Difference unclear," Cook said. "Possibly fictional. Artifact unifies or supersedes conventional physical laws."

"So the Artifact makes us heavier, does it? It would be a very unpopular Artifact back home."

"Miller," Cook said, "I am not Dr. Jay Cook."

"Of course you're not, Jay. And neither am I. But you're one of these future people, aren't you, Jay?"

Cook studied him. "Belief imperative for action, Tony Miller. Jay Cook no longer controls this body."

"Well, you have to admit that's a tough one to believe."

"Concrete proof unavailable. Describe behavior of so-called Cook herenow."

Miller smiled. There was no need to be diplomatic now, not with death approaching. "You're acting nuts," he said.

Cook nodded. "Insufficient preparation-download time. Warning received of impending Bodhi action. Regret. Cook persona imitation inadequate."

"I wouldn't say inadequate. Just—"

"Insane?"

Miller patted Cook on the arm. "You hit your head, Jay. It's perfectly natural. Be as crazy as you want. I don't care, really."

Cook was silent for a moment. Then, "What is required to convince you?"

"That you're from a future culture, sent back to take over Jay Cook's body and save the universe by grabbing a mystical Artifact?" Miller laughed. "It boggles the imagination, Jay."

Cook nodded, appeared to think hard. "Proposal," he said. "Pretend to believe."

Miller blinked, surprised. "Why?"

"If Artifact is product of insanity, you are about to die. If story is truth, you have chance to survive."

Miller shook his head. It was starting to sound right, and that worried him. "If you're from the future, why can't you tell for sure what happens here?"

Cook looked pained. "Probabilities only. Multiple futures."

"Well, what probabilities are we looking at?"

Cook looked away. "Miller has one chance in seven of survival."

"Ouch," Miller said.

Cook looked back and grabbed Miller's arm urgently. "Highest tested odds, based on simulations using fourteen million test subjects."

"Fourteen—"

"Fourteen million," Cook said. "Run through identical simulation. Miller scores highest of all. One in seven."

Miller laughed. "It's nice to know a future society thinks so highly of me. What about you, Jay?"

"Cook does not survive," he said. "Twice only in fourteen million simulations."

"You seem pretty calm about that."

"Artifact sole importance," Cook said. "My mission parameters were find Artifact only. Miller must rescue Artifact, escape."

"How do I do that?"

Cook shrugged. "Answer variable. Important only that you do it. *Preserve Artifact*."

The islanders around them were falling silent, their laughter and cheerful joking trickling to a stop. Miller looked ahead. Fifty yards in front of him the path ran straight into the rock through a chest-high opening, leading inside the volcano—and into his death?

"These other people—the Bepos?"

"Bodhis," Cook said impatiently.

"The Bodhis. Why haven't they tried to stop us?"

Miller looked at him pityingly. "They have. Is herenow island culture typical of region?"

"No, but—"

"Native culture past-time bent by Bodhis to cause failure of attempts to rescue Artifact. Miller—ultimate time cusp herenow. Commitment to action required."

The line jostled to a halt. The Chief and her cronies

began a soft chant at the low doorway. Something thudded into Miller's back. He glanced behind him to see Pirate, sneering at him and whispering something that didn't need a translation. He thumped Miller again with the butt of a spear.

Miller blocked the spear with a hand and turned his back to Pirate. The guy was getting on his nerves. Even if Cook was as crazy as he sounded, it would be fun to try to screw up Pirate's sadistic pleasure. And on the remote chance that Cook, or whoever/whatever he was, was telling the truth . . .

"What do I have to do?" Miller asked.

"Rescue Artifact," Cook said. "Escape."

"Escape with the Artifact? Why?"

"If Artifact captured, Bodhis will attempt to destroy."

The Chief raised her voice, making a powerful command, or a very pushy request, of Ku. "This thing is obviously important to the islanders. Wouldn't it be easier to destroy it instead of trying to take it away?"

Cook shuddered and looked panicked. "Destruction of Artifact is Bodhi triumph. Time-space shattered, Bodhi simultaneous all-time herenow imposed. New reality, Miller. Or no reality. Either way, disastrous."

"So if the thing breaks, that's the end of everything?"

"Not end," Cook said grimly. "Highest probability indicates transfiguration to random. Seventy-two hours for possible correction, then entire line of time-space broken, reassembled in random no-order fashion."

"*Broken?* Just like that?"

"Just," Cook agreed. "Simulation indicates very small chance of successful intervention at Bodhi homespace before seventy-two hours."

"Bodhi homespace? Their headquarters? Where is it?"

Cook gave him a bleak smile. "Herenow designate, thirty-eight, one-twenty-three."

"What does that mean, thirty-eight—" Miller started to object. But Cook just spoke louder and faster.

"Coordinates! Do not fail, Miller. Absolute! Current probability nexus favorable. Homespace invasion low probability operation."

"But if I get there in seventy-two hours, I could fix it anyway?"

"Extremely low probability," Cook repeated. "Herenow optimum action point."

"And where is it?"

But they were interrupted as the Chief's voice peaked and was joined by the Elders and then rest of the crowd. They were answered by a loud rumble of thunder. Miller glanced up. A low finger of dark cloud approached the cone of the volcano. As he watched, a tongue of lightning licked out. The Chief shouted one more sentence to Ku with her arms raised and then bent down to enter the volcano.

The Elders followed her, one by one, and the villagers began to move slowly toward the doorway. Pirate pushed roughly at Miller to move him forward.

"Crisis immediate," Cook said. "Will you do it?"

11

CHAPTER

Miller's answer was cut off before he could even form it. They had arrived at the low opening into the volcano, pushed roughly by Pirate and a little more gently by the other guards, but pushed nonetheless. Cook went right through; Miller, much taller, had to bend almost onto his knees to enter.

Inside, Miller stood up again—slowly, since in the dark of the tunnel where he now stood, he could not at first be sure if he could stand without hitting his head.

His eyes adjusted to the dimness quickly; the Elders were standing at intervals of about fifty feet, each of them holding a lighted torch. Once again Pirate bumped him from behind. Miller didn't react, except to move off down the tunnel. It appeared to be a natural vent of the kind volcanoes sometimes developed, the ground bumpy but relatively level, polished by generations of scuffling feet.

The walls, and even the floor and ceiling where Miller could see them in the reflected light of the first torch, had a dull shine to them. He rubbed a hand against the near wall and glanced at his palm; sure enough, the wall left a dark gray smear on his hand.

"Lead," he said to Cook. "The walls contain a very high concentration of lead."

Cook nodded. "Necessary to shield influence of Artifact," he replied. "But not totally effective."

Miller looked around him. "What do you mean?"

Cook dragged his right arm slowly up level with his head and let it fall. "Heavy."

"I noticed that before," Miller said. He lifted his own arm. "It's worse."

"Closer to Artifact," Cook said.

And indeed, Miller could feel the sensation of weightiness growing on him as they dragged down the dim hallway. And then, as he watched the nearest Elder, standing at the side of the tunnel with her torch, he had the strangest sensation that all motion had stopped, that they were suspended between moments. Abruptly, with a flicker of accelerated movement, time returned and they walked quickly past the Elder.

"What just happened?" Miller asked.

Cook shrugged. "Artifact," he said.

Miller felt a coldness growing on the back of his neck. *It can't be*, he thought. *There's got to be a perfectly good explanation.*

"Stress," he blurted out. "Stress is causing the illusion of—of—" He stopped, unable to think of what to call it.

"Scientific mind accepts evidence, not conjecture," Cook mocked him.

"But—" Miller said, and stopped. He took a very deep breath and let it out slowly. *There is no thought, only the breath, the chi, the movement . . .*

It didn't work. The scientist in Miller's conscious mind was fighting frantically for a foothold, but he was falling, falling, into the rough darkness of his own subconscious, his dream mind, his lizard brain, where all such things were possible, where Cook was telling the truth and was a being from a strange future inhabiting the body of Jay Cook, and some thing, some *Artifact*, was waiting for them ahead and had the nightmarish power to control time, space, gravity—

A series of blasts on a conch trumpet knocked the crazy thoughts away and Miller breathed again. *My mind is off. My whole system,* he told himself. *The stress of death approaching, that's all. It's turned on a switch in my psyche—perfectly natural.*

But what if Cook was right?

Another blast came on the conches. They'd arrived at a door into what looked like a massive inner chamber.

As Miller stooped and crossed into the new area—moving quickly to avoid another love tap from Pirate—he noticed a glow, as though from a natural light source. The sun must somehow be reaching them, in the bowel of the mountain. And as he straightened up and looked around, he was stunned by two things:

The first was finding he was right. There *was* a glow of natural light. He stood on a ledge that ran almost halfway around the huge inner cone of the volcano. Below him was a smooth floor of cooled volcanic rock, and above him a large circle of sky was framed in the lip of the volcano's peak. A small slice of the sun was just visible on the far side.

The second jolt was an almost physical blow as he looked down at the floor beneath the ledge he and the others stood upon. The sensation of overwhelming heaviness was much more powerful here, and again he felt a strange flickering of time. The Chief raised an arm, and it seemed frozen there in midair for hours. Then suddenly, with no transition, the arm was no longer in the air and the Chief was standing several feet from where she'd been.

Miller blinked. Another thump fell on his back and he turned—slowly, then quickly—to see Pirate snarling at him.

Pirate pointed his spear down at the floor below the ledge and said something. His words were harsh and low, and then whipped out with the speed and pitch of a chipmunk. But the meaning was clear, as was the man's triumphant sneer. Miller turned and gazed down.

There, below him, where the rock floor within the volcano stretched away for about fifty yards, he saw a strange, dully flickering sphere. It seemed about twice the size of a basketball, and resembled a giant ball bearing, as if it had been machined. Its color was shifty, uncertain, but nearly always dull and pulsing with a strange light. Or was it just the reflection of the torches above it? Miller wondered. And how was it possible for it to reflect when it was so dull? Except now it wasn't dull, it was . . . what? Shimmering, then not, then—for less than a heartbeat—alive with brilliant color that hadn't been there at all before . . . and then it seemed to be almost everything all at once, impossible to describe, impossible to look at without a sense not just of disorientation, but of the destruction of all meaningful reference points—time as well as space. Up, down, there, later—all these concepts lost their meaning in the presence of this . . . *this* what?

"Artifact," breathed Cook beside him, sounding impressed for the first time since they'd left Runa Puake. "*Artifact*," he repeated.

The thing changed again, while somehow staying the same, and then with an intense and sudden jolt, the conch horns came again—but now he could *see* the sound rushing at him like hard, rounded stones—

—which again turned back to the notes of the trumpet.

Miller felt sick to his stomach. He had no idea what was going on, and for the first time since he'd been a boy, he felt afraid. Not of impending death, nor of a very great power he could not understand, but of what that *thing* on the rocky floor below might mean.

Cook was telling the truth.

The *thing* was the Artifact, a primal object that ordered and controlled all of time and space, coveted by two future powers and placed here by one group so that the other could maneuver *him* into taking it.

In fact, he was so overwhelmed by the implications of what he'd experienced that it was quite a while—or was it?—before he noticed what covered the rest of the floor beneath the ledge.

Bones.

Human bones.

Hundreds of skeletons, partial skeletons, skulls, femurs, piles of teeth and finger bones—all scattered across the floor as if they'd been emptied out of a giant box and flung down like dice to roll and slid to a stop wherever they could, by random chance.

The bones were in all stages of decomposition. Looking down from where he stood, he guessed the most recent were only a few years old, while the oldest were no more than piles of dust still imbued with the faintest remnant of human shape.

There were very few relics among the bones; no scraps of cloth or ornaments. It was as though they'd all been picked clean. Far from the Artifact, toward what seemed to be a small opening leading off the floor, there was a scattering of spears and throwing-sized rocks and a large cluster of bones that seemed to have been felled by the weapons.

The rest of the skeletons looked like they'd simply been hammered flat while running. The bones were fanned out from the Artifact, none any closer to it than fifteen feet. The only thing Miller saw below, other than the bones, spears, and the Artifact, were four rectangular panels of a strange material he couldn't identify. They were clearly man-made, but from this distance it was impossible to say what they were.

And at this point, it didn't really matter.

The conch trumpet sounded again, and Miller looked up. The Chief was frozen with her arms in the air, the light from above ran down the spectrum to red, and he felt the Artifact flicker a tentacle out at him. The trumpet blast came at him like the taste of a coppery mango, and the murmur of the crowd around him was like sour gum balls. Pirate grabbed his arm with fingers that sounded like marbles in a grinder and pushed him forward with a sound like a wave hitting a pile of wineglasses.

". . . Artifact." Had Cook said this several minutes ago? Or was it only now, as the tentacle of strangeness retreated, that Miller could register the words as his senses unscrambled. Again he felt Pirate's fingers on his arm. Another of the warriors had Cook in a similar, gentler, grip.

The Chief called out something with a rising inflection; the crowd yelled back in unison. The Chief nodded and, still speaking, turned toward the Artifact. She waved an arm three times; the crowd murmured something with each wave, and then they were all looking at him.

Pirate squeezed his arm, trying to twist it back as he hissed something in Miller's ear. One of the words was the same as something the Chief had said, and Miller recognized it as a Polynesian word with the K transposed to a T and the R to a B. It meant *bare* or *uncovered*. He did not have to spend much time trying to work it out, for Pirate immediately began to tug at his shirt.

Miller had had enough. He turned and knocked Pirate's arm down with the cutting edge of his hand. It stung; Pirate hissed with the pain of it and glared at Miller. He started to raise his spear, but one of the other warriors placed a hand on his shoulder and murmured something in a reproving tone of voice. Pirate kept his hate-filled eyes locked on Miller, but he nodded and backed up half a step. He motioned with the spear for Miller to undress.

Miller glanced around. Every eye in the cavern was on him and Cook. Two of the Elders were chanting; one of them dribbled his fingers across the head of a small drum, while the other held a stick tipped with feathers up to a torch and lit it on fire, waving the stick to the four cardinal compass points.

Cook began to undress. With only a slight hesitation, so did Miller. There was no point in resisting for mere body modesty. He was totally powerless, surrounded and outnumbered by these people to an overwhelming degree. If they wanted to, through sheer weight of numbers they could pin him to the ground and strip him in a matter of seconds.

Besides, there was a more interesting problem at the moment. Since none of the skeletons had even a scrap of fabric on or near them, the fact that he and Cook were being forced to strip probably meant they were about to be sent down to the Artifact. If he were going to survive the ordeal—and he had every intention of doing so—he needed an answer, quickly.

He leaned his head toward Cook. "What killed them?" he asked. He heard his voice slither down the scale to a crawl and then saw it change to particles. Cook was surrounded by millions of tiny globs of light, like small fluorescent BB's. The globs coalesced into the taste of lemon pudding and dribbled into Cook's ears. Cook turned to him with a movement that smelled of hot machine oil.

Four highly polished marble cubes cascaded from Cook's mouth and Dopplered at Miller, turning into a cold blue rain that fell on him as, "The Artifact."

Miller shook his head. The light in the room slid back up the spectrum, and he was hearing normally again.

"How?" he said. "How did the Artifact kill them?"

Cook opened his mouth. It stayed open for a long time but nothing came out. There was no sound, no motion, no time.

"Unclear," Cook finally said as time unfroze. "Too many options."

"Shit," Miller said.

"Main probability," Cook said.

"What?"

"Promise, Tony Miller. Promise to see Artifact to safe position."

"Safe where?" Miller asked.

"Tahiti real-time. GECO contact at airport."

"How do I find them?"

But before Cook could answer, the guards grabbed him by the elbows and dropped him off the ledge.

12

CHAPTER

"Cook!" Miller yelled. He pulled free of Pirate and looked over the edge.

On the floor, twenty feet below, Cook, on all fours, struggled to regain his feet. At first Miller thought he was injured. But as Cook strained to stand as if fighting a heavy backpack, Miller realized that he was simply behaving like he was a great deal heavier; closer to the Artifact, his gravity had increased.

For a moment, Miller forgot to breathe. He looked again at the hundreds of skeletons. All of them appeared to have been hammered flat. All were sprawled out in a spread-eagle posture. And the closer to the Artifact, the more extremely were they spread.

"Gravity," breathed Miller. "It's gravity!"

He leaned over to yell at Cook. A hand grabbed him from behind, but he shook it off. "Cook!" he called.

He was interrupted by another blast of the conch trumpets. All eyes went to the Chief. She took a red-feathered spear from an attendant and raised it over her head. She spoke in a voice as hard and clear as the trumpet, and then, so no one could fail to understand, she pointed beyond the Artifact.

Just on the other side of the Artifact, Miller saw the outline of a doorway, backlit by daylight.

The meaning was clear. Make it through the doorway and you're free.

And judging from the bones, nobody had made it yet.

The heavy gravity field generated by the Artifact had smashed them all to paste. And now it was Cook's turn.

Miller tried again to warn him. "Cook—" But it was too late. Cook, on his feet now, had begun to stagger away from the wall.

The crowd noise rose as the villagers egged him on with a two-syllable chant. Miller didn't bother to attempt a translation. He leaned out as far as he could and called again. "Cook!" But the noise was too loud. Cook, moving away, couldn't hear him. Miller put all he had into one earsplitting yell: "Gravity!"

If Cook heard, he gave no sign. He moved slowly, keeping his distance from the Artifact, studying it as he made a half circle out to the middle of the lower floor. He went no closer than he already was, but Miller could see that his steps were dragging and the extra weight was close to exhausting him already, after only a few minutes.

Halfway across, Cook swiveled his head to look up at the ledge where the Chief stood. Then, with an almost comical double take, he looked down at a point under the Chief's perch, at floor level. Miller shaded his eyes and strained to see. At first he could make out nothing at all. Then he saw it.

A second doorway.

Whether it led out of the volcano and to safety or just into another room didn't matter. It was a way out, a way to get off the floor.

Cook realized it, too. He took a step toward the doorway. But before he could take another, the villagers' chant turned ugly, like a crowd at a boxing match when they suspect a fix. He took another step, and they began to pelt him with rocks. Covering his head with his arms, he tried another step, but the shower of debris was now so intense he could not move. He took a step backward and the rock shower stopped.

Cook stepped forward again: rocks. He stepped back: the rocks stopped.

He looked up at Miller and shook his head. He pointed toward the Artifact, and Miller nodded helplessly. Cook looked at him for a long moment, until the crowd began to sound angry again. Then, half lifting one arm in a wave, he turned toward the Artifact and began to walk.

Except *walk* was not the word for it. With each step closer, Cook's movements got slower, heavier. He was frowning in concentration, keeping his eyes fixed on the Artifact as if for some clue.

Sweat poured from him and onto the rock floor. Miller, even from his spot on the ledge, could see that Cook's breath was rapid and shallow, like a man with emphysema. But Cook moved closer, and closer still.

He was almost halfway to the Artifact when his legs gave out. He did not fall over so much as simply collapse toward the floor. Miller could see from his expression that Cook thought he was still walking when he looked at the ground, was surprised to see his hand was resting on it, and tried to get up.

He couldn't. He tried again, but the weight on him was just too much. He began to crawl forward on all fours, panting desperately for air. The crowd was yelling now, sensing the end, straining forward with excitement.

Cook lifted his head with tremendous effort and looked around. His eyes fixed on one of the four strange rectangular panels that lay on the ground. For a long moment he stared at the panel, panting. Then, with a colossal effort of will, he turned to look at Miller.

Cook's tongue hung from his mouth, swollen, and his eyes were bulging. His breathing was painful for Miller to watch, coming in short, rapid gasps that were obviously not doing the job. His face was red and swelling; he was clearly near death, and Miller knew there was not a damned thing he could do about it, except look into his friend's eyes and share this last moment with him.

But Cook had more in mind than a last glance. Using almost the last of his strength, he turned very slowly to face the rectangular panel, then turned back toward Miller. When Miller did not respond, Cook repeated the movement.

The crowd began to throw rocks again. Very few of them came close; they were mostly stopped by the gravity field. But a few of the villagers—Pirate among them—were strong enough to arc their rocks very close.

One of them smashed into Cook's leg and he collapsed. He tried to straighten again onto all fours, but another rock caught him on the back and the amplified weight of it crushed him to the floor, face first. For a moment he didn't move. Then he slowly began to crawl on his belly, dragging his inert legs behind him, moving toward the rectangular panel.

Why? Miller wondered. Why were the panels so important that Cook had invited the hammer-smash blows of the rocks? What was their significance?

Cook was nearer to the panel now. But he was also ten feet closer to the Artifact, and the proximity was proving to be too much. His crawl slowed, then stopped. His fingers scrabbled at the rock floor for a few moments. Miller could see his back heaving spasmodically as he fought for breath. Then he was still. A small pool of blood seeped from his nostrils and began to puddle around his head.

The Artifact chose that moment to freeze time again. For what seemed like hours the picture was frozen: Cook on the floor, head resting in blood; the Chief with her spear upraised, red feathers standing out; the crowd on its toes in excitement.

Then time flickered into gear again. Cook was still as he'd been, but the crowd was in a new position now, one of anticipation. And all eyes were on Miller.

The Chief nodded to the trumpeter. Once again the conch blasted, and again the Chief raised the red-feathered spear over her head. She repeated her short, strong words and pointed to the doorway beyond the Artifact. Pirate grabbed Miller's arm, almost glowing with eagerness. He twisted and began to shove Miller toward the edge.

The death of Cook, the strange and completely unsettling reality of the Artifact, and Pirate's drooling anxiety to see him dead, all combined to overwhelm Miller. He snapped.

Pivoting quickly on his heel, he caught Pirate's

wrist and twisted it into an armlock, driving a knee into the man's groin with the same motion. Pirate dropped his spear and doubled over in pain as Miller took Pirate's elbow with his other hand and levered Pirate face first into the rocky floor of the ledge.

He put a foot on Pirate's neck then, maintaining his hold on the arm. "That's enough," he said, bending so Pirate could hear him. "*Botaoa*," he added, making a guess at what the word "enough" might be in this island's dialect.

Pirate struggled and Miller increased his pressure; Pirate hissed in pain, but stopped moving. Then Miller felt a sharp sting on his right arm as one of the other guards nudged him with the point of a spear. Blood ran down Miller's arm now. The guard jerked his head, indicating that he had to release Pirate. Reluctantly, he did.

Pirate stood, brushed himself off, and stepped toward Miller with an evil gleam in his eye. There was a small trickle of blood running from his nose, and his lip and cheek were scraped and cut, too. Clearly he planned to even the score. But the guard with the spear stepped between them. He spoke one short, sharp sentence. The words were simple, and Miller was almost sure he understood.

"No," the guard said. "His meat is for Ku."

Pirate stood still for a moment, still eager to avenge himself upon Miller. The conch sounded, however, and Pirate turned toward the Chief, who was glaring at him. They locked eyes for a long moment. Then Pirate shrugged, stepped back and retrieved his spear, pointing it at Miller. He nodded down to the floor where Cook lay dead.

Miller didn't wait to give Pirate another chance.

With a quick smile, he said, "Say hello to Yuki for me," and was rewarded with a flush of anger from Pirate. It wasn't much, but that, and the good feeling he still had from driving Pirate's face into the rock, would have to be enough.

Miller turned and began to climb down off the ledge.

The crowd called out its approval as he made his way down with no "help" from the guards. Miller barely heard them. His mind was racing furiously, trying to find some handle for the problem of the Artifact, some way to think about the thing that would allow him to understand it enough to survive it.

It didn't matter right now what the Artifact was, or whether Cook was truly a future being sent to find it or just a deranged Jay Cook. All that mattered was that the Artifact was here and it was lethal. And he could either approach it and find a way to survive, or let the crowd stone him to death.

Gravity, he reminded himself. It increased gravity. The closer you got to it, the heavier you got. And you couldn't stay away or the crowd would pelt you with rocks.

So you had to move closer, which meant you had to get heavier. Which meant that he might last a little longer than Cook had, but sooner or later he, too, would be crushed by his own weight.

He was only a little more than halfway down to the lower floor, and already he could feel his weight increase. It seemed he was carrying an extra seventy-five pounds.

Miller looked down. He was about six feet above the ground now, normally not much of a drop. But if he jumped down at this weight, he might sprain an ankle, or even break one. He carefully moved farther down, until he was only a few feet above the floor. Then he stepped off the wall. His weight had increased again. It was an effort just to turn and take a step away from the wall.

The wall. The lead in the wall acted as a shield . . .

Stupid thought. He couldn't break off a piece of wall, couldn't get behind it, couldn't even stay close to it or he'd be stoned to death.

Think! There has to be a way.

But if so, there was no evidence that anyone else had ever found it. How could he hope to succeed where hundreds, perhaps thousands, of others had failed? What did he think made him special?

As if it was a voice answering a direct question, Miller remembered Cook saying, *Miller has one chance in seven of survival.*

One chance in seven. Not great odds, but at least they were odds. It said he could do it. He could beat this thing, if only Cook had been telling the truth. Or—what was the other thing Cook had said? *If story is truth, you have chance . . .*

So why not assume it was true? If it wasn't, he was dead. If he believed in what Cook said, he had a chance. A documented, predetermined chance.

Believe, then, Miller told himself. Everything Cook had said about the Artifact was the truth. It was a device of unknown origin that could alter time and space. Cook had been sent from the future to locate it, and he, Tony Miller, had been chosen to save the thing from Cook's enemies because he could do it. Computer simulations gave him a one in seven chance of success.

Simple. Believable. More than enough to pin his hope of survival on.

Sure.

But it was what he had. And as the villagers began to sound unhappy with his lack of movement, he took a deep breath—how many more of those did he have left?—and stepped forward.

He began a slow shuffle in the same arc Cook had tried, not getting closer to the Artifact, but at least moving so the rocks would not come raining down upon him. Moving his feet just enough, shuffling forward as his brain whirled.

Cook knew, he told himself. *Cook was from the future. Cook knew.*

But what had Cook been able to do with his knowledge that was any different from all the others who'd died here? Cook's body was right there, lying next to the weird panel, dead like all the others.

He'd died trying to reach the panel.

Cook knew.

The panel.

The panel!

13

CHAPTER

Miller began to move toward the rectangle of strange material. He knew now that he had to reach it if he hoped to survive. That was what Cook had been trying to tell him, and he'd been reaching out for the panel when he died. It was the key to survival. Miller was not sure why, but he knew he was right.

He slid his feet forward, working as hard as he ever had just to keep going without pitching onto his hands and knees. He was only ten feet or so closer to the Artifact, but the difference was overwhelming. His heart was pounding like he was sprinting at the end of a marathon, and his lungs felt ready to explode. He was forced into a kind of hunched-over shuffle and knew that with another significant increase in gravity he might not be able to stand any longer.

He shuffled. Slowly, the pressure built along his spine, down his legs. He felt light-headed. His feet were killing him, and he thought how dumb that sounded. *I'm about to be killed by a gravity field, generated by a—a whatever—and I'm thinking how my feet hurt*, he thought. *I need my head examined.* For some reason that seemed funny, and he almost giggled out loud. *Feet hurt? Have your head examined!*

He shook off the thought. He needed all the concentration he could muster just to keep his feet moving. He was closer now to the Artifact, and his knees buckled with every step.

He was closer to the panel, too. Miller could plainly see the rectangle of strange material now. He'd seen something like it before, not too long ago . . . When? He knew it was important, but with the crowd yelling and pounding, his head throbbing and his legs about to crumple under him, it was almost impossible to think. He took another step closer to the rectangle—and unfortunately, another step closer to the Artifact.

Miller went down. He caught most of the force of his fall—a shocking force, as if he had fallen from thirty feet in the air—on his hands. But his arms crumpled, too, and he pitched onto his face as the crowd roared.

Slowly, he pushed himself up onto his hands and knees. His vision blurred for a moment and he wiped at his forehead: blood. The fall had opened a large cut across his brow and the blood was pouring into his eyes. He tried to wipe it away, and succeeded, at least for now.

In addition, his left wrist felt badly sprained, and his knees, now supporting a body weight that must be close to five hundred pounds, would not take much more. His lungs were pumping so hard and so fast that he could feel the tendons between his ribs knotting up, stretched to their breaking point.

But none of that mattered. Not now. Because Miller

had seen something as he pitched forward onto his face, seen something on that chunk of odd material just before he toppled over.

A logo.

A stylized DNA molecule, with three glowing strands instead of the normal two.

Now he remembered where he'd seen something like the material of the rectangle before: on the crashed spaceship that Cook said had brought the Artifact to this island.

And now he knew why Cook had almost literally given his life to make him aware of the material:

The sheets of it scattered around the floor of the volcano must have been part of the packing case the Artifact had traveled in. Which meant that whatever the Artifact was radiating, it couldn't get through the material.

It would shield him. Save his life. Get him out of here.

Miller moved toward the rectangle.

As he did, the crowd began to growl. It was clear now that he was headed for the rectangle and not toward the Artifact, like he was supposed to do.

The villagers did not like it. It was not just that they would be cheated of their spectacle; Miller knew it was usual in Polynesia to believe that an improperly performed ritual or sacrifice was worse than none at all. They were half afraid that the gods would be furious if he did the wrong thing, that it would be disastrous: the crops might fail, the volcano might once again erupt.

The rocks began to fly.

There was absolutely nothing Miller could do about it except keep crawling forward. On his hands and knees, under three times his normal weight, he could no more dodge the rocks than fly. With his head low and all his concentration on reaching the rectangle, he couldn't even see them coming. He just had to hope he stayed lucky.

He paused for just a second to lift his head and look at the panel, now only fifteen feet ahead. He could make it. He *would* make it. He took a deep, cleansing breath and tried to slow the awful violence of his heartbeat.

A rock crashed to the ground next to him. It was not a large rock, but with the tripled gravity, it smashed itself to powder as though it weighed a ton. Several more fell, inching closer to him. A spear clattered down, closest of all, the shaft shattering on impact. Without looking, Miller knew it had been thrown by Pirate. He began to move again, crawling as fast as he could. It wasn't fast, but it made it that much harder for the villagers to hit him. And with Pirate actively trying to kill him, speed had become more important than stamina.

Ten feet. Only ten feet to go. Then five. Then—
AAAaaaaahhhh . . . !
Pain ripped through the calf of his right leg and Miller collapsed face first onto the stone floor. Numbly, panting with exertion and the incredible pain, he fumbled a hand back to feel his leg. On the floor by his thigh he felt a broken wooden shaft of some kind and he dragged it in front of his face. It was a split spear shaft.

Thinking hard through the red mist of agony, Miller pieced it together: the rest of the spear was in his leg. It was causing the pain. He closed his eyes, tried to clear his mind. Then he took a deep breath and pushed himself upward. It took all his strength, and halfway up he nearly passed out when he scraped the piece of spear still in his leg against the ground. The pain was worse than when the spear had entered his leg, but he held on and continued to push himself up until he made it to a sitting position.

The broken wooden shaft stuck out of the back side of his calf. The bronze spear head, flattened from impact with the ground, was half in and half out of the other side of his leg. The spear had traveled through the fleshy part of the calf muscle, missing both bone and major artery.

But if somebody had wanted to design a leg wound that would cause maximum pain and disability without death or permanent damage, they could not have done better than what the spear had accomplished. The phrase "Just a flesh wound" popped into Miller's head. It would heal in a few weeks with no lasting damage—but first he had to survive the next five minutes.

From his sitting position he leaned forward and began to crawl again. He could do it, just barely, by dragging the wounded leg, taking the weight on the knee. Slower—but he was almost there.

The crowd noise rose to a pitch where the sound had a physical impact. Miller could feel it throbbing in his wounded calf and torn forehead as he dragged his body forward.

Five feet, three feet, two . . . he reached a hand out to touch the rectangle and pitched forward onto his face again, falling onto the smooth and odd coolness of the material. He felt it suck the warmth from his face, and he didn't like the feeling.

Once again he pushed himself to a sitting position with unbelievable difficulty. For a moment he just stared. He'd made it. He was touching the panel, the thing that would save his life, get him out of here. It was all going to be all right again.

Miller raised an incredibly heavy hand to his head. It was throbbing, with the gravity and with the crowd noise. His sight dimmed and he thought he was going to black out. His heartbeat had settled into a steady thrum; it was pounding so fast he could hardly hear the individual beats. He heard the crowd, as though at a great distance, snarling and yelling their displeasure. *But why aren't they cheering?* he thought. *I made it, didn't I? I'm here at the panel. I'm going to make it out of here—*

A rock smashed down beside him. The tip of it just grazed his hand where he was leaning on it, and he felt the little finger break. A chip of rock flew off and lanced into his arm just above the wrist. The sudden double blast of pain brought him back from the edge of unconsciousness.

Miller looked up. Above him, on the ledge, the crowd leaned forward, pouring fury and rocks down on him. The Chief stood rigidly, watching him like some old stone carving, and Miller could see the great stone heads in the set of her features.

He looked to his right and again locked eyes with Pirate. The warrior stood on the lip of the ledge, glaring down at him with his teeth bared, looking almost like he wanted to jump down onto the floor and challenge him.

Let him come, Miller thought, grimly amused. As if anybody would willingly climb down here onto the killing floor.

The rocks were coming closer, and Miller knew it was now or never. As much as he could with his head pounding and his ribs aching as if about to split open, he took a deep tai chi breath, centering himself, bringing his focus back to the task at hand. He felt the blood pouring off his forehead, off his arm and his leg. With his increased heartbeat it was squirting out of him much faster than it normally would. He knew he didn't have much time.

It didn't matter. He didn't need much time. He grabbed the edge of the panel and lifted. It was light, even here in the triple gravity. He slid it sideways, its edge dragging along the floor, until it stood between him and the Artifact.

Instantly, he felt the difference. It was as if he'd been lying under a boulder that was now rolled off him. His heart slowed, his breathing was easier, and he quickly gasped in several deep, sweet breaths.

The taste of the air nearly made him drunk. It seemed like the best air he'd ever breathed. But he didn't have the luxury of sitting still to enjoy it.

Holding the panel firmly with both hands, Miller stood up.

The crowd fell silent.

Miller was not in the least theatrical. Even his lectures back at Berkeley were known for being a bit dry. But as he stood, in this place where no one had ever stood before, he could not help a small dramatic gesture. Holding the panel firmly between the Artifact and himself with one hand, he slowly turned to look from one end of the crowd to the other.

They stared back at him with dumbstruck awe. Not one of them—not the Chief nor any of her Elders, not Pirate, none of them—could look at him and speak. In the memory of their people, no one had ever seen what Miller was now doing. No one had ever hinted that it was even possible.

Miller felt savage triumph as he watched them. He was surprised at the power and sweetness of the feeling, and he took a moment to let it wash over him. Then he turned deliberately away from the villagers and faced the Artifact.

He could not resist looking at the thing. He was so close to it now, and standing on his feet gave him a much better look. But to see it he had to take his head out of the shelter of the panel, and the resulting blast of pain nearly sent him to his knees again.

Miller crouched behind the rectangle and began to slide forward, dragging the panel along the floor, covering as much of his body as he could. The posture was difficult, straining his injured leg almost to the limit, but it was better by far than exposure to the Artifact.

In total silence he moved forward until he felt the edge of the panel thump against the Artifact. He carefully leaned the rectangle against it and stood up, looking around. The villagers still seemed unable to move or speak. Miller took advantage and quickly limped around the floor, gathering the other panels of the strange material and carrying them back to the Artifact. He discovered that they slid together, interlocking to indeed become what he'd assumed was the packing case that must originally have contained the Artifact when it was brought here.

Miller rapidly fit the pieces together, and in a few moments the Artifact was once again crated, harmless. There was no way he could see to lock the panels into place, but they fit snugly, and he would worry about securing them later. When it was done, he turned again to face the Chief.

For a moment the old woman stared back at him.

Then she nodded once and slowly, carefully, went down on her knees and bowed to him.

Like a row of dominoes tumbling over, the entire crowd of villagers followed suit. They all fell to their knees and bowed to Miller with stunned reverence.

All but one.

Pirate remained standing, clenching and unclenching his fists, teeth bared, chest heaving with barely controlled rage. In the sudden quiet of the large room, Miller thought he could hear the man's breath whistling in and out.

Pirate locked eyes with Miller.

Miller glared back.

He deliberately challenged the bad-tempered villager, trying with his stare to rub the man's nose into it. Pirate had been nothing but mean-tempered and hostile, working overtime to make him die, and die miserably. And now he'd lost. Miller was a god now, and there was nothing Pirate could do about it. Nothing at all.

But nobody told Pirate he was helpless. With a last hissing breath, he grabbed up a spear, gave a war cry, and jumped down onto the floor of the volcano.

And then, without pausing, he charged Miller.

CHAPTER

Miller had only a moment to brace himself and then Pirate was on him, charging maniacally forward with the spear leveled. Miller just managed to push the spear aside before it would have impaled him through the chest, and then he took the full force of Pirate's body. His wounded leg crumpled under the other's furious charge, and he was down, on his back, struggling to keep Pirate off him. Pirate lunged again with the spear, and Miller barely managed to roll away. With all his strength he brought his good leg around and swept Pirate's legs out from under him.

Pirate fell. The spear clattered away to the side. Miller struggled to stand and take advantage, but he was too slow. Pirate was up again, on the balls of his feet, ready. Miller backed off a step.

Pirate jumped at him, and Miller launched a kick at his stomach. Pirate pushed it aside and threw a fist at Miller's head. If Miller had not rolled the other way, the fist would have landed hard; it still grazed him and made his ears ring.

Then Pirate was directly in front of him, launching a salvo of punches. Miller blocked and ducked, landed one of his own to the center of his opponent's stomach and took one on the arm that numbed his elbow.

For a moment it was a fairly even contest, but Pirate was fresh and Miller had just been through a hellish ordeal and had no reserves of energy. He could feel his strength melting away. He was barely able to lift his arms to defend himself. Pirate recognized Miller's condition and backed him up step by step, until Miller came up against the case shielding the Artifact.

Exhausted and blocked, Miller was trapped, and they both knew it. All Pirate had to do was step in and finish it. Instead, he paused a moment to gloat, regarding Miller with a wolfish smile of victory.

And in that moment, Miller stepped to one side and lifted the panel of the Artifact's packing case.

Pirate was hurled to the floor. He looked like he'd been hit by an invisible piano dropped from fifty stories up. Crouched behind the other protective panels, Miller watched as Pirate's body slowly spread out across the floor under the increased weight. No one had ever been this close, only one step away from the Artifact, and as its full power was unleashed on Pirate, he had no more chance than a snowflake in a blast furnace.

Miller watched with growing horror as Pirate's body puddled outward, taking up twice its normal space as it flattened, spread, and turned to a red paste. Pirate could only gasp once, gurgle, and die as his face was sucked into the spreading red pool along with the rest of his body. His bones collapsed, and the remains were no more than a quarter of an inch thick.

Miller slid the panel back into place.

He was still horrified at the gelatinous mess before him that had been a man a minute ago. True, the man had repeatedly tried to kill him, but he'd been a man nonetheless, and Miller was no murderer. He looked away.

Above him on the ledge the conch trumpet sounded. Miller looked up to the Chief. She raised her arms, the right one holding the red-feathered spear, and waved the spear three times across the silent crowd. Then she very carefully broke it over her knee and began scattering handfuls of the red feathers as she ripped them off the broken shaft.

Miller limped slowly over to Cook's body. It was not liquefied as Pirate's was, since it was much farther back from the Artifact. But it was flattened and badly beat up. Between the pounding Cook had taken from increased gravity and from the rocks, and from being taken over by whatever the strange being from the future had been, his remains would have called for a closed casket service.

But there was no casket, and in any case Miller needed to look at his friend's face to accept what had happened. So he stood and looked down at what was left of Dr. Jay Cook.

Oddly, the face now looked more like his friend than it had since they left Runa Puake Island. There was some peace showing on Cook's face now, some sense of quiet. Maybe not much, but more than Cook had had when they arrived here.

Miller buried Cook on the beach, facing northeast,

back toward Berkeley. It was a silly, sentimental gesture, one that would probably have embarrassed his friend. Cook had had no particular attachment to Berkeley; to him it was just the first place to have the good sense to offer him tenure.

Miller was just as surprised by his action. When he was done pushing the dirt over Cook's body, he stood for a moment, just looking down. He didn't pray, although he felt an odd urge to say *something*. He just stood for a moment, feeling foolish, then turned away and walked back to the village.

The Chief and her Elders were sitting in a circle in the center of the village. They were not talking, and they didn't seem to be doing anything beyond simply sitting.

Around them, throughout the village, the rest of the people were just sitting, too; or lying down with their faces covered, or leaning against the doorways to their huts. The whole village seemed to be in a state of profound shock.

It occurred to Miller that they probably were. He had killed their god, and they knew of no other. The Artifact had been the anchor of their existence, the central provable fact in their system of belief, and he'd taken away its power.

What would they believe in now?

Miller walked slowly to the center of the village. All eyes followed him; not with hostility or anger, but not with joy, either. No one could say how he should be treated; there had never been anyone like him before. He was the god-slayer, and no one knew whether he was just a lucky man or if he might be a god himself.

Miller stood next to the Chief. She looked up, then away. He sat down next to her. She still said nothing, and between his exhaustion and the fact that he was still struggling with the dialect, Miller had nothing to say, either.

The Chief pulled a twig from a mound of dirt and began to scratch at the ground idly. *"Amota, Ku,"* she said. *Goodbye, Ku*.

It was true, then. They didn't know what to do about their dead god. Of course, he was not sorry that he'd killed Ku; it had been Ku or him. But Miller did feel some responsibility for the people, and could not leave them in this state. Other cultures had sickened and died out completely under less strain. And this particular culture had already strayed so far from the Polynesian norm that it would be impossible to nudge it back again.

But what to do? The logical course was to replace the fallen god with whatever had vanquished it. In this case, that meant the Great God Miller. Stone statues in his image. Blushing virgins dragged naked before him. Offerings of fruit, fish, shells piled high in front of him. Universal adoration and reverence. The thought made him want to puke.

Besides, he couldn't hang out and play god the rest of his life. He had to get off this island, get back to Berkeley—and publish! My God, the things he'd discovered, on Runa Puake as well as on this island. His career was absolutely *made* when he published all this.

Not just the sociological stuff, but the Artifact. What was it? How did it work? All he knew was that it was incredibly powerful, and it stood the laws of physics on their ears. If he could get it studied properly, in a lab, what might they learn? What incredible benefits for mankind might be locked up in the thing?

It would not just make his reputation, it would give some meaning to Cook's horrible death, make his name last as co-discoverer. And anyway, he'd promised Cook, or whoever Cook had been, that he'd see the Artifact to safety. Whether to the safety of an agent from the future at the airport in Tahiti, or the Physics Lab at Berkeley, remained to be seen.

He had to leave, as soon as possible, and get back to civilization. But he could not leave the island to rot away in despair. What if they followed the path of Easter Island and Runa Puake, and literally ate themselves out of existence? If he could stop it, he must.

So how did he give these people something to replace what he'd taken?

Miller got up and walked along the beach, still limping on his injured leg. He waded out waist deep, letting the saltwater soak through his wounds. It stung at first, but it cleaned them, and soon began to soothe the pain.

He waded back to shore, still turning over the problem. His plane was pulled up safely where he'd left it, and he sat in the shade of the wing.

All right, Miller, he said to himself, *this is a perfect final exam question. Given the previous culture and how it died, what can replace it without killing this microsociety?*

An hour later night was falling, and he had his answer. The details had to be worked out, but the rough outline would work.

Miller searched the nearby forest and found wood. He dragged it down to the beach, his wounds throbbing. He was exhausted and he hurt like hell all over, but this had to be done, and done tonight. Using a cup full of gasoline to start the blaze, he soon got a roaring bonfire going on the beach.

He took an empty five gallon gas can from the storage area of the plane and, sitting cross-legged beside the fire, began to drum on it. He chanted all the snatches of Shakespeare he could remember, all the old poems ("Oh, once there was an elefunk who tried to use the telefunk"—it sounded surprisingly impressive), and then songs, nursery rhymes, pages from his doctoral dissertation—anything at all he could think of to keep an imposing rhythm going.

After a while he heard footsteps and glanced up at the path. A young boy stood there, watching him curiously. Miller thumped extra hard, told the boy, "Tomorrow and tomorrow and tomorrow, creeps in this petty pace from day to day. And all our yesterdays have lighted fools the way to dusty death . . ." It sounded solemn, even scary—even to Miller.

The boy took off, running as fast as he could back to the village.

The Chief came back first, then the Elders. Within half an hour they were all there, watching him, none daring to approach him, but none wanting to miss anything, either.

Miller poured it on. He let the words burble out of him in great streams of consciousness, building them to a fever pitch just as the fire began to die down to the coals. And when he judged the time was right—partly because he couldn't think of anything else to say—he stood slowly and carefully, raising his arms to the heavens, his back to the people from the village.

Reaching carefully to the waistband of his shorts, concealing his movements from the villagers, he pulled his flare gun, taken from the plane's stores, and fired it into the air.

He had meant the flare gun to be a dramatic touch, something to make it look like he was communicating with the gods. Just a little parlor trick to impress people who had never seen anything like it before.

The response was all he could have wished for. As the flare arced out over the water and up into the sky in a beautiful red streak, the people murmured and stepped nervously away from him. A few fell to their knees as if to worship him.

Miller tucked the pistol back into his shorts—and quickly changed his mind; it was hot enough to raise blisters. Instead he dropped it by his feet and kicked sand over it. Then he turned to face the Chief.

In a few hours, using his sparse knowledge of their dialect and a stick to trace ideas in the sand, Miller outlined the new "religion." It was simple, and as similar to the old one as he could make it.

The basic idea was that he, as a representative of the gods, promised that one day Ku would return. Until then, the people must show that they were worthy by keeping to his ways. And they must, in addition, welcome all strangers with hospitality, because one day one of the new arrivals would be Ku, coming back in disguise to test them.

In the meantime, he told the Chief, he had to take the old Ku back to the land of the gods, so all his brothers and sisters could make him well again.

The Chief was impressed. Miller could not be sure whether she believed him or not, but the old girl was politician enough to recognize a way out of a major crisis when she saw one, and she quickly agreed to all that Miller said and then announced it to the people.

Their culture had changed, but the people were still

Polynesian. They adapted to change quickly—and they marked all events of major importance the same way. Within a half hour of the Chief's announcement, a major party was under way around the bonfire on the beach.

Miller knew he had to stay for a while, just to be politic. And out of common politeness he had to drink a certain amount of the native beer, too. It was stronger than he'd assumed it would be. A lot stronger. And they kept passing him big bowls of the stuff, and he had to take a sip each time; it would have been rude not to.

When the time came that he knew he had to lie down or pass out on the beach, he found that his legs were no longer working properly. Probably from the strain, the injuries—he really hadn't had that much beer, not that much at all.

And because the natives were such a polite bunch, really, underneath all that sacrificing stuff, they cheerfully helped him up the path to the village. Very nice of them, really. And they seemed to be having so much fun helping, he let them think he really needed their help. It was really just the leg wound, of course. He could walk if he wanted to. He was fine. Never felt better. But he hated to disappoint them by being able to walk. Let them help, God bless 'em all.

They took him to a hut he thought he recognized—he *did* recognize it. It was Pirate's hut. Sure, the old thing about when you kill somebody you get all their stuff. He could use it to sleep in, very nice place really. Damned nice of them.

His eyes felt a little dry and sticky, probably from the heat of the bonfire. He closed them for just a second to get them wet again. It felt good. Very good. Cool, peaceful, pleasant. And it stopped the awful spinning Pirate's hut was doing.

When he opened his eyes again, the villagers were gone. There was no sound in the hut, and Miller assumed he was alone. Far away he could hear the noises of the dying party, down on the beach. The cool night breeze was blowing across him. It felt wonderful, riffling across his bare skin . . .

Bare skin?

But he had been dressed when he flopped down here, just a minute ago. What had happened to his pants, his shirt?

Miller sat up and looked around the room. It wasn't the best idea he'd ever had, since the room began to spin again. He closed his eyes, and a cool hand pressed against his forehead.

"*Pala'aka batow,*" the soft and musical voice said. *Lie down.*

Miller blasted his eyes open. It hurt. He was looking into the gently amused eyes of Yuki, who was trying to push him softly back down onto the sleeping mat.

Miller's first thought when he saw her was, *My God, but I'm naked.*

His second thought was, *My God, so is she.*

He let Yuki push him back down.

15

CHAPTER

He was having a dream. It was a good dream, and he didn't want to wake up from it until he saw how it turned out. But between the bright sunlight kicking at his eyelids, and the fact that some kind of fragrant weight had caused his arm to go to sleep, he finally opened his eyes.

And the funny thing was, the fragrant weight on his arm was Yuki, naked and in his arms, and that had been the dream, too.

It really happened, he thought. *All of it—even this.*

He slid a hand lightly down her back. It was like rubbing silk. She sighed and then murmured softly, arching against him. He let his hand rest on her buttocks, not wanting to wake her, not sure how she would be in the light of day.

But as he looked at her, he became aware that her eyes were open, looking into his. *"Patao . . . ?"* she murmured. *Again?*

"Patao," Miller agreed.

It was a week before Miller was ready to go. He told himself that he needed the time to heal after the ordeal in the volcano. But he was also more than half in love with Yuki, although he could not admit it to himself. He tried to picture her married to him, at a faculty wives' cocktail party in Berkeley, and the image frightened him.

He could teach her to dress, and wear makeup, and talk about books and music and the other wives, but who would she be then? Not Yuki, the independent, sensual woman he knew now. Her attitudes and outlook could not survive in "civilization."

She belongs here, he decided. *And I do not.*

And so he made himself and his plane ready. Daily, he checked the radio in the plane for a weather forecast, but either there was still damage from the tsunami or he was too far away. Perhaps there was some fringe effect from the Artifact. In any case, he got nothing but static.

So he prepared the best he could without the radio, and on a day as perfect as all the others, he was done. The plane was loaded, the gas tanks were topped off, he had food and had refilled the water bottles from the island's spring.

Last of all was the Artifact. Miller did not want to go anywhere near the volcano floor, with its bodies and bad memories. But he had to take the Artifact with him, and it was in the volcano. He made himself go back along the trail, down the tunnel and onto the ledge.

From above the floor it looked much the same. The hundreds of years of bones were still scattered like a leaf pile blown by a strong wind. *Maybe I'll come back*, he thought. *We could learn a lot from those bones.*

Perhaps the people who brought the Artifact here—

the GECOs, was that right?—maybe their bones were here, too. What advances could the biotech people make from studying future DNA?

Right now he left them alone. He still felt like he was too close to being one more pile of the bones himself, and he had no wish to touch them or disturb them in any way.

Miller climbed down onto the floor and crossed over to the packing case containing the Artifact. He'd brought a roll of duct tape from the plane and used to it secure the box. He hefted it. It was surprisingly heavy for containing something only twice the size of a basketball. It easily weighed over a hundred pounds.

It would have been hard to move it out of the volcano and down to the beach under the best of circumstances. With a bad leg, it was a murderous trip. Miller did not want any of the villagers to help him—he would have preferred that they didn't know what he was doing—and so he had to do it himself. He was drenched with sweat and panting when he finally got the crate into the plane and tied it down.

He cross-braced the crate and tied it carefully into the center of the plane's cargo area, making sure it was secure. When he was done, he plunged into the surf and just floated for a while, letting the water soak out the aches and the fatigue. He was ready to go. He should leave soon, in the morning, get out of here and back to the world. He knew that.

But he waited one more day for no reason at all. It was hard to leave such a beautiful place—and Yuki.

And that night, after they made love one last time, he had a nightmare.

In his dream he heard the rumble of thunder and a

voice crackled at him, "Now do they come. Go back."
And then the Bodhis dropped on him from the clouds.
They were tall, wispy-thin figures draped in white,
whipping toward him like a herd of banshees, and he
could not flee them because wherever he turned they
were already there. When he sat in a chair to rest, the
chair wrapped around his arms and turned into a Bodhi.
And when he opened a door to run, the door metamor-
phosed into a Bodhi, and then the doorstep, too, and
they were all over him, surrounding him, shaking him
hard—

"Miller!" Yuki said. She had learned his name and a
few other English words, as he had learned more of their
dialect. "Miller!" she repeated, shaking him and then
slapping his face.

He opened his eyes to her face, the hair cascading
off her head and framing her eyes and her sharp, high
cheekbones. She was so beautiful that for a moment he
forgot the nightmare and just stared at her. She slapped
him again.

"Okay," he said, taking her hand. "Okay." She
looked at him with concern for a moment, then
shrugged and curled up against him again.

He could not get back to sleep. The dream had both-
ered him, and he was sure it was more than just a random
collection of dream images. It was his subconscious
reminding him that he was in danger.

He hadn't seriously considered the threat Cook had
warned him about. He'd been too busy recovering,
relaxing, enjoying the fact that he was alive. Besides, at
this point it was difficult to accept the reality of all that
Cook had told him. He had to remember that, logically
speaking, a glowing orb with extraordinary powers—

which might be at least partly hallucinatory—did not actually imply two warring cultures from the future, either one willing to do anything to secure the Artifact. These things didn't happen, especially not with Tony Miller, Ph.D., in the middle of it all.

But the Artifact was real. It was all that Cook had told him it would be, and more. Was he being foolish to accept the Artifact and not the warning that went with it? It existed; was it really any more of a stretch to believe the rest? And if the rest was true—what terrible danger was he in? What awful risk was he exposing Yuki to, and the other islanders, by staying here?

By morning he'd made up his mind. He knew he had to go. He wasn't completely convinced, but again it made more sense to *act* like he was. If there was a chance that the Bodhis were real—and the Artifact said there was a chance—then he had to go before they could find him.

Dawn came with Miller still wide-awake. He was tired, and oddly rattled by the dream. He was not in the best shape for a long plane flight, but he was determined to go today. By his reckoning, he was about five hours from Tahiti. He should make that easily, well before dark, and with plenty of fuel to spare.

He shared a last breakfast with Yuki—fresh fruit, some of the native bread, springwater—and headed for the beach. She followed him down to the plane, and when they got there, Miller was surprised to see that what looked like the entire village had turned out to see him off.

The Chief stepped forward, her arms raised. She came to Miller and embraced him warmly. Each of the Elders followed and imitated her.

Then Yuki stepped up to him and kissed him passionately while the villagers cheered and hooted. She stepped back, whispered, *"Amota,* Miller," and leaned in again to drop a necklace over his head.

Miller looked at it. The necklace was beautiful, made of polished hardwood, mother of pearl, and a handful of the precious red feathers. Dangling from the center, woven into a small rope net, was a large ball bearing, probably from a ship's engine, which Miller realized was meant to represent the Artifact.

He caught Yuki's eyes and raised the necklace to his lips. Then he held her one last time, giving her back a kiss as passionate as the one she'd given him.

And then he climbed into his plane and started the engine. With the Artifact secured within its packing case, there was no trouble. The engine warmed up with a smooth and steady purr. When it was ready and Miller had finished his preflight checklist, he released the brake and rolled the plane into the water.

He taxied the plane out to the edge of the lagoon and turned back toward the beach. The wind was coming straight off the shore, and there was plenty of room to take off, so he gunned the engine and pointed the nose right back at the beach.

For safety's sake he aimed to the right of the knot of villagers there to see him off, and as he banked the plane, he could see them off to the side, a large cluster of people jumping up and down and waving, and, standing quietly to one side, the slim figure of Yuki, looking up at him without moving as he passed overhead.

The image stayed with him most of the way to Tahiti. He was surprised and disturbed to discover what the native girl had come to mean to him. He tried to talk himself out of it. They were from two totally different worlds. Hell, they didn't even speak the same language. Completely unsuited to each other.

But instead he kept remembering the light in her eyes, the unbelievable silkiness of her skin, the softness of her smile, which hid the strength of her personality. And he wondered if he'd been stupid to leave her behind.

But as he approached Tahiti he made an effort to put Yuki and her island out of his mind. The strange-looking crate in the cargo space behind him was proof enough that he had other things to think about, and he ordered his mind to concentrate on them.

He would land and try to find Cook's contact at the airport. Or would he? The urge to keep the Artifact for study was overwhelming. Miller was an academic, after all, and the thing in the crate was a unique object, so completely singular that nothing even close to it had ever been seen anywhere, as far as he knew.

Could he give it up, on the vague instructions of somebody who was either deranged or visiting from the future, when so much good could come of studying it?

He thought, too, of his nightmare of pursuit by Cook's enemies, the Bodhis. He'd expected them to try to stop him before now—how, he didn't know, but he hadn't expected the completely uneventful flight he was now completing. If they hadn't come after him by now, they probably weren't coming.

Maybe it's all a bunch of crap, Miller thought. *No Bodhis, no GECOs—just this Artifact.*

Because if they hadn't come after him yet, it didn't make sense that they would hit him in a populated area like Tahiti. And he could now see the big island ahead of him on the horizon.

He'd made it. He was safe from all the devils, imaginary or real, who he had been told would pursue him. They hadn't. He would land in Tahiti in ten minutes, and that was the end of it.

He tried the radio one more time: still nothing but static. It didn't matter. He could practically see the airport already. He reached to turn off the radio—

Time froze.

The feel of the plane's controls in his other hand was like crust on lemon pudding and the radio crackled like jagged crystals.

"Now do they come. Go back," the radio said.

Exactly what he'd heard in his dream. Word for word.

"Quickly," the radio said.

And then time returned to normal. Miller finished the motion of turning off the radio and looked around him. Everything was normal. The light of a beautiful afternoon streamed in, the shore of Tahiti was ahead.

So what had just happened? What was The Voice, and how had it had repeated what he'd heard in his dream?

"The Artifact," he said to himself. That must be it. Residual hallucination from the Artifact. It was just a last twitch, one small tendril of whatever it did. And it didn't matter, truly. Soon he would be on the ground and the thing would be out of his hands. He felt a small bubble of elation rise up inside him and he smiled.

"Ha!" Miller said aloud. "Home free!"

That's when the storm came up out of nowhere.

16

CHAPTER

Directly ahead, between Miller and the island of Tahiti, the air shimmered. The water below went dead flat and turned a dull gray-green. The shimmering turned to wavering shadows, then wispy threads of cloud, and in less than a minute a huge black thunderhead boiled toward him.

Out of nowhere, literally out of a clear blue sky.

Within moments it was a vast, wild storm, roiling with huge thunderclouds, crackling with massive lightning and deafening thunder. And in spite of the fact that Miller's instruments told him the wind was behind the plane, the storm was charging straight at him, at a speed approaching seventy miles per hour.

"Damn it," he muttered, knowing exactly what it meant.

They had found him.

He didn't even have time to think about what that might imply before the storm was on him, all around him, tossing him like a feather through the raging currents of wind and enormous cumulonimbus clouds.

Miller tried to bank around the storm, sneak out to the left and head for the airport from the side. But the storm was either too quick or too massive. Perhaps both. In any case, it snatched at his plane and threw him straight down. He fought the controls and just barely escaped crashing into the ocean.

At this level the rain was beating down so hard he couldn't see more than twenty feet ahead—but because of the smashing impact of the rain, the wind was less.

Miller gambled. He knew what the topography looked like ahead, and his little plane was far better equipped to deal with heavy rain than with hurricane force winds, thunder and lightning.

He decided to fly blind, by instrument, no more than ten feet above the highest wave crests in the ocean below him. He was still buffeted by wind, but the rain beat down the worst of it, and it was not as severe at this low altitude as in the clouds above. He had a chance here.

If the storm stayed like this, he could make it to the coast of Tahiti. After that—well, he would see. But if he could make it to the coast, he would survive, even if it meant ditching, splashing down into the shallow water off the beach and walking in. He would survive.

Then, miraculously, he was out of the storm, and he saw the beach, no more than a mile ahead. The sun was shining and people were playing on the sand, swimming in the lagoon. Having the vacation of their lives, with no thunderstorm raging around them.

Miller pulled back on the yoke and began to climb. If the storm had let him go, he would make the airport, make a safe landing and preserve the Artifact.

He'd made it up to about fifteen hundred feet when

the storm came back. This time it did not tease him with windblown games of toss-the-plane, and it did not slap him with rain.

This time the storm came out shooting the big guns.

CRA-ACK!

A bolt of lightning snarled through the air inches from the wing tip. Miller jerked the plane away from it.

CRA-ACK!

Another bolt, on the other side now. Miller pulled the plane away, back to his original course.

CRA-ACK!

Again, on the same side as the first.

Miller was being herded. The storm was pushing him wherever it wanted him to go.

Just to experiment with that idea, he turned the plane left.

CRA-ACK KA-BLAAMM!

Definitely a bad idea.

Lightning smashed into the wing, racing down the radio antenna and into the instruments. Blue flame arced out onto Miller's hands.

"AAaahh!" he bellowed, letting go of the controls for just a moment. In that instant, the wind got under the plane's tail and pushed it into a dive.

Miller grabbed the smoldering controls and tried to pull the plane out of its downward plunge. More powerful gusts of wind pounded the plane from side to side and he could feel the fuselage twisting in ways it was not meant to do.

Below him he saw the control tower of the airport. As he watched, several bright red vehicles raced out of a hangar and headed for the spot where his plane was pointed. The rescue crew. Good to know they were on the ball. He hoped he wouldn't need to find out just how good they really were.

With just a few hundred feet to go before impact, Miller began to pull out of the dive. The storm fought back, hitting him with furious cross winds. The fuselage twisted more—he could feel it in the controls, *see* it in the way the wall beside him moved—and he was sure something would give.

It did.

Just a second before he pulled out of the dive, he heard a loud *TWAANG!* behind him and the plane lurched to the left. At first he thought the rudder cable had broken—but the plane responded when he tried to straighten out and continue his climb. But behind him he heard another *TWAANG!* and now the plane lurched in the other direction.

Again he straightened out, and this time heard a ponderous sliding sound from behind. And as the lightning crackled around him in an all-out fireworks display, Miller realized what had happened.

The Artifact.

The Artifact had broken out of its tie-down. It was sliding around loose in the cargo area. And an object of that weight could crash right through the side of the plane if the craft were tossed around violently enough.

And it was.

As if it knew exactly what it was doing, the storm threw everything it had at Miller's plane. The huge gusts of wind tossed him up, down, left and right. With each crazy slide, he heard the crate behind him shift, then smash into the fuselage or bulkhead. It was just a matter of time before it broke through and fell to earth.

And then what? He didn't know if the Artifact

could be destroyed—but suppose it could be? Cook had said it was built to impose a logical order on time and space. If it was destroyed, what would happen? Nothing at all? Something unimaginable? Even Cook had been unable to guess.

The plane was plunging downward again, and Miller could no longer think about the Artifact. He was fighting for his life.

Just before the power dive was about to take him into the control tower below, a massive updraft grabbed the plane and flung it, hard and fast, straight up. And as the nose shifted to its skyward point, he heard the noise he'd been dreading all along.

BOOM-CRUNCH! The Artifact slid straight back to the tail section, probably the weakest area, and smashed the bulkhead. The plane was whipped by wind, and Miller fought to level off but was again thrown straight down—*CRASH!*—and then up again.

And this time, when the Artifact hit the back wall, there could be no doubt. With a crushing, splintering crash, it broke through the fuselage and was falling.

The plane tilted crazily, then leveled off without the weight of the Artifact. The storm blew out as if somebody had turned off a switch, and Miller again had control of the plane.

He turned in time to see the crate holding the Artifact. It was falling straight for the center of the landing field. Any second now . . .

Miller was holding his breath, eyes glued to the falling crate. What would happen?

And though he was braced for *something*, nothing could possibly have prepared him for what actually occurred.

The box fell toward the ground, and then it hit—

The lights went out.

In the dark there was nothing; no form, no sensation, only dark and the presence of Idea. And Idea grew, gathered itself, and—

The crate hit the ground and—

The sky was rusty brown, the land beneath him was the same color, and nothing lived here. Nothing could possibly live here, with the dim dead sun hanging so low and huge in the sky, and the horribly dry, rusty air cutting at Miller's throat and lungs, choking him, and—

The crate hit the ground, and—

KA-BAM! Miller's plane was tossed upward, outward, mingling with all the atoms that would ever be and—

Where the crate hit, the ground turned as bright as the sun. Enormous, hot waves of energy rippled outward, as if waves of water were racing away from a huge rock dropped into a lake. The energy waves rippled, spun through the spectrum in every possible color, gaining speed as they moved outward, until they were racing so fast they became invisible.

Suddenly, lightning bolts began to rain down on the Artifact, from the clear blue sky above. Dozens, hundreds, thousands of bolts of sheer energy smashing into the Artifact and the ground around it. Miller's hair stood straight out from his arms and legs as well as his head.

The plane bucked, twisted, and went dead.

Not just the engine this time, but everything; the instruments, the dash lights, everything.

A huge explosion from the Artifact rent the air and—

Reality flickered.

It was as if a veil had been whipped by wind and then split in half. Miller was staring down at the airport—but it was deserted. Weeds grew up through the tarmac and—

Flicker.

Lightning smashed into the Artifact and—

Flicker.

Miller was flying over a swamp. Something large lifted its head up to look at him, and then returned to feeding with no interest. With shock, Miller recognized it. It was a brontosaurus. *But that's not—*

Flicker.

Lightning smashed at the Artifact.

Flicker.

The red desert. Miller held his breath, hoping he would not be stuck here.

Flicker.

A crowd of naked people with bluish skin and feathered crests shaped like Mohawks stared up at him. He stared back, losing altitude now, and—

Flicker.

Lightning smashed at the Artifact.

Another of the huge explosions; more shock waves raced out, gaining speed until they vanished, and Miller was flicked through two dozen realities so rapidly he couldn't even see what they were. For a heartbeat each, he raced through bright light, darkness, tremendous weight, a numbing vacuum where he fought the panic of being unable to breathe; then bright colors, loud noises as if someone were spinning a radio dial through dozens of channels without pausing—

A three-dimensional, all-encompassing wave of color, sound, taste, and sensation raced across the field at Miller. He tasted lemons, rusted blueberry, the hot spark of cinnamon mixed with fire on his skin, and the sound of flutes; time stopped as the flavor of rich earth burst on his tongue wrapped in the sound of hundreds of great church bells and the feel of cold Vaseline on his skin—

FLICKER!

The runway was coming up at him, and instinctively, without time to think, Miller steered the plane carefully into a dead stick landing, coasting to a stop in the center of the field, with weeds growing up all around him.

For a very long time, he didn't move.

Didn't dare to.

He sat, waited for something to happen, waited for his heart to return to normal, for his breath to stop sounding like a dying old man wheezing and gasping for every breath, for the sweat to dry off on his palms.

He waited for even one small hint at where he was and what had just happened.

Nothing.

And finally, when he thought he could move without exploding, he unbuckled his seat belt and opened the door. He swung his legs out and dropped to the ground, amazed at how much it *hurt*, how every muscle seemed to be twanging, tight and aching.

He took a deep breath and looked around. There was no sign of the control tower—unless that heap of rubble over there . . . ? Miller stepped toward it, far enough to see that, if it *was* the control tower, it had been in ruins for many years. Weeds grew up through the debris, and a small tree was perched on the slope of the ruins.

He shook his head. Anyway, he was down. The storm was gone, there were no signs of more explosions or flickers—whatever they had been. He was on the ground, in one piece, and, for the moment at least, he was safe.

Which was probably more than could be said about the Artifact.

Reluctantly, Miller started to walk in the direction where he thought the crate had crashed to the ground. But was it even here? Or Now, or whatever/wherever he was? Perhaps he should start saying it the way Cook had, "herenow." Was the Artifact, or whatever might be left of it, herenow?

Clearly, he was in the future. The state of the airport told him that. It wouldn't have existed at all in the past, and it had been kept up properly in the present. Somehow, the Artifact had launched him into the future—a hundred years? two hundred? Impossible to say. He didn't have a clue what the Artifact could do, or why. Even Cook had been uncertain about that.

But reality still existed. It was all around him—a bird flitted past to the tree on the rubble mound. Insects buzzed, a breeze blew gently over his face. Whatever else might have happened, the Artifact had not destroyed everything, as Cook feared it might.

In fact, it was such a beautiful spring day that it was impossible to believe anything bad whatsoever had happened to reality—*herenow*, he reminded himself. So maybe the Artifact was perfectly all right. After all, what would it really take to harm a thing that powerful? There was no way to know—but surely it would take more than falling a few hundred feet from an airplane and getting hit by lightning.

He hoped he was right. If the Artifact was damaged—What had Cook said? "Time-space shattered." Whatever that meant, it clearly hadn't happened. "New reality or no reality," he'd said. Well, if this was the worst of the new reality, it would be all right.

But wait—hadn't there been something else? Something about a time it took before the effect took hold? He tried to remember, but when Cook told him, they'd been marching into the volcano to what he was sure was certain death, and some of the details weren't clear to him now. It had been, what; seventy-two hours? He thought that was right. Seventy-two hours before it all locked into place.

Miller checked his watch. Only ten minutes since he'd landed. It seemed like coming through that last strange storm had happened in another lifetime.

So, seventy-two hours from now he had to be somewhere—no, *before* seventy-two hours. And Cook had given him the coordinates. But what were they? Thirty-something, one-hundred-something . . . But north or south? East or west? He didn't have a clue.

Well, it didn't matter. The Artifact would be fine, he was quite sure. It was too nice a day.

He rounded one last patch of weeds a foot taller than he was and saw the Artifact—

—or what was left of it.

The pieces of the packing crate were shattered, blackened, splintered and tossed all over.

So was the Artifact.

There was a large scorched area, blackened and buckled pavement with tendrils of smoke still rising from it. A layer of debris had been tossed around the area for twenty or thirty feet in every direction.

And that was it.

Miller felt his legs give way, and he knelt at what seemed to be the epicenter of the blast. A few pieces of something glittered at him through the dirt and scorched pavement. He poked at one, about the size of a kid's marble. It ran through the color spectrum and he picked it up. His hand seemed to freeze, and then feel heavy, but nothing like what he'd experienced in the volcano. Just a tiny twitch, less noticeable than a mosquito bite. But it had to be a piece of the Artifact. All that was left were a few fragments like this one.

Miller stood wearily and put the fragment in his pocket, although he wasn't sure why. Souvenir of disaster. And worse to come.

Seventy-two hours. To do what? Go somewhere he wasn't sure of, do something he hadn't been told, with what Cook had said were very low odds. No kidding, low odds. It was impossible.

But he had to try.

He started heavily toward his plane. Maybe if he pulled out the charts he would recognize the numbers. Thirty-something one-hundred-something could only be a few places in the world. With luck, he could rule out most of them as being in mid-ocean. Whatever was left, it had to be someplace odd people could do their business without attracting attention. That ruled out a lot of the land surface, too, in his time.

Thinking about it, he grew almost hopeful. Maybe he really could find this place. And if he could get there in time, who knew? Maybe he'd figure out the right thing to do, too. Cook's people might even send someone else to help—why not? They could travel in time.

He heard something then, off to the right, partly

whipped away by the wind, but still clear enough to identify.

It was a woman's scream.

It came again, closer this time.

And behind it came another sound: the sound of horse's hooves galloping, pursuing, and the shouts of the hunter.

17

CHAPTER

Lots of people scream, **Miller thought.** *All the time, for a lot of different reasons.* It didn't have to mean the woman was in danger. He'd heard similar screams before at fraternity parties. Miller tried to reason with whatever was making the hair stand up on the back of his neck at the sound. He had the urge to crouch down, hide behind something, as if some ancestral memory was telling him: *The enemy is coming.* But that made no sense—there was no enemy. At least not on horseback.

Besides, he was somewhere in the future. Wasn't it more reasonable to assume that the sound of horses meant some kind of amusement, and not primitive warriors chasing down a screaming victim?

So he tried to feel casual as he turned away from the plane and walked toward the sound he'd heard, telling himself it was good news to find other people so quickly, people who could tell him where/when he was, and perhaps how to get home.

Maybe the airport had fallen into ruin because these

people traveled through space and time nowadays. That would make sense. Cook said that they had mastered time travel in the future. Why bother with the upkeep on an airport when you could travel through time?

The more Miller reasoned it out, the more certain he became that he was about to meet Cook's people, perhaps the very contact he was supposed to have met when he landed.

That made him pause for a moment. He could not hand over the Artifact. There wasn't enough of it left. Would they believe his wild story about a storm?

But all that was forced out of his mind by what he saw ahead of him. At the far edge of the runway a forest had grown up to the pavement. Bursting out of the tree line and to his left was a sight that stunned him nearly off his feet.

A clot of men, perhaps a half dozen of them, ran from the trees pell-mell. One of them paused to whirl a sling and let a rock fly at some unseen target still in the trees. The others ran as if the Devil himself was after them. And other than their weapons, the men were completely naked.

Naked and painted blue.

Celts?

But if this was the future . . .

Three more figures raced from the trees. The first was a woman, luxurious red hair spilling across a dark, hooded garment. She held her arm as if it had been injured. The two warriors behind her kept their backs to her, facing the woods with their swords held ready. As Miller watched, one of the rearguard warriors fell, an arrow sprouting from his chest, and the last one turned to urge on the woman. Then, with a bloodcurdling yell, he charged back into the trees, waving his sword.

The woman hesitated for a second and called after him. But even from his distance, Miller could hear the yells and the clash of steel just within the tree line.

In the meantime, one man in the small group of warriors in the front turned and came racing back to the woman. As the woman tried to step back toward the trees, he grabbed her, threw her over one huge shoulder, and ran for his comrades.

Moments later a line of horsemen burst from the wood to bear down on the Celts. And once again Miller held his breath, feeling dizzy and completely lost. Because the silhouette of this new group was unmistakable. From the sharply protruding armor on the shoulders and the angled horns on their helmets, down to the distinctive leggings and the banners flapping behind them, there could be no doubt of who they were.

Samurai warriors.

Samurai warriors, chasing a group of primitive Celts.

And the whole melee was headed straight at him.

There is a time to analyze and wonder, and a time to run for your life. Miller had absolutely no doubt that right now was a prime example of the second option. He turned and ran for the plane.

The soreness in his muscles had magically disappeared. He dove back through the pilot's door and began to scrabble through the plane for some kind of weapon. Anything at all. Ah! The flare gun—where was it? Damn! Had he left it half buried in the sand on Yuki's island? No, he remembered distinctly. He'd loaded it into the plane, stowed it behind the water jug.

He fumbled the two gallon water container out of the way, dropping it onto his toe. He cursed at the pain—but *there* was flare gun!

Miller grabbed for the gun and the small bag of shotgun, shell-shaped cartridges. Only four left. With trembling fingers he shoved a cartridge into the gun, put the spares into his shirt pocket, thrust the gun into his waistband, and climbed back into the pilot's seat.

And as Miller popped into view in the cockpit, so did a head of flaming red hair. The woman in the robe, the one who had been carried from the woods, was beside the airplane now. Her burly companion set her down and, as Miller appeared, the man stared at him.

Miller held up his hands and tried to think of what he might say to assure the man of his peaceful intentions. "Pax," was all he could blurt out.

It was enough. The warrior shoved the red-haired woman at Miller, panting out an amazingly lyrical-sounding sentence, and ran back toward the charging Samurai. As he ran he pulled a sword from his baldric and swung it over his head with an ululating war cry.

Miller jumped down from the plane and held out a hesitant hand toward the woman. She did not even see him. Instead, still holding a bloody wound on one arm, she focused all her attention on her warrior. Miller turned to watch, too.

The warrior made it no more than fifty feet before the first Samurai was on him. The Celt raised his sword and began to shout a challenge.

The Samurai, who seemed unarmed, halted his horse in front of the Celt. With amazing speed he reached behind his neck. A gleaming long sword appeared, a flash of light arced toward the Celt, and in the blink of an eye the other warrior's head was rolling across the ground. His headless corpse tottered for a few seconds, spouting blood from the neck, and then toppled over.

The woman beside Miller gasped, a look of horror on her beautiful face. She stepped forward, a shout of rage forming on her lips, and raised her arms, the injured one with some difficulty. But as she did, Miller heard the hoofbeats again. Beyond the Samurai, the rest of his troop was galloping into view.

Miller took the woman by the waist and swung her down into the slim protection offered by the airplane. She hissed at him.

"Please," he whispered. "I can't fight them all. And neither can you." She didn't understand, of course, but she didn't shout or stand up, either.

The cluster of Samurai thundered by on their horses, chasing the fleeing line of Celts. They did not appear to notice Miller and the woman.

The Samurai with the sword got off his horse and lifted the warrior's head from the ground by its hair. He examined it, appeared pleased with it—especially the long blond mustache

—and hung it from his saddle.

This was too much for the woman. She slipped out from under Miller's arm and stepped away from the plane, toward the Samurai with the head.

She raised her arms above her head and began to chant. Miller couldn't understand the words, but the tone was clear; it was a curse.

The Samurai watched her for a moment, amused. Then he sheathed his sword, carefully wiping the blood off the blade on his tunic. He turned to the horse and took down a bow and quiver of arrows. He nocked a shaft.

The woman slammed her wrists together, ignoring what must have been considerable pain from the wounded arm, and shouted a series of syllables. As her voice lifted on the last syllable, the Samurai's horse reared, whinnying. It ran its shoulder into the Samurai, knocking him down, and galloped madly away, eyes rolling.

"How the hell—" Miller said in amazement.

But the Samurai was back on his feet, nocking the arrow again and aiming at the woman.

With a bellow, Miller dove for her. He swept an arm at her legs and knocked her to the ground as the arrow whipped through space where her head had been. There was a *spong-thunk!* followed by the noise of a dribbling fluid, and Miller turned to see that the arrow implanted in the plane's fuel tank. Gasoline was streaming across the cracked tarmac.

"Come on," he said to the woman, pulling her by the hand. "We've got to get out of here!"

She didn't resist, but she didn't help much, either. Miller got the idea that dying in battle was okay with her. She was entitled to her opinion, but he didn't happen to agree.

The Samurai nocked another arrow. Miller pulled the woman around to the other side of the plane and crouched low to see what the warrior was doing.

He was, in fact, being sensible. Miller saw his feet approaching cautiously. He was now holding his sword instead of the bow, and stepping toward the plane with the razor-sharp blade held at the ready.

"This is our chance," Miller whispered.

The woman looked back at him. Her eyes were lively, sparkling with rage and battle lust. She shook her head to indicate she hadn't understood him.

"Come," Miller said, again grasping her hand. She

nodded and stood up, taking a deep breath. To his horror, Miller realized she was about to bellow something at the Samurai, probably a challenge or an insult, and he quickly clapped a hand over her mouth. "Shhh!" he signaled.

She bit his hand. He pulled it away, shook it, then used it to show her he was unarmed. "Look," he said, waving a hand at his shorts and ragged shirt. "Nothing to fight with. Not even a big rock. We've got to make a run for it." She looked dubious, and glanced longingly in the direction of the approaching Samurai. "No," Miller said firmly, urgently. "There's no chance. Come on." He held out his hand, nodded at the ruins of the control tower.

She still looked doubtful, but did not resist when he took her arm—the good one—and led her at a quick half crouch away from the plane.

Miller made for the rubble at an angle that blocked the Samurai's view of them. They were only twenty feet from the relative safety of the rubble heap when the warrior came around the tail end of the plane.

"Yamay, Ainu!" he shouted, and sheathed his sword in favor of the bow and arrow again. He took careful aim, and, even at this distance, Miller knew he would not miss. One of them was about to die.

The Samurai paused and looked down at his feet. He shook one of them, irritated; Miller saw something splash off. He was standing in a puddle of gasoline from the punctured fuel tank.

As the Samurai raised his bow one last time, Miller whipped the flare gun out of his waistband and fired.

It was a lousy shot. He'd meant to hit the puddle of fuel, to scare the man into dropping the bow and running away with singed eyebrows.

Instead, he hit the warrior squarely in the chest. The man was thrown backward from the impact of the twelve-gauge flare. His whole body rolled through the pool of gasoline, his silk tunic soaking up the fuel like a sponge. In less than a second the man was burning like a bonfire.

He made no sound at first, simply burned, stood up, fell to his knees, struggled halfway up again and then let out something between a gasp and a squeal.

And as he fell over, the entire pool of spilled gasoline blossomed into an inferno. The sheet of flame raced back toward the airplane.

"Run!" Miller shouted, grabbing the woman by the hand again and pulling her around to the far side of the rubble heap.

They had just made it to the shelter of the fallen tower when the plane exploded. A hot wind whistled overhead, and a trickle of dirt and small rocks cascaded down the slope above them. A rock the size of a golf ball bounced off Miller's head.

"Ouch," he said, and the red-haired woman looked at him.

Miller felt an almost physical impact from her stare. Her eyes were cat-green and alive with intelligence, compassion, and strength. She held a hand out to his head, palm first, and moved it around until she came to the spot where the rock had hit.

"It's nothing," he said.

The woman shook her head and smiled at him. Miller smiled back and took a moment to study her.

Aside from the fact that she was beautiful and seemed intelligent, there was very little he could guess about her. If she was, in fact, a Celt, then her robe would indicate that she was a Druid, a learned and holy person. That would explain why her companion had willingly given his life to give her a chance to escape.

Additionally, she wore a thick gold necklace—a *torc*; the name popped into Miller's head from his brief studies of the Celts in graduate school—which also indicated that she was a person of some rank and importance.

She had been studying him, too, and now their eyes met once again. She lifted a strong and graceful hand and placed it on her chest, next to a beautifully worked brooch. "Mara," she said.

He gave her a small half bow. "Tony Miller," he replied, and they smiled at each other.

In the distance, the sound of the battle lifted up; a huge shout, followed by the most god-awful caterwauling, wheezing noise. Then the hoofbeats came closer, closer—and as Miller and the red-haired woman peeked out around their rock and dirt barrier, the Samurai warriors galloped past, back toward the forest. There seemed to be a couple of them missing, and one of the remaining warriors slumped over in his saddle, both arms folded across his stomach.

The caterwauling grew closer, pursuing, and Mara stood up, yelling curses at the fleeing Samurai, who galloped on without slowing or turning around, heading for the shelter of the tree line.

Behind them Miller saw their pursuers. In a steady and unhurried march, a ragged line of fifty or sixty warriors approached. In front of them came six or seven others who seemed unarmed, but held something at their chest . . .

Of course! Bagpipes! That was the caterwauling. The pipers were leading the troops into battle.

And now it was Mara who took Miller's hand and led him to her people.

18

CHAPTER

The Celtic village was on a bluff overlooking a small river. The bluff had been worked upward into an earthwork that merged at the bottom with a stout wooden wall. Dominating the enclosure was a large stone tower, set in the middle of the round walls. Four large, cone-shaped thatched roofs poked up around the tower, and smoke came from the peak of two of them. A narrow gate, just wide enough for one person on horseback, was cut into the steeply banked earthwork.

"*Oppida,*" Mara said, the way one might talk to a child. She nodded her head at the village. "*Oppida,*" she said again.

A shout came from the small hut perched on top of the gate and a robed man leaned out, waving happily at Mara. She called something back and he grinned.

In the village, a warm sprawl of children, people, dogs and other animals, came to meet them. There was laughter of relief, then anxiety and tears as the people noted who had come back and who hadn't. One young woman pushed her way through to Mara, her face a mask of worry. She grabbed Mara's arm; it was the wounded one, and Mara winced, gently removing the woman's clutching hand.

The woman spoke earnestly and Mara nodded, reaching into her robe and taking out what looked like a plant. The young woman clapped her hands together with relief and urged Mara to follow, now. Mara nodded. She turned to Miller. "Tonymillahr," she said, and beckoned him to follow.

The young woman led them through a scattering of smaller huts to one of the large buildings and down to a far dark nook. It was all one large, open room, with a fire pit in the center. It smelled of smoke, humanity, cooking; not an unpleasant smell, but a powerful one.

Miller looked around at the place. What an amazing treasure trove of knowledge it was. His colleagues who specialized in the European Bronze Age would have traded their tenure to poke around in here for fifteen minutes. Museums bragged about Celtic collections that would fit unnoticed in one small area of this building. He saw things lying carelessly on the floor that he'd never seen before except under glass on a velvet cushion. And yet they were tossed here and there, common objects, part of a daily life that had once covered most of Europe.

Europe—and this was supposed to be Tahiti. The strangeness of that thought brought him crashing back to the present—the *herenow*, he reminded himself, letting the word bring the urgency washing over him again.

His plane was gone, and along with it his charts, and all hope of finding the Bodhi stronghold and reversing the disaster caused by the Artifact's destruction. All over the world, would there be bizarre pockets of oddly assorted cultures from across time and space? Or was that just the beginning? Were fresh and even more unlikely disasters waiting to unfold, things he couldn't even guess at?

His mind whirling around the possibilities, Miller walked right into Mara's back. She had stopped at a small pallet on the floor beside the far wall and was looking down, frowning with concern.

On the pallet lay a golden-haired girl about seven years old. Her eyes were closed and her breathing labored, and even from ten feet away Miller could see the red flush of fever on her cheeks. The young woman—the girl's mother?—was speaking to Mara in a low and urgent voice. Mara nodded and knelt beside the girl. She placed a hand on the girl's forehead and closed her eyes. She stayed like that for several minutes, unmoving, then stood up briskly and said something to the young woman, who immediately hurried away, returning moments later with a small metal brazier containing a few glowing coals.

Miller watched as Mara took a small bronze pot and boiled water in it over the coals. She took a few leaves from the plant she'd removed from her robe and crumbled them into the water, then dropped a few more directly onto the coals and wafted the smoke toward the unconscious girl.

When the water had boiled for a few minutes, the young woman raised the child to a sitting position and helped Mara force the liquid between her lips.

Miller watched with wonder. This explained why a woman of Mara's importance had wandered away into danger. She was the Healer. She'd been looking for this herb, to heal the girl.

And it seemed to be working. When the tea was gone, they laid the girl back down again. Mara placed a hand on the child's forehead and again closed her own eyes. As Miller watched, the flush left the girl's cheeks and her face relaxed into what looked like a restful sleep.

Mara opened her eyes, stood, and spoke quietly with the mother, who nodded and embraced Mara with gratitude.

Mara smiled and returned the hug, then led Miller back outside. He turned once to see the mother kneeling beside the girl, holding her hand with a small smile and crooning a lullaby.

That night the village—*oppida*, Miller reminded himself—celebrated the successful return of their Healer. In the center of the enclosure the men built a huge bonfire, and the women set large kettles of fragrant stew to cook on the coals. Grinning young men rolled out great wooden barrels filled with beer, sampling just a little as they set them upright a stone's throw from the fire.

Just before dusk a great roar went up from the gate and all the children ran to look. A hunting party returned, children yelling and dogs barking at their heels, with a huge boar slung on a pole, which they quickly gutted and threw over the fire on a large spit.

By full dark the party was going strong and Miller was in the thick of it. He was impressed with the way the Celts accepted him, a total stranger, without hesitation. They all seemed open and friendly, refilling his clay mug with beer, showing him to the choice bits of stew, helping him to a good slice of boar, making him feel completely at home.

Some of it, of course, was gratitude for the man who had saved their Healer. But there was more to it; Miller had the feeling that he was genuinely welcome, that these people believed in hospitality. He didn't look like them, dress like them, talk like them, or even think like them, but they tried to make him feel at home.

But though Miller tried to be gracious in return, a sour mood had overtaken him. He found it nearly impossible to put out of his head the image of a clock ticking down.

Sixty-eight hours.

Sixty-seven hours, forty-eight minutes.

Sixty-seven hours, thirty-nine minutes.

Sixty-seven hours, thirty-eight minutes, twelve seconds . . .

He sipped the beer, working hard at clearing his mind. There was nothing he could do about it. It was out of his hands. He'd tried as hard as he knew how, and they had been waiting for him with their monster storm. It was not his fault. It was not, goddamn it, even his *responsibility*. They couldn't just draft him without so much as a pretty please and thank you. What the hell did he care about their damned Artifact? It was nothing to him; wouldn't affect his tenure, his salary, the size of his overflowing graduate seminar on Oceanic migration . . .

It would only end the world. Big deal.

But it wasn't his problem! He hadn't asked to be chosen for this, and had no interest in being chosen.

He just had been. And he was the only one anywhere in the world, as far as he knew, who could do anything. That made it his responsibility. It was like finding a kitten on your doorstep. It didn't matter if you didn't want a kitten; it had chosen *you*, and that was all there was to it.

There was still nothing he could do about it. But he knew he had to try.

Miller looked around for Mara. She had been talking with one old man for some time now, and he spotted her across the fire, still speaking with him. The old man was bony, string-thin, with a powerful jaw and a large nose. A few wisps of white hair struggled off the pink skin of his head. He wore a robe like Mara's and leaned on a staff, his eyes closed, nodding his head rhythmically to whatever Mara was saying.

Miller sighed and looked into his mug. He shouldn't be sitting here, drinking beer like a U.C. sophomore on spring break. He should be doing something, anything. There was too much at stake, he had to . . . to . . . Well, something, damn it. Anything. But he didn't have a clue what to do, where to start—he didn't even know why it was all up to him. He felt like he was on a ship headed for an iceberg and somebody had just told him he'd been appointed captain.

He didn't like this beer. Yuki's beer had made him happy. This stuff was tragic.

Miller stood up and smiled politely at the inquiring looks of his two neighbors. He walked away into the darkness by the village wall and stared up at the stars. They seemed remarkably large and bright, much more so than in Berkeley, and there were so many more of them. There was a tang to the air, too, that tasted crisper, better, than the stuff he was used to. There was, in fact, an overall sense of difference, of *foreignness,* to everything here, which he'd never experienced in all his world travels.

It hit him in his guts that he really was in another time and place. Not just reconstructing, computer-imaging, postulating for publication. He was there. He was really there, in the middle of *history*, and he wanted to go home. And he knew he couldn't, not without some miracle, a helping hand from some outside source he couldn't even imagine.

A hand fell softly on his shoulder and Miller almost jumped out of his skin. Mara was smiling up at him, a gleam in her eyes that was more than reflected starlight. She looked at him for a long moment, her smile fading. She reached out her hand and lightly touched his forehead. Then she moved her hand down to his chest and held it there, two inches from his heart, as if searching for something.

Her eyes met his again, and there was a warmth and compassion to her expression that gave Miller the impression that she knew how he was feeling. She spoke softly, lyrically, and though he could not understand a word of it, he felt sympathy in her words. He nodded. "Thanks," he said.

She looked at him a moment longer, then patted his arm, took him by the hand and led him back to the fire.

When he'd walked away moments ago, it was a raucous gathering, as one might expect. There had been half-drunken singing, groups clustered around men telling what were obviously bawdy stories, even a good-natured wrestling contest. Now, as Miller returned to the fire on Mara's arm, the mood was different. Everyone had found a place to sit, leaving an open space near the fire, and the noise level had come down about fifty decibels. There was a feeling of expectation in the air. As he and Mara approached, people made a space in the front for them.

Mara pushed him to a sitting position, then sat next to him, patting his arm and saying something soothing in her wonderful, lilting way. And then the crowd went suddenly quiet. Not a sound could be heard except the crackling of the fire and, from behind them, the slow shuffling of two pairs of feet.

Miller looked back. The old man, the one Mara had spoken with at such great length, was slowly moving through a path the crowd made for him, leaning on his staff, working his way to the fire. His eyes were half closed and his brow was knotted, as though he was thinking hard about something.

"Seanachie," Mara whispered to him. Miller knew the word: *seanachie*, the bard, the storyteller. That explained the Druid's robe he wore, and the great respect with which he was treated.

Behind the *seanachie* came a boy, no more than fourteen, carrying a three-legged stool and a Celtic harp. The boy set the stool down near the fire and the *seanachie* spoke sharply to him. The boy blushed, moved the stool three or four feet farther away from the fire and helped the old man sit. When the *seanachie* was seated, the boy handed him the harp and sat behind him on the ground.

The old man stroked the strings thoughtfully, frowned at the boy behind him, and adjusted the tuning on one of them infinitesimally.

Satisfied now, the old man began to stroke the harp. He spoke softly, and Miller could almost hear the crackling of energy as the crowd strained forward to hear every syllable.

For a few moments the old man strummed and spoke softly. Miller gradually became aware of the subtle

rhythm in the *seanachie*'s words. And then the old man's
face grew drawn and pinched and he began to cough.
Miller was afraid the old man would pitch off the stool,
overcome with his fit. He looked quickly around, looked
at Mara, to see why no one moved to help the *seanachie*.
But they were all transfixed, leaning forward with lips
parted, barely breathing. Miller noticed now that the
coughing was rhythmic; with a shock of wonder he realized that it was part of the story.

The old man went on, his voice rising, hitting the
cadence for emphasis, dropping away again, coughing
for one more verse. When Miller had heard the word
Mara several times, he finally put it together. The
seanachie was telling the story of the sick girl, Mara's
search for the herb to heal her, and the encounter with
the strange and terrifying warriors in the woods.

The music clamored, and the old man's voice rose
to go with it. Miller could *feel* the clash of swords, the
rattle of the arrows, the hopelessness at being so desperately outnumbered, the gallant retreat. There was brav-
ery in the old man's voice, and the music hinted at
sacrifice, noble death. Miller looked at Mara and saw
tears rolling down her cheek. She repeated one of the
words the *seanachie* had used several times, and Miller
guessed it was a name, one of the fallen warriors.

And then he heard the old man say, "Millahr," and a
flutter went through him as he realized he had now
entered the story. All eyes in the crowd swung to him,
then back to the *seanachie*. The rhythm changed; it
became lighter, slightly comic. The old man did a wonderful imitation of Mara trying to persuade someone of
something, and with a shock of nausea Miller heard the
seanachie's voice answering back in *his*, Miller's, voice.

He was saying something petulant, sounding worried, refusing.

The crowd laughed, nudged each other. Mara's voice again rose over the jangle of the harp strings, countered by the slightly whiny Miller. The crowd laughed again.

Miller's cheeks grew hot. The old man was clearly making sport of him, and he couldn't understand a word of it, couldn't speak to defend himself against whatever was being said.

But then he felt a hand cover his. Mara patted his knuckles and gave him an encouraging smile, and as she did, the music changed again.

Miller refocused on the *seanachie*. The music's rhythm of the telling grew more urgent, and the old man's voice clearer, harder-edged, more strident. He had clearly come to the climax of the story, and from the sound of it, some great warrior named Miller was tearing things up. He felt the blood mount to his cheeks again, but it felt better this time.

Mara's voice in the story grew an edge of panic, while Miller's grew calmer, more commanding. And then it was all the great warrior Miller, and to the real Miller's wonder, the *seanachie* performed an extremely creditable imitation of the flare gun firing, the screams of the dying Samurai, and the explosion of the airplane.

The crowd gasped, glanced at Miller with covert awe, and bent their attention back to the *seanachie*.

The man knew his audience. He brought his voice all the way down now; Miller recognized a chorus from the beginning of the performance, repeated now with irony, and repeated again with humility. The *seanachie*'s voice rose, the music fell away, and then the old man's voice soared far above them all, above the fire and the village and all things human, out among the stars. Finally, the voice died away to a whisper as the harp gave out one last soft chord that seemed to linger forever.

And then there was silence. The *seanachie* bowed his head, totally spent, and his young assistant leaned forward to hand him a mug, from which he sipped sparingly.

As if that was the signal, the crowd erupted. They were all on their feet in an instant, shouting and applauding wildly, and grabbing Mara and Miller in exuberant bear hugs. And it dawned on Miller: He was a hero. It didn't matter to these people that he had caused the Artifact to be destroyed, couldn't figure out what he was supposed to do next, and was drinking beer again instead of battling impossible odds to do things he couldn't even imagine. To these people, he was the great warrior who had saved their Healer. He was Miller, the Hero.

Now if only he could feel like it.

19

CHAPTER

That night Mara came to him in a dream. Miller felt guilty, since he'd been thinking of her as he'd tottered off to bed, long after the many toasts with his new friends, long after he showed them a few of his martial arts tricks, long, long after the great fire had died down to a bed of dull red coals.

He remembered thinking, as Mara finally led him off to show him the guest hut, that she really was a fine-looking person, especially for a Druid. And the guilt had stung twice as hard, since he was still thinking about Yuki, and anyway, making love to Mara would be like sleeping with a nun—wouldn't it? Because she wore that robe, and . . . and anyway, she had just clapped him on the shoulder and shoved him in the door, where he'd found a pallet of clean grass and a beautiful wool blanket waiting for him.

And he'd lain awake just for a few minutes, amused at first at the thought that this was two nights in a row that he'd been up drinking, and he almost never drank back home . . .

Home.

Where was home now? *When* was it? Would he ever see it again? It wasn't perfect, but it was his life; could he possibly get it back? It didn't seem likely—but then, nothing that had happened to him in the last two weeks seemed likely if you looked at it. Maybe there was still a chance . . .

Without a way to get anywhere, except his legs. Without a map, without, for God's sake, any faint notion of *where* he was supposed to go or what he was supposed to do when he got there. He glanced at his watch. The numerals glowed faintly. Sixty-four hours, seventeen minutes. On top of everything else, there wasn't any time to do all the things he didn't know how to do . . .

And so it was not a terribly happy Tony Miller who finally sank into sleep.

He didn't know how long he'd been asleep before the dream came to him. But it was very clear, and not at all illogical, like so many dreams. Mara's face swam in front of him, and he felt guilty because he wanted to see the rest of her, maybe without that bulky robe; and she seemed to know that, from the understanding smile she gave him. And she leaned close to him, her moist lips parting softly, and she spoke.

"Thirty-eight, one twenty-three," Mara said. "Home, sweet home." She reached a hand down toward his face and he closed his eyes, anticipating the caress—

Miller sat bolt upright on his pallet. He was panting, a thin coat of sweat had formed on his forehead and he felt a chill in the air. Around him the snores of other men echoed off the walls. In the distance a dog barked and someone was retching.

Thirty-eight, one twenty-three.

Miller never for a second questioned that it meant *something*. But what? What the hell did it mean, and why had Mara appeared in a dream to tell him?

His breath was slowing a little now and he made an effort to shake off the nightmare feeling, the sense of unbearable urgency, that the dream had left him. And why should that be? It was just Mara, telling him some numbers. Why the perception that it was so vitally, earthshakingly important? The only thing he could think of with that kind of urgency to it was as good as over, the business of locating Bodhi headquarters within . . .

Miller looked at his watch. Sixty-two and a half hours. And then it was all over no matter what.

That was the only number that mattered: sixty-two and a half. Not some nonsense from a dream. He needed to get a grip. Clearly, it was no more than an anxiety dream, like the one he'd had his first year of teaching at Berkeley, where he'd been halfway through his favorite lecture in front of the huge freshman Intro to Anthro class and looked down to discover he wasn't wearing pants.

Reflexively, he felt for his pants. He was still wearing them. But the small lump of Artifact was missing from the pocket. Miller felt a powerful stab of panic, but he fought it down. It was just a rock at this point. It didn't matter. Still, he felt the loss very deeply.

Puzzled by this, he rubbed his neck and realized the necklace Yuki had made him was gone, too. What was happening? Was he really being robbed, here in a Celtic village? From what he knew of the culture that was unthinkable—but the two items were missing. How? It was possible that somebody had taken them while he slept, but as far as he knew only Mara had been close enough to him.

Mara—the dream came back to him. It had been so compelling, as if she had really been there, almost as if he had really opened his eyes from sleep and seen her standing over him. So real—and it now seemed so important. What had she been trying to tell him? What had the dream meant?

Miller shook his head. What was he thinking? It was pure anxiety. Mara had been in the dream because he'd fallen asleep thinking of her. And the numbers were random; they meant nothing, they'd just been generated by . . . by . . .

By what? Did dreams generate random numbers or images? He didn't think so. Usually they didn't create anything, they only combined what was already there, burbling away in the subconscious. Why should he have numbers in his subconscious? He was an anthropologist, not a mathematician, not a number-oriented person at all. That's why he always forgot things like his own telephone number or zip code; why he'd forgotten the numbers Cook had blurted out to him, the coordinates to Bodhi headquarters that—

Time stopped.

Not the way it had when the Artifact had stopped it, no. This time it was purely subjective. Time stopped only in his head. Miller held his breath and tried to stop the furious pounding of his heart, concentrating on nothing but his breath, his heartbeat. It worked, and Miller let out the breath.

Thirty-eight, one twenty-three.

The coordinates.

The location of Bodhi headquarters. It had to be.

The subconscious never forgot. It had been trying to kick the numbers back upstairs into the conscious mind, and chose Mara to deliver the message.

It sounded right, it *felt* like the numbers Cook had blurted out to him. For no logical reason, he was sure they were the right coordinates.

And so what? Where in the world was 38–123? He didn't have any idea whatsoever, not even an idea of how to find out. He was in, what, third century Northern Europe? They didn't even have maps, let alone latitude and longitude. Having the numbers was no help if he didn't know what they meant, where they were telling him to go. And the dream had given him no hints at all about—

Home, sweet home . . .

All right, Miller, he told himself, *if you're going to believe in messages from dreams, let's go all the way. The numbers that came from your dreams really are the coordinates of the Bodhi headquarters. Fine. So "Home, sweet home," clearly had to mean something, too. Right? No problem.*

What?

Well, all right. It could mean Mara's home. Which meant he was there, at the right place. Which meant the Bodhis were a bunch of third century Celts.

Nope.

Or it could mean *his* home. Either where he was born or where he now lived, in Berkeley.

Berkeley? Was it possible?

Miller closed his eyes and thought hard. A few years back the university had made a film to show to prospective students. They'd done a clip of his graduate seminar on the evening he discussed the cultural context of hula dancing. He jokingly referred to it as the "Swimsuit Issue" of the seminar.

Only slightly embarrassed, he'd gone to see the film when it was finished. It had begun with a huge flourish of music and then a voice-over. An important-sounding announcer had droned on about the campus, located in the San Francisco Bay area along the thirty-eighth parallel, with a few well-chosen and interesting examples of other things on that same parallel.

Home, sweet home . . .

Could it be?

Were they really located in Berkeley—*his* Berkeley?

Miller thought about it. If there was one place on earth where a cult would not be disturbed or even noticed, it was California. Within a stone's throw of the campus there were a number of ashrams, spiritual retreats, New Age think tanks, holistic centers—everything from spiritualism and Buddhism to UFO worshipers.

Yes. It could be. It definitely could. It made sense.

Miller lurched up off his pallet and ran for the door.

If Mara objected to the uproar when Miller stood at the door to her hut and called out in the early hours of the morning, she did not show it. One of the warriors present had barred his way, but backed off and stood at a distance with the others when he saw it was all right with her. After all, Miller realized, he was a hero; and he had a strange and powerful weapon, and anyway, if the Healer didn't mind, it was all right.

The hard part for Miller was thinking of a way to communicate to Mara what he needed. He'd said *pax* to the warrior at the plane, and that had worked. The Celts had some contact with the Romans, he knew. Perhaps it was the way to go with Mara. He was certainly better with Latin than with Celtic.

"*Marum,*" he said. He made wave motions with his hand to indicate the meaning, *sea*.

She pointed to herself and lifted an eyebrow. "Mara?" she asked.

"No. Mar-*um*," he said. "*Marum.* Ocean. Sea. Water—*aqua*?"

She shook her head and said something in a voice still rough from sleep. Whatever the exact words, it was clear that she wasn't getting what he was trying to say. He tried again.

"*Marum.* Mar—Mare? Uh, damn it, large body of water," he said, trying as many hand gestures as he could think up. "A place where there are boats. Boat. I need a boat. Ship. Bark, brig, sailboat. Uh . . ." The word *coracle* came into his head. He knew it was descended from the Welsh word for that kind of small, round boat the northern Celts had favored. He shrugged and tried the word.

"Coracle. No, by God, *curagh*!" he said as he remembered the Gaelic.

Mara cocked her head. "*Corwgl?*" she said, cupping her hands together to make a small rounded boat with a pointed prow. She rocked her hands to show the boat on the ocean.

"Yes!" Miller exulted. "*Corwgl,* by God. *Corwgl!* Boat!" In his excitement, he took her hand, and she smiled and pulled it away.

"*Corwgl,*" she said. She pointed to the sky, mimed the sun coming up. Then she took his hand and made the two fingers of her other hand walk. The meaning was clear; in the morning, I will take you there.

Miller stood, gently lifting her up with him. "Now?" he said, pointing at his watch to show urgency. But of course that meant nothing to her. He hopped on one foot, then the other, like a child who had to pee. "Now?" he repeated, pulling her toward the gate.

She studied him for a moment. After all, the dangers of night travel were plentiful, especially with unknown enemies out there, like the Samurai. Miller tried as hard as he could to pantomime urgency, *Now, let's go,* and Mara finally nodded. She held up the palm of her hand, indicating he must wait a moment, and went back into her hut.

And now Miller really was almost hopping on one foot in his anxiety. The idea of a boat offered such a slender chance to begin with that it was almost better to simply relax and live out his life as a hero among the Celts. But it offered a tiny chance, and he had to take it.

He had reasoned that, if Samurai and Celt could be side by side, there must be some lump of future thrown into the mixture somewhere, too. And if that proved true, there might, just *might*, be something at the seaport fast enough to get him to the coordinates in time.

When Mara came out again, she was dressed for traveling, with her dark, hooded robe and a heavy shoulder bag. She beckoned and led Miller toward the gate. The warrior who had stepped forward before, now appeared at Mara's elbow, and the other warriors closed in. Mara glanced at them and was met with a look of such fierce determination that she merely smiled and bowed her head. It was clear that the men of the *oppida* were taking no more chances with the safety of their Healer.

20

CHAPTER

It had been a fine spring evening when they left the *oppida*. But as they got close to the coast, the temperature continued to drop until Miller could see the frost in his breath. The last small stream they crossed was frozen over with an inch-thick skin of ice.

Miller shivered. He was still dressed only in his shorts and thin tropical work shirt. He swung his arms vigorously as he walked to keep himself warm, but it didn't seem to help a great deal. The Celts didn't seem to mind; they wore wool shirts and long pants, and in any case they were more used to the cooler temperatures.

But it did seem to bother them that it was getting cold now—not the temperature, but the timing. It was supposed to be spring. And as the sun came up they all begin to notice things that seemed wrong. One of the men had paused to examine a shrub. He snapped off a branch and called to the others. They came back to him and looked at the branch, conferring quietly for a moment before showing it to Mara.

Miller stamped his feet and rubbed his arms, and
Mara looked up at him. Then she said a few words to
the men. They looked doubtful, but she repeated her
words firmly, and they reluctantly agreed.

Mara turned and beckoned Miller onward. They
continued to move through a changing landscape; there
was what had to be a gum tree, right next to an oak. A
row of eucalyptus trees made a fringe for a small water-
hole in which an otter splashed.

And finally Miller smelled the fresh, clean salt of
the ocean ahead. They walked around a row of tall pine
trees that whispered in the salt wind from the sea, and
there it was, spread out below him.

They stood atop a rocky bluff, perhaps a hundred
feet above the ocean. But it was not Tahiti's warm and
gentle ocean, with its long slow breakers. This one,
whatever it was, roared in against a sharp row of rocks
and crashed into huge towers of cold spray. Even here
on top of the rocks Miller could feel the far-flung
droplets of water on his face.

He stood and looked. It was an impressive view—
but as far as he could see in either direction, there was
no sign of a seaport. No sign of anything at all but the
relentless surf pounding on the sharp rocks of the
coast.

Behind him Miller heard the men, muttering rest-
lessly. He turned; they were knotted together a few steps
back from the edge, looking anxiously at him and at
Mara. She reassured them with a hand signal and spoke
a few words to Miller, ending with an upward lift, as if
it was a question. Miller thought he understood her to be
asking, Well then? Is this all right?

"Corwgl?" he asked her. "Where are the boats?"

Mara hesitated, looked at her men, then shook her head. She pointed down to where a long arm of rock stuck out into the water, creating a small but snug bay. Clearly, the boats were supposed to be there, but there was no sign that anything had ever been there except birds and moss.

Miller's heart sank within him. There was no way to know how they had missed the port, whether in the past or the future, but it was not there. No port. No boats. No hope of getting to the Bodhi sanctuary on time.

Perhaps either up or down the coast he would hit on something, either in this time or by shifting to another, however that worked. In any case, there was no need to keep his Celtic friends any longer. They didn't like this strangeness, and their looks said that one or two of them thought it had something to do with him. They wanted to go home, to be safe again in their *oppida,* where things were familiar and easy to understand. Not standing on a *wrong* cliff with Miller, a man they knew to have strange powers of some kind and who might very well be leading them to some devilment.

So Miller took Mara's hands and pressed them into his. "Thank you," he said. "From here, I will find my own way."

Mara pressed his hands back and kissed him on both cheeks, speaking something that might have been a charm for a traveler. Then she reached into her robe for something and, stepping forward, she placed Miller's missing necklace back around his neck.

"My necklace," Miller said. "What—"

He picked up the pendant in front, where Yuki had woven the ball bearing into a mesh. It was gone now. In its place was the chip from the Artifact.

Miller looked up at Mara. She smiled at him and stepped back. She raised her arm in benediction and returned to her group of warriors. Miller waved to them, too, thanking them for their help.

One of the warriors stepped forward and pressed his wool shirt into Miller's hands. "Thank you," Miller said with a slight bow. He wondered if he was expected to offer something in return, but the man turned away before he could.

Another man stepped forward and gave Miller a knife. The blade was razor-sharp bronze, about eight inches long. The handle was a deer's horn, worked and smoothed to have a grip that felt perfect in his hand. He looked up at the man, touched by the gifts. "Thank you," he said again, feeling the inadequacy of the words. "Thank you all. For everything."

And then they were hurrying off through the unsettling woods. Mara turned and looked back at him once, just a glance, and then they were gone.

Miller was alone, in a land that was strange even to the people who lived here. He had no idea where he might be, or when, and not a clue where he should go next. He shivered, shrugged into the wool shirt, and moved out onto the cliff as far as he could. He looked hard to his left. Something seemed to reflect light there, just for a moment, but it could easily have been the crest of a wave, a wet rock, anything.

To the right he saw nothing at all. He looked left again, and even though the small blink of light was not repeated, he decided to go that way.

Miller turned away from the edge—

—into blackness.

He could hear a *thump* echoing in his head and he

felt a numbing pain in his forehead that matched it. Another blossomed in the pit of his stomach.

And then he was falling.

The bright agony of smashing into rocks jarred Miller from his unconsciousness. He opened his eyes; nothing but dark rock in front of him, cradling his face.

He struggled to turn over. His left arm was not working exactly right. It hurt a lot, between the wrist and the elbow. But he got turned over and lay on his back, looking up.

He was on a small ledge about twenty feet down from the lip of rock where he'd stood looking up and down the coastline. Above him he saw no sign of what had attacked him. To his side the ledge extended only a few more inches beyond him before dropping off sharply to the rocks and the water below.

He had been very lucky. Now he had to stay that way if he wanted to live.

Miller struggled to his knees, fighting dizziness and keeping his good arm pressed against the rock face for balance. He scrabbled with his one hand and finally found a small chunk of rock jutting out. He pulled himself slowly to his feet, clinging to the rock face and pressing his face in against it to keep far from the edge of the ledge.

He stood with his eyes closed for a moment. When most of the dizziness passed, he opened his eyes. What he saw almost made him lose his balance and fall over backward.

Miller was staring directly into what had to be a gang graffiti. It was the same Day-Glo colors they had used in his day. There were only two differences, in fact, between what he now saw and what he'd seen sprayed onto the walls back in Berkeley.

The first was that, instead of saying, *CHACO* or *42 DUKES*, this graffiti showed a symbol Miller knew very well, as did everyone even remotely interested in archaeology. It was the ancient Egyptian symbol for Osiris, Lord of the Underworld, God of the Dead. Underneath was written, *ZOID*.

The other small difference, the one that had nearly knocked him off the ledge, was that this gang sign was three-dimensional.

No matter from what perspective Miller looked at the graffiti, it gave the illusion of standing straight out in sharp relief. He passed his hand through it from several angles; it was just an illusion, but a nearly perfect one.

But what did it mean? The 3-D graffiti was clearly from the future—what did a future gang have to do with ancient Egypt? What was *ZOID*? And how did the graffiti get halfway down this cliff, and why?

Again Miller reached a hand out to touch the symbol. It still startled him when his hand passed through the 3-D illusion. But it startled him even more to hear a hard chuckle above him.

Miller looked up.

Standing on the edge of the cliff and apparently looking down at him were two futuristic figures. There was a weird familiarity to them, and Miller gaped and blinked until he got it: They looked like comic book heroes.

Both were dressed in identical dark and glistening body suits that either revealed hard, muscular bodies underneath or created the illusion of them by careful contouring. Shoulder pads stuck out sharply, and the suits were topped with half helmets that included tinted goggles.

"Nasty fall, eh mate?" one of them said.

"Come on up, then," added the other.

The accents were Australian.

Miller stared.

"He's one of them dumb brutish ones," the first one commented.

"Can't be," the other said. "He's not naked and painted blue."

"We could fix that," said the first, and they both laughed.

"What do you want?" Miller asked them.

"It talks," said the first. "Lovely."

"We don't *want* anything, mate," the other said reasonably. "If we did, we'd have taken it, wouldn't we? Now climb on up."

"Come on, then, have a go at it," urged the first one.

Miller looked at the two on the cliff top. There was nothing about them that inspired trust, and he was pretty sure they'd knocked him down here to begin with. If he climbed up, they might very well just push him off again, making sure that this time he didn't land on the ledge.

"Thanks," he said at last. "I'll stay here."

"Get up, you silly shit, or I'll bloody well have your ragged arse for tea."

"Come and get it," Miller said politely.

"I bloody well will."

"Fine," Miller said, sitting cross-legged on the narrow ledge. "I'm not going anywhere." He began to examine his latest wounds. Feeling had started to come back into his arm, but it was mostly pain. Still, he could move the fingers and make a fist, so he was reasonably sure it was a sprain and not a break.

Miller glanced up. One of the two thugs on the cliff top was still raving at him. The other appeared to be trying to calm him down. For a moment it seemed to be working, but Miller knew his position was still not a good one. He couldn't stay here on the little ledge forever. Sooner or later it would occur to them to throw rocks. There were some very big ones up there, which they could simply roll off one at a time until he was paste.

He couldn't go down; the cliff face below him juked inward at a sharp angle and there were no handholds that he could see, nothing but the jagged spears of rocks waiting at the bottom. And he couldn't climb up with those two waiting for him. They could kick him right off again, or capture and torture him, or whatever they wanted.

That reduced his options somewhat. And he couldn't even outwait them. They had warm clothes, a good safe place to sit—and one of them could go for food while the other waited. He could not even stretch with any safety.

On the plus side, he still had the bronze knife the Celts had given him, and he could move his injured arm a little better. And of course the— No damn it, it was gone. He scrabbled frantically through his waistband and all his pockets, but he could not find the flare gun anywhere. It must have fallen out when he was dumped off the cliff.

Maybe I should try to outwait them, he thought. *Maybe they'll get bored and go away.*

But they didn't sound bored. In fact, their voices were rising again and the angry one appeared to be working himself up into a real rage. He pulled away from his partner's restraining hand and began to kick at the ground, shouting insults and challenges at Miller.

The quieter one stepped away from his friend and smiled down at Miller. "He doesn't like you," the banger said. "He goes all mental."

"I'm sorry to hear that," Miller replied.

The quieter one looked fondly at his partner, who was kicking a hole through a small tree. "Terrifying, in't he?" And then he looked straight at Miller and said, in a different voice entirely, "Go with them, Miller. But do not trust them."

Miller stared.

"If you survive, they can help," the Voice said.

It was the same gang-banger, but it was as though someone else was using the man's larynx. The words were cool, remote, detached from any feeling, and yet they seemed to hang there in time and space with a force and presence Miller had never heard before.

"Uh, excuse me?" Miller stammered.

"I said, terrifying, mate. Scarey-like," the banger said in his regular voice. He wagged a finger down at Miller. "You need to build up your word-power, you do."

He appeared completely unaware that he'd said anything else.

But if he hadn't—where had the words come from? Was it another possession, Miller wondered, like what had happened to Cook? Were Cook's people trying to get him a message? Or was it their enemies, the Bodhis? How could he tell? For that matter, considering all the pain and strain he was experiencing, he could have imagined the voice.

"Okay," Miller muttered to himself. "Think binary. There are always only two choices." Number one: Believe the voice, whatever its source. Number two: Don't believe it.

If the words were part of some trick the bangers were playing on him, what was the point? Why should they bother? Once the angry one calmed down, they would both realize they had him and could do whatever they wished with him, whenever they wanted.

So the highest probability said the other voice hadn't come from the banger. That left either Cook's people or their enemies. But again: If it was someone who wanted to destroy him, why bother? He was as good as dead sitting there on the ledge.

So whoever the voice belonged to, there were pretty good odds that it represented a genuine offer of help.

Miller shook his head. The logic worked, but in his gut he found it hard to believe that it had happened and that it was good advice.

But let's say I imagined it, he thought. *What if it's my subconscious, then, telling me to go with them because it spotted a way out that I don't consciously see yet?*

And again, against all common sense, the answer seemed to be to climb the cliff and face the bangers.

Okay, Miller thought. *I'm cooked either way. It might as well be on my feet.* He stood up and stretched, trying to get all the feeling he could back into his arms and legs. Then he looked up again.

The raver was still invisible, his angry voice rasping on out of Miller's sight. The other man stood and watched his mate. Miller could see his back. Sprayed on the back of the jacket was the same Osiris symbol as in the graffiti.

Miller climbed. When his hands finally found a hold on the top, a pair of steel-toed boots appeared under his nose.

"A wise decision, sport," the calm one said. He allowed Miller to pull himself to his feet on the cliff top.

But as Miller stood up, the angry one charged him. Something flashed in his hand, and Miller instinctively jumped back. With an angry hum, the weapon slashed through the space where Miller had been.

Miller held his bronze Celtic knife and waited for the next move. It came quickly; the banger leaped high into the air with a kick for Miller's head, slashing downward with his laser knife as Miller dodged the kick.

Miller ducked the blade, too, and managed to nick the other with the tip of his blade before the man whirled on the balls of his feet and lunged again. Miller parried with his blade, but the banger slashed and the blade fell in half, leaving Miller holding the horn handle and very little else.

The banger snarled. "Bloody caveman, with yer bloody little toy knife," he said. "This here's a real weapon—how'd you like to see yer liver?" And with the last word he spun in again.

Miller jumped and managed to slam the heel of his hand against the other's wrist. The laser knife spun out of his fist, and Miller jumped the man before he could pick it up again. He kicked hard at the pit of the man's stomach and his opponent doubled up, out of breath. Miller pounded him on the head and the banger went down.

Stooping quickly, Miller grabbed for the futuristic weapon. But as he did, he felt a blinding stab of pain in his shoulder and heard the second banger speaking softly.

"I don't think so, mate," he said.

More pain bloomed in Miller's head, and he heard

the angry banger, gasping for breath, but staggering over to him anyway. Miller felt the steel-toed boot slam into his ribs and tried to twist away from it. And then he heard the hum of the laser knife again and the man's gasping voice in his ear.

"Kiss it goodbye, you bastard," the banger grunted out. And as Miller tensed, waiting to feel the blade slash across his throat, he instead heard a strange *whoosh*. Then the light was blotted out, something heavy fell onto his head and again across his chest.

And then it was all darkness.

21

CHAPTER

Miller woke up in darkness. He could feel several moist spots on his body, which seemed strange because his mouth was so dry. The idea of a sip of water seemed the most wonderful thing he could imagine. There was also a lot of soreness in his body, most of it centered in the spots that felt damp.

In a minute he would move one of those suddenly very heavy hands on the end of his long, ponderous arms and feel around, find out what the wetness was. But right now it seemed like too much trouble to move at all.

A hand touched his forehead and then retreated. A moment later there was flare of light. Mara knelt beside him, propping a torch into a crack between two rocks. They were in a shallow cave, just big enough for the two of them.

Mara moved her hands back to Miller, to the moist spots. He looked down to see that they were his wounds, each covered with some kind of herbal poultice. And to his amazement they were not bloody, gaping holes. As Mara moved the moss away, he saw small spots of scar tissue. He was nearly healed.

"What happened?" he asked her, surprised at the weak and raspy sound of his voice.

Mara ignored his question. Instead, she closed her eyes and held her left hand over each poulticed area, for a minute or so. Heat came from her hand, and somehow Miller could feel the wounds healing further, pulling together, mending.

He closed his eyes again.

When he opened them again, the torch had been extinguished. Against the mouth of the cave he could see Mara's silhouette. Two larger shadows leaned in and he could hear them speaking in rough, low tones: the warriors who had accompanied her; he recognized one of the voices.

From the outlines of their heads, nodding down and to the left, Miller guessed they were telling Mara of something outside. She responded quietly and came back into the cave. The warriors slipped away into the darkness.

Miller sat up, and Mara quickly put a cool finger on his lips, whispering something to him that he guessed was *Be quiet*.

Now he could hear voices; they were moving closer and—were they speaking English? Yes, he could make out a word or two. It was English.

With an Australian accent.

Miller jumped to his feet—and sat down again, hard. The cave had a very low ceiling, and he'd smacked the top of his head directly into it.

Mara pressed back against him, placing her hand on his lips again, urging him to be quiet.

There was a shout outside that sounded like, "Hoy!" And then a small battle erupted. Miller heard the rattle of Celtic swords and the hum of the laser knives; and then he could smell the seared flesh and singed blood from the bangers' knives, and a great shout went up from the Celts.

Then the sounds began to move away. Miller held his breath and took Mara's hand, giving it a squeeze for luck.

In a few minutes the sounds had moved far out of earshot. Miller tapped Mara and motioned her out of the way. "Stay here, keep quiet," he said, pantomiming his meaning as much as he could. She nodded, and he crawled to the cave's mouth.

Miller looked carefully out of the cave before moving forward. He was amazed at how good he felt. Either he hadn't been as badly hurt as he thought, or Mara's powers were extraordinary.

He listened carefully at the mouth of the cave; nothing. When he thought it was safe to take a closer look, he crawled out, just a few feet, to see better.

"Well, well, well . . ."

Miller looked up. Standing above him was the calm banger, partner of the angry one. His arm was in a sling and there was some blood crusted on it.

"Lookit here," the banger said, and behind him four more of his mates moved into view, dressed in the same kind of body suit. "Zoid was right," the man said. "This one really is a caveman."

"He's the one did for Zoid?" rumbled one of the newcomers, a man nearly twice the size of the others.

"That's him," the first banger agreed happily. "Nearly had me as well," he added, holding up his injured arm.

"You tried to kill me," Miller protested.

The bangers looked at him with pity. "You were on our turf, dear," the injured one said. "Think we'd ask you in for tea?"

The huge banger stepped forward. "We're going to have to tear you up a little," he said. And he reached a huge hand to grab Miller.

Instinctively, Miller knocked the hand away and stepped sideways into a fighting stance.

"Hoy," the giant said. "He's a proper bastard, in't he?" And he spit into his hands and began to circle Miller, looking for an opening.

Miller circled, too, wondering how he could possibly fight somebody seven feet tall who apparently knew what he was doing. And he was quick, too; Miller barely stepped away from a lunge that he hadn't seen coming.

But the giant's second lunge would have gotten him if he hadn't slipped. Because behind him in the cave he heard a sound.

Mara was coming out.

Even the giant's eyes left Miller, and Miller looked, too. It was a sight well worth seeing.

Mara stood in the cave mouth, her green eyes flashing, looking every inch the warrior queen. She held a bronze dagger in her hand and appeared to be ready to use it.

For a moment all the men just stared. Then the injured one cackled. *"Eee-hah!"* he said. *"Ab-so-fuckin'-lutely.* I like a piece with some spunk, ey? Don't just lie there, ey?" And he cackled again. "Come on, sweetheart," he said, stepping forward and holding out his good hand to Mara. "Let's you and me have a little fun."

"No!" Miller said. But the giant stepped between him and Mara, and there was nothing he could do.

Mara said nothing, simply stood motionless, watching the banger approach. He stepped closer, reached for her hand—

And with a movement too fast for Miller to follow, Mara whipped her knife up and around and into the banger's neck, the only clearly vulnerable spot in his armor.

The banger looked very surprised. He frowned, turned to face his friends, said something that sounded like, "Keck. Keck . . ." then he fell face forward onto the ground and didn't move anymore.

Mara stepped back to her original position, knife held ready, and said something that sounded like a polite challenge. She was clearly inviting the others to try their luck.

The other bangers stood motionless, and for a moment Miller was sure they would explode into violence.

But then the giant burst into loud laughter in a high and squeaky voice. The others stared at him, then they, too, began to laugh.

It was not reassuring laughter. In fact, in some way it seemed more threatening to Miller than screams of anger would have been.

"Spider," the giant said to one of the others, when he'd stopped laughing. Spider just nodded.

"Now then, missy," the giant said, and stepped toward her. She turned to face him, knife ready, and as she did, Spider jumped her from the back.

Before Miller could do anything, Spider's laser knife was at Mara's throat and he had knocked her bronze knife out of her hand.

"Now, then," Spider said, "shall we kill her before, or after?"

"You'd do a dead girl?" one of the others asked with disgust.

"They don't talk so much," Spider explained.

"The girl is mine," Miller blurted, without stopping to think.

The giant swung around to stare at him with amusement. "Oh, is she," he said. "Why, we had no idea, did we, mates? We're awful sorry, yer worship. Can I kiss the ring now?"

The others laughed, and Miller realized he'd put both feet into it. Unless he could pull off a colossal bluff, he was in even worse trouble than he'd been before he spoke. But what bluff did he have? Unless . . .

"Let's do him first, any road," Spider said.

There was a general murmur of agreement, and they turned to face Miller, except Spider, who kept his grip on Mara. And the giant one looked right at Miller and said, in a clear voice that was not his own, "Tell them you're Set."

Miller stared.

"Osiris's brother, Set," the Voice urged. "Tell them."

"I'm in the mood for a go-round," the Giant said, in his voice now. He snapped out his laser knife. "Have me a whittle."

Miller could not have defended himself at all if the Giant had attacked. He was still reeling in shock.

What was the Voice?

He had heard it twice now—no, *three* times. The radio had spoken to him before he hit Tahiti—was that the same thing? And on the cliff the Voice had told him to go with the bangers, but not to trust them. That had turned out to be the right move.

And now it was telling him to pretend to be an Egyptian god? Brother of Osiris, whose mark these thugs all wore? But Set had tried to kill Osiris—was he being set up? And if so, again, why not just kill him? He was totally in their power.

"Go on," the Voice said, this time come from Spider. Miller whirled to look at him. "It's your only chance," it said.

No one else gave any sign that they had heard anything. The bangers shuffled slightly closer, readying their weapons. And the moment was on him. He had to fight hopelessly, with his certain defeat meaning the rape and eventual death of Mara, and the loss of the last hope for restoring the awful mess the Artifact's destruction had created.

Or do what the Voice told him to do.

Without knowing why, or what It was. Or what it wanted.

Miller took a deep breath and looked at the circle of armored super-goons closing in on him. What choice did he really have? He certainly didn't have any other ideas. *If this doesn't work, I'm history,* he thought, and then he couldn't help thinking it was an ironic choice of words, in this new world where future, past and present were one and the same. *But it has to work.*

He did his best to work a small, superior smile onto his face. His lips were dry and cracked and it hurt to try, but he hoped it was convincing.

"I wouldn't do that if I was you," he said.

"Yes, but you're not me," the giant replied.

"You're not really any of us," Spider added. "So just who the fuck are you to tell us what to do, mate?"

"Set," Miller said. "Brother of Osiris."

There was an instant, and, to Miller, very gratifying stunned silence. "Go on," the giant said doubtfully.

"Pull the other one," Spider added, but he was just as uncertain.

For the moment it was a stalemate. Miller's bluff had gained them some time, if nothing else. It was working, just as the Voice had suggested. By claiming to be Set, the brother of Osiris, he had put them off balance and, with luck, bought himself and Mara a safe passage through the bangers' territory.

"I am Set," he repeated. "Brother of Osiris. Let us go now, or face my wrath—and my brother's."

"Can't be," the giant said.

"But he is supposed to show up some day," one of the other bangers said. "What if this is really him?"

"We could just kill him," Spider suggested. "Say we made a mistake."

"We'd be for it then," another warned.

"For certs," the first said. "Osiris'd have our balls for a necktie."

"Which he will anyway," the giant said. "Zoid and Sookie both dead and nothing to show?"

"So why not bring him this bastard?" Spider said. "Say it was all his fault."

"Hoy, that's it," one of the others said.

"And what about her?" the giant asked, nodding at Mara.

"Take her with," Spider said.

"Yes," added the first. "If it's his wife, Osiris'll want to see her, too."

"Good-o," Spider said.

"What, just take 'em both?" the giant said. "Let 'em see everything?"

"Got a better idea, mate?" Spider asked him.

"I'd still like to kill 'em both," the giant said.

"Well, you can't, all right?" Spider told him. "Because if you do, Osiris will eat your liver, won't he? And mine, too. Now give over, mate, and let's shove off."

"All right, all right," the giant grumbled. "But if Osiris doesn't want 'em, I got dibs on killing 'em. Fair's fair."

"Fair's fair," Spider agreed. "Come on, then."

22

CHAPTER

It was not a long trip, no more than forty-five minutes, but the landscape changed at least twice. They started off in a Northern European winter, where the cave was, and after only about fifteen minutes of walking they were in a warm spring day with the smell of cherry blossoms wafting into their nostrils. But that soon changed to winter again, a harder, bleaker, unclean winter, with only a few miserly patches of scrub brush scattered around, and a great deal of rusty dirt and half-eroded rock. Dirty snowdrifts leaned against the rocks, and patches of unhealthy-looking ice lay in the shadows.

Throughout the journey Miller stuck as close as he could to Mara. He didn't really know if his presence was any comfort to her, but he felt he had to try. Several times she looked around covertly, carefully, and Miller guessed she was looking for her warriors. He didn't know if they could track her here, but there were enough of them to handle this party of bangers if they could.

Unless the bangers had some other weapons hidden besides the laser knives, which were basically useless for anything but infighting. They acted so cocky, so confident—perhaps they did have something else, guns of some kind. If so, the Celts would be slaughtered.

Perhaps luckily, the question was never answered. They arrived at a ravine that wound back and forth for about a quarter of a mile before dead-ending at a rock face about twenty-five feet high. A grayish snowdrift was piled to the sides, but where it touched the rock face it had melted, leaving small greasy puddles at the foot of the stone slab.

Spider stepped forward and put his hand out toward the rock. Miller heard a humming sound, and a bar of light passed horizontally over Spider's face. Retinal scan? Miller wondered. Whatever it was, it recognized Spider. The stone wall peeled away to reveal a long metallic tunnel, sparsely lit, and straight for as far as Miller could see.

They entered.

"Welcome to Duat," Spider said with a mock bow as Miller and Mara passed through the door. "The Land of the Dead. Enjoy your stay." And he laughed at them, joined by the others.

Miller was faintly surprised that they were carrying the Osiris legend this far. It was working in his favor to this point, but he was under no illusions; it could change quickly and brutally, depending on the whim of the leader, the ruler of Duat. This Osiris, whoever he was, must be an interesting person to fuse gangsterism with Ancient Egyptian theology.

But "interesting" was not going to help. Some kind of superfast plane or boat was what he needed. Miller glanced at his watch; forty-five hours left. If he could somehow work a deal with Osiris, or whatever his real name was, there was still time. In a jet, the trip would take no more than five hours, and these people had to have something like a jet, something fast.

But what did he have to make a deal with? Other than his watch, he was without possessions. He had knowledge, but this Osiris obviously knew as much as or more than he did about Egyptian mythology. And as for any other area of knowledge—well, this slice of the world was obviously from the future. They must have access to things he could only dream about.

There was only one thing he knew that Osiris did not: why the world had suddenly twisted. And he knew how to stop it. Osiris would certainly see that it was in his own best interests to help him get to California and reverse this whole thing.

And anyway, he had no idea what kind of person Osiris was. If he were open to reason, maybe he would just release them. Maybe they could just walk away.

The hallway arrived at a wall that Miller couldn't see. The illusion that the corridor went on indefinitely was just that—an illusion. More light bars scanned them, and a hidden panel snapped open to reveal three guards, armed with what looked like very deadly rifles. They were several times the thickness of a conventional rifle and wrapped in tight coils of insulated wire. The guards instantly swung these weapons to cover Miller and Mara.

"It's all right," Spider said. "They're with me." The guards didn't move. "For Osiris," he added petulantly, and the guards lowered their weapons and disappeared behind their panel again.

The corridor took a sharp left and dead-ended again after only a few steps. A wall slid across the opening where they had entered, and then the small room began to move downward—an elevator.

Mara clutched at his hand with alarm, and he did the best he could to reassure her. "It's all right," he said. "This won't hurt us." But she didn't look convinced.

The room dropped, quicker and quicker, and then slowed to a stop. The door hissed open again. The temperature was immediately much hotter, and heavy with moisture that had a faintly metallic odor to it. The bangers adjusted a control on the belt of their suits—for coolness now, instead of warmth, Miller guessed.

Beside him, Miller heard Mara gasp in either awe or consternation, and he could feel her wobble with shock. He turned to her. She seemed to be all right, though taken aback. She was staring out the door, and he swiveled around to look. And then his jaw dropped, too.

They were looking at an underground world of incredible complexity. The stone walls of the chamber stretched upward at least a hundred feet, and at their top a series of clear pipes about the width of a school bus fanned out and disappeared into the far walls. They seemed to be filled with liquid, but Miller couldn't even guess what they were for.

Below the pipes stretched a slum. People were sprawled in front of vile-looking heaps of rag and paper, obviously their beds. Most of them seemed too listless to move, and only glanced up at Miller's group as they passed by. But a few of the stronger ones scurried about stealing the choicer bits of cloth from the weak ones. As Miller watched, one of the weak ones fought back; the predator stealing from him slammed a sharp piece of metal into his back quickly, and then, looking around to make sure no one else was coming to challenge him, he quickly rifled the dead man's belongings.

Miller felt Mara shudder beside him, and he turned to her. Their eyes met, and he slowly shook his head. What kind of world was this, where hundreds of people just watched as someone was killed for a heap of rags?

The bangers led Miller toward a huge black marble facade at the far end of the chamber. It was carved so that a pyramid jutted out in relief; at its top was a three-dimensional eyeball that sparkled and crackled with energy, seeming to turn and look in all directions at once. The rest of the facade was decorated with hieroglyphs, prominently featuring Osiris and Isis. And at the very top, behind the eye, Miller saw the clear pipes coming out of the top of the pyramid. Whatever the pipes were, they seemed to originate inside the pyramid.

They were once again scanned by the light bars before the massive doors opened. Then they were in a large chamber, decorated with what at first looked like bas relief murals. But as Miller passed the first panel, he realized they were all painted with the same three-dimensional paint that he'd first seen in the graffiti on the cliff face. He recognized a couple of the panels; they were taken from *The Book of the Dead*, an Egyptian guide to the Afterlife.

And at the far end of the room, on a raised platform, was the source of the glass tubes. It was a large, water-filled chamber from which all the tubes emanated. An airlock led inside, where a small car waited.

Spider led them up to the platform, and the door to the airlock hissed open. He waved a hand grandly, beckoning Miller and Mara to enter the small car inside. "Your barge to the City of the Dead, milord," he said.

The giant snickered and gave Miller a shove from behind. "Get in," he said.

The car bobbed slightly in the water as they entered. Mara gasped and grabbed Miller's arm as the doors slid shut. He led her to a bench, and she stared out the window, obviously terrified.

Water swirled against the car, sounding like a massive toilet flush. The car jerked and bobbed for a moment, and Mara dug her fingernails into Miller's arm hard enough to draw blood as they bumped, wobbled, and slammed into one of the pipes. Seconds later, the car shot straight up, whisking them away at an incredible rate of speed.

Through the triple filter of the water, the window, and the pipe itself, it was difficult to make out any details of the passing scenery. Miller got an impression of bleakness with rare slashes of color. There seemed very little movement, even in those areas where there were large groups of people.

Twice they came to junctions, where the pipes split into three or four different routes. Each time, the car slowed down and bumped the walls a bit before sliding into the open line and speeding away again.

Miller wondered why a mass transit system would be designed this way. Surely there were more efficient methods of transportation. This was the future, after all. Did Osiris use water just to carry out the imagery of the story cycle? What had Spider said, "barge to the City of the Dead"? And so the system used water so the car shuttles would simulate barges, with transparent pipes so people could see that these barges actually went to

Osiris? Was that it? Miller was skeptical. He thought there had to be more to it than that.

What about the water itself? Was it possibly a by-product of something else—say a power plant? Maybe it was used to cool a hydroelectric or nuclear generator, and then piped throughout the whole underground world to provide warmth. And then the shuttles simply took advantage of something that was already there.

And of course, the system did not really need to be efficient. The cars were small, able to hold only fifteen to twenty people at a time, and they passed no others that Miller could see. It was not really mass transportation at all; it was elite transportation. That fit in with the little Miller had seen of this bleak and deranged place.

The car came to a third junction, this one much larger than the others. They slowed, and then slid out into a massive chamber. This time the car bobbed to the surface, and began to move toward one end of the chamber. Off to one side Miller could see the docking area for the cars, and beside it, perhaps twenty times as big, he saw another dock. A fleet of what he assumed to be minisubs bobbed at their moorings here. A horde of slaves moved through the subs' airlocks, whipped and kicked by guards wearing the same costumes as Spider and the giant. They piled their loads on the dock and went back for more without pausing.

The loads were made up of all kinds of loot; bales of goods, huge and heavy crates and boxes, cartons and cases of every kind. Many had obvious water damage, but no one seemed to care.

Another line of slaves piled the goods onto carts and hauled them toward a large door at the far end of the dock.

There were hundreds of the subs, shaped like squids, with a long cargo area, a bulbous crew nodule that could probably hold up to five, and a cluster of grabbing arms at the front. But grabbing arms for what?

Salvage?

Or piracy?

Were the submarines predators, or did they salvage goods like vultures from the already-dead on the ocean floor? Miller guessed it would be a little of both. They could move in packs and take advantage of any target of opportunity. If it was already dead, so much the better. If it was alive and weak, that made no difference.

Miller thought about a culture that could survive as an opportunistic feeder. First, there would have to be plenty of opportunity. It would be a world in which the general order of things had broken down, and one strong leader could impose his will.

Was it some natural disaster that had caused all this? Nuclear winter, or a polar shift? Possible—after all, it had been awfully chilly outside for Australia. Perhaps another ice age had dawned, and this was a transition culture, living from the ruins of the old one while evolving into something new, adapting itself into . . .

Into what? A society where an elite few lived off the blood of the many? And why Osiris? Why should the whole system be based on a mythology that was three thousand years old? There were far stronger images that could be used to control a populace. Why should a leader who could create all this—a considerable achievement in spite of the system's brutality and oppression—choose Egyptian theology as his ruling tool?

Miller didn't have enough puzzle pieces to figure it

out. And in any case, it could all be at the whim of the leader, this Osiris. Maybe he just liked Egyptology.

"How we rule the seas," Spider said to him. "Right there, them submarines."

"I've never see anything like them," Miller said, fishing for information.

"'Course you haven't," Spider said indulgently.

"They look very fast," Miller said.

"Fast?!" Spider said. "Fast ain't even in it, mate. These things can *fly*. Eat up the distance like nothin' else."

"What do you get with them?"

Spider winked. "Whatever we want, mate. Whatever is, you know, available."

The car bumped against the dock. Whatever the answer to the puzzle of this culture, he would see the next piece soon.

They were offloaded onto the dock, and the giant marched them past the slaves, laboring in their long lines.

"That's the lucky ones." The giant grinned at Miller. "Maybe you'll get lucky, too, eh?" And for emphasis he kicked one of the slaves in the kneecap, kicked him so hard that the man's leg bent backward and he collapsed to the dock in agony.

A guard ran over and examined the fallen slave. He looked up at the giant with an expression of disgust.

"Bloody hell, mate," the guard said. "He's bloody useless now, in't he?"

"Sorry, mate," the giant said. "It were an example, like."

And he pushed Miller onward as the guard kicked the injured slave into the water. There was a splash, followed by a furious thrashing. Miller looked back to see a powerful swirl of water, a spout of red, and the slave's body disappear, dragged under by something large and powerful.

Spider leered at him as he turned back, thoroughly shaken. "Care for a little swim, mate?" he cackled.

They passed off the docks and into another long hall. This one was far more ornate than any of the others. Even half sickened by what he'd seen so far, Miller could not help being impressed with the degree of ornamentation. And as far as he could tell, it was all authentically reproduced, or—

A horrible thought hit Miller. What if this was the real stuff? What if this culture of scavengers had rummaged through the Valley of Kings in Egypt and gutted the Great Pyramid, the Sphinx, the hundreds of tombs, just to decorate this passage?

He tried to tell himself that didn't matter, that stealing from the long dead to spruce up the future was a thing that had no impact on him, but he felt it deeply anyway.

He was still fretting about it when they arrived at an enormous black door, trimmed in real gold.

"All right, then," the giant said, clearly nervous. He smacked Miller on the arm. "Just keep yer bloody piehole shut, mate, and show some bloody respect, hear?"

He looked so anxious, this enormous, brutal man, that Miller couldn't help feeling apprehensive, too. And then the huge doors began to roll slowly away. Miller felt his mouth go dry.

At first all he could see was a stunning, blinding amount of gold; the entire room appeared to be nothing but gold, trimmed with the divine blue of Egyptian deity.

The doors rolled open farther and a row of guards stood glaring at them. They were dressed in the same superhero body suits, but theirs were trimmed in gold and blue.

And then the doors rolled all the way open, and Miller's heart lurched into his mouth.

There he was.

Osiris.

23

CHAPTER

Miller was still trying to blink the blinding dazzle of all that gold out of his eyes, so for a moment he almost convinced himself it was an illusion. But his eyes adjusted and he was still seeing the same thing. No matter how unbelievable it was, it was there.

Sitting in the exact center of the far end of the room on a raised dais was the god Osiris. Not a punk in a suit, not a thug dressed up. It was Osiris, an exact replica of the wall paintings Miller had seen. He was larger than a human being. He held a tall golden staff and was draped in white linen. His blue skin, the color of the room's trim, set off a large, slanted pair of green eyes.

Oh. And there was a beak.

And a feathered crest.

For just as the original Osiris had been a hawk-headed god, so was this one. And right now the green hawk's eyes stared unblinking at him.

The head turned marginally, with the boneless grace of a real hawk turning its head, and Osiris stared at

Mara. Then the green, unblinking eyes came back to Miller. It was totally impossible to read any kind of human feeling in that face, beyond a kind of general hunger. Miller tried to look back just as boldly and remember that he was, after all, that thing's brother. But it was incredibly difficult not to collapse into a heap on the floor. He felt his heart pounding and he was unable to swallow.

For a long moment Osiris stared. Then, in a hesitant voice with a powerful Australian accent, the god spoke.

"Brother?" he said. Miller heard uncertainty in the voice and rejoiced.

He had a chance.

If there was uncertainty in Osiris, then *he* was faking it, too. And therefore he could never be sure that somebody else claiming to be the same thing was an impostor, too.

Whatever biogenetic miracles he had used to look like the real Osiris—the hawk's head, the amazing temple, all of it—Miller knew Osiris's claim was every bit as fraudulent as his own. And confronted with his assertion that he was Set, Osiris had to play it safe.

And so Miller said nothing.

He simply stared back, watching the other for weakness, waiting to see if the all-powerful Osiris would break first and rush to fill the accusatory silence in the room.

He did.

"Well," Osiris said, in that oddly inappropriate voice. "Come to see for yourself, have you? Well, as you can see, brother, I am alive."

Miller said nothing.

Osiris laughed. "Oh, it was a right proper fuck-over

you did me, brother. Seven great pieces, I was. It hurt, too."

Osiris was now sounding him out, Miller guessed, to see how much he actually knew. The legend said that Set had murdered Osiris, his own brother, by chopping him into *fourteen* pieces—not seven. Set's consort, Nepthys, and Osiris's wife, Isis, had teamed up to sew him back together, thus guaranteeing him immortality. But he had stayed below, in the Underworld, and ruled the dead. His son Horus was placed in charge of the living.

Miller knew he must finally speak and answer the challenge.

"Fourteen pieces, brother. As you know. And it was the price you willingly paid to guarantee your immortality."

The hawk head nodded slightly. "True enough, brother. True enough. A price you have yet to pay," he added slyly.

"I have paid," Miller said. "Betrayed by my own wife, banished from my land, forbidden a throne of my own."

"Been wandering, have you?" the hawk sneered. "Well, now what? Come to grab for my throne again, is it? Well, have a go, brother. Go right ahead. Go on, try for it."

"I choose not to," Miller said.

Osiris studied him for a long count. "What do you want?" he finally asked.

"To speak with you about something that concerns us both. Alone," Miller said.

Osiris laughed. "Think I'm afraid, is that it? I don't need the guards. They're just for show, make the boys feel useful. I reckon I can handle myself."

"I just want to talk," Miller repeated.

Osiris nodded. "All right, then," he said. "Take off, you lot," he told the guards.

The guards looked confused and hesitant. "Go on," Osiris said. "You heard me."

Reluctantly, the guards filed out of the room.

"Them, too," Miller said, nodding at Spider, the giant, and their other captors. "The woman stays with us."

"Gang up on me, eh?" Osiris said. "All right, then. Take off," he added to the giant's group.

The giant left quickly, willingly, with a worried backward glance at Miller. In just a few moments the black doors slid closed behind the last of the bangers. Miller and Mara were alone with Osiris.

"Well, brother," Osiris said. "Let's have it."

Miller studied the hawk face, wondering how to play his only card. But Osiris's face gave nothing away, and Miller realized he would just have to feel his way through this and hope he got it right the first time. There wouldn't be a second chance.

"Maybe you've noticed that things have changed outside," he said. "Out in the land of the living."

"I've noticed," Osiris said peevishly. "That's why I had the boys out. Scouting, like. Marking our turf. Looking to see what's what. Oh, I noticed, mate. I surely did." And then the great hawk head cocked at an angle and studied Miller. "What do you know about all that, eh?"

"If I tell you," Miller said slowly and carefully, "I want one of your submarines."

"A submarine," Osiris said curiously. "What for, eh? Why a submarine? Why not half my kingdom? Why not riches, eternal life, all that, eh?"

"Because I can still reverse it. Keep these changes to the world from becoming permanent. And I'm the only one who can do it."

"Are you, then? The only one. Well, well," Osiris said, looking at him thoughtfully. "What was all this about being my brother Set, then?"

"I had to get in to see you," Miller said. "I needed to keep your men off balance long enough to get to you."

"Clever lad," Osiris said. "So you're no longer claiming to be an ancient Egyptian deity, eh?"

"I'm no more an Egyptian god than you are," Miller said.

"'Course not," Osiris said with a laugh.

"I know you can see the advantage to getting your world back to the way it was," Miller said with confidence. "All of this strangeness and uncertainty gone. Back to ground-level reality again. Your world restored to what it should be."

"Wouldn't that be a pisser?" Osiris said, sounding more like an Australian gang-banger and less like a deity of any kind with each moment.

"But it has to be done now," Miller said. "I need to get to California in less than—" He glanced at his watch. "—less than forty-three hours."

"That a fact?" Osiris said.

"It is," Miller said. "Or I won't be able to stop everything from staying broken up like this. So with your permission, let's have your men take me to one of those submarines. Unless you have something quicker."

"Oh, I do, mate," Osiris assured him. "I absolutely do." And he picked up a handle-shaped object beside him and flicked it into life—a five-foot long laser blade. "This ought to do," he said.

He stood up and swung the blade. "Nice balance," he said. "Much quicker, too. I'm afraid I have to tell you, mate. I don't bloody *want* the old world back."

Miller was stunned. "Don't—"

"Absolutely don't. The more fucked up everything is, the better I like it. Back home they were starting to gang up on me, pull together. That'll never happen with this new setup. And if you say it's the same way the world over, that gives me a big advantage. Might even carve out a bigger piece this go-round. No, I like things this way, mate. I really like it." He stepped closer to Miller and swung again. Miller ducked reflexively. "And I can't have some bloody twink tiptoeing around and saying I ain't the actual Osiris, now can I?"

Osiris took a huge step toward Miller and swung the blade. Miller shoved Mara hard to one side and rolled the other way. He could feel a hot wave of air slice past him a few inches overhead.

As Osiris came back with a backhand, Miller dove forward, again rolling under the blade and coming to his feet on the far side of Osiris.

"Acrobat, are you?" Osiris said. "Good-o, bit of exercise for me." He twirled almost faster than Miller could see, and, stamping in the style of a classic fencer, drove the point of the blade straight at Miller's breastbone.

Miller dodged to the left, throwing his hands out to push the blade aside by reflex, and jerking them away just in time to avoid searing the flesh off his bones.

Osiris chuckled. "Give it up, you spry bastard. You're in the City of the Dead, remember? You can't leave it alive."

He swung again; Miller jumped back, but almost

too late this time. In fact, it would have been too late if he hadn't tripped on the step up to the dais and slammed flat as the blade hummed overhead. But now, sprawled on his back, helpless, it looked like it was all over.

Osiris didn't pause to gloat. He lifted his crackling blade straight up—

—and turned around without swinging, startled, as a crash sounded behind him.

Mara had grabbed up a ceremonial urn by the door and heaved it at Osiris. It had missed him, but it gave Miller a few seconds of precious time. He crab-walked backward, away from Osiris, and his hands came up against something—the golden staff. *Better than nothing,* he thought, and lurched to his feet, holding the staff at the ready.

Osiris was still looking at Mara. "It's always the crockery with them, in't it?" he said sadly. "I was married once, mate. Believe it. And it was always the crockery. Must be something in that X chromosome. Never found out for sure with me wife. Not even after the dissection. And now this one. Beautiful vase, too," he said, and turned back to see Miller with the staff. "Hello," Osiris said. "Give 'er a go, mate, but I have to warn you it's useless. Can't kill what's already dead, you know."

And he lowered the sword, closed his eyes, and held his arms out in a sacrificial pose.

"If I can't kill it," Miller said, gripping the heavy golden staff, "I'll settle for beating the crap out of it." And he stepped forward and swung with everything he had.

Miller was braced for a bone-jarring blow. But to his astonishment, the staff went right through Osiris and out the other side, and Miller swung with it, the force of the blow swiveling him all the way around and down to the ground, to a seat on the dais.

But the staff had *hit* Osiris—that is, it had hit where he was standing. And it had gone through him like he wasn't even there.

"That's impossible," Miller said.

"Well then, you fuckin' well dreamed it, didn't you?" Osiris sneered. "This is the Underworld. *My* world, sport. My rules." He leaned forward and pulled Miller up by the shirtfront. "And what I say goes. All of it."

Miller was still stunned, but grappling to recover. *A hologram, that's all,* he thought. *That's how he manages to do it like that. Let the staff go right through him.*

But he knew a hologram couldn't grip his shirt with fingers as strong as these were; could not, in fact, grip at all. A hologram was a three-dimensional projected image. In practical terms it had no mass, no physical existence, beyond what an equal amount of normal light would have.

So how was he doing this?

Osiris gave him no time to think about it. He shook Miller, hard. "And I say," Osiris said, "that your visit is *over*." And he threw Miller against the wall.

Miller took most of the shock on his arms, but still tapped his head against a golden knob sticking out from a mural, and he slid to the floor dazed. He shook his head, trying desperately to clear out the cobwebs and think.

He can be a hologram—or he can be solid, he thought.

Osiris scooped him up and raised him high overhead.

But can he be both at once?

He'd managed to hold onto the golden staff, and as Osiris cocked his arms back to fling him again, Miller swung the staff hard at Osiris's elbow.

The staff passed straight through—

—and Miller dropped right through Osiris's grip and fell to the floor with a stupefying thump.

He can't do both at once, Miller exulted as he fought for his breath and struggled to regain his feet. "Open the door!" he shouted to Mara behind him. He couldn't tell if she understood, but he did not dare take his eyes off Osiris.

"Your rules, is that it, Osiris?" Miller taunted.

"Too right," Osiris snarled, and jumped forward.

Again Miller swung the staff, and then leaped back. Osiris swung his blade, and Miller felt Mara's hand on his spine as he jumped back again. She tugged at him, and before Osiris could attack again, they were through the door. Miller tugged at the massive portal and it slid easily shut on perfect bearings. He jammed the staff through the handles to hold the door shut and turned to Mara.

"Let's get out of here," he said.

But she was looking behind him, her eyes wide with fright, and she called out his name in warning. "Millahr!" she said, and he whirled back to the door.

Osiris was passing easily, smirkingly, through the solid doors.

"My rules it is," he said.

"Run!" Miller urged, and grabbing Mara's hand, he fled down the hall.

They hurtled down another of the seemingly endless hallways. Over his shoulder Miller caught a glimpse of Osiris. He was striding along, in no great hurry. He seemed to be humming.

"Watch yourself," Osiris called cheerily. "Watch for that bump, it's a right bastard."

Miller turned around. Ahead of him, as far as he could see, the hallway was empty, deserted, practically featureless. The floors and walls were smooth, without bumps of any kind. Osiris was obviously taunting him. *He's so confident*, Miller thought, *that he's not hurrying, he doesn't seem worried—*

He and Mara slammed into an invisible wall. Stunned, Miller staggered to his feet and felt around.

"Warned you, didn't I?" Osiris called, much closer now.

Like the one they had passed on the way in with Spider and the giant, this wall was an illusion, showing an endless hallway ahead, when in fact it was solid and hard. Miller groped for the real opening and found it on the right. He tried to pull Mara to her feet, but she was unconscious. A thin trickle of blood ran down her forehead from where she'd slammed full-force into the wall.

Miller glanced at Osiris, only about fifty feet away now and closing fast with his unhurried stride.

"Here I come, ready or not," Osiris said.

There was no choice at all. He couldn't leave her. Grunting with the effort, still wobbly himself, Miller stooped and got a shoulder under Mara's midsection, lifting her in a fireman's carry.

He staggered away as rapidly as he could, down the hallway, looking frantically for someplace to run to, anyplace at all. If he could find a room or another corridor to the side while Osiris was still out of sight around the corner, he had a slim chance of gaining some time.

As if the walls had heard him, an open door appeared on the left. It was dark inside, but Miller lurched in anyway. Banged up as he was, and carrying Mara, he couldn't go much farther without a breather.

But as he hurried inside and across the floor, the door banged shut behind him and brilliant lights came on, flooding the room with the same dazzling golden glow as the throne room.

"Peekaboo," Osiris said from the far end of the room. "Tricky bastard, aren't you?" He shook his head. "A little too tricky, if you ask me, mate. You'll come to no good end."

And before Miller could more than gape at him with despair, Osiris waved a hand.

"About now, I should think," Osiris added.

The floor beneath them shimmered, then disappeared, and Miller and Mara plunged straight down into darkness.

24

CHAPTER

The fall was a brief one, but long enough for Miller to regret nearly everything he could think of—all he'd said, done, and especially *not* done in the last few weeks. But before he could really wallow in the dreadful guilt, they fell out of darkness and into a dim light. Miller just had time to recognize the submarine unloading docks a hundred yards away, and then the water closed over their heads.

Somehow, he held onto Mara, and as they plummeted down into the chilly water, he felt her arch her back and buck several times. She had obviously regained consciousness, but too late to keep from inhaling water. Miller tried to slow them, and she waved her arms feebly, and soon he was kicking hard for the surface, his lungs bursting and Mara's movements slowing to almost nothing.

But after he broke the surface and gasped in a lungful of sweet air, he managed to squeeze an explosive cough out of her, then another, and soon she was gasping for air, too, as he held her head above the water. When she'd recovered a bit, he helped her out of her heavy Druid robes; they would quickly pull her under if she tried to swim in them.

Underneath the robes, Mara was wearing a simple wool shift, plaid and a bit worn. Without the robes, Miller was surprised at how young and slender she looked.

He looked around for a way out of the water. It was cold enough for hypothermia to hit them both within a matter of ten or fifteen minutes. But the chamber looked featureless, except for the docks. And as he began to swim toward them, motioning to Mara to follow, he saw the guards beating a slave, and he remembered what he had seen before.

A body falling into the water and disappearing instantly. Yanked under by something huge and hungry.

And whatever it was, it was in this water.

Miller stopped swimming so abruptly that Mara ran into him. She spluttered and said something indignant in a questioning voice. He pointed ahead to the docks. Mara nodded. Miller made a shark mouth with his hands and growled as he mimed something big chomping down.

Mara smiled.

He shook his head. "No, damn it, it's not funny," he told her. "There's a *thing* in the water. Maybe more than one." He repeated his chomping gesture. "It'll get us, Mara. If we swim over there, it'll get us."

Mara smiled again. This time she added something that sounded reassuring, and began to swim toward the dock again.

"Hey!" Miller called after her. "Damn it, it's dangerous!"

But she kept swimming, and eventually Miller swore and went after her. He was a good, strong swimmer, and in spite of her lead, he caught up with her after she'd covered only about a third of the distance to the docks.

"Mara," he gasped out, reaching out a hand and placing it on her shoulder. She turned and looked at him, an eyebrow raised. "Damn it, girl," Miller said. "That thing will get you."

She smiled and shook her head. She said something that sounded like it was supposed to be reassuring. In short, she wasn't worried about any mean old monster.

And to make it absolutely clear to an increasingly frustrated Miller, she held up a necklace she was wearing around her neck. It had been hidden by the robes, but with them off, it hung down across her collarbones. It was very pretty, some beads hung on a leather thong, and a large pendant of intricately worked silver hanging at the center.

"An amulet," Miller said. "You're not worried about being eaten by a sea monster, because you're wearing an *amulet*."

She nodded her head and resumed swimming.

"Come back, damn it, that's just primitive superstition—you'll be eaten alive!" She wasn't listening, and the gap of black water between them grew larger.

Miller took off after her.

"Damn it, Mara," he gasped. She was about fifteen feet ahead of him because of her head start. He was closing the gap easily, gaining on her, when he saw it.

Cutting through the water, headed straight for Mara, was a very large dorsal fin.

"Mara!" he bellowed, surging forward to try to stop

her—why, he couldn't say. The thing must be so large, judging from the fin, that both of them would be no more than a light snack for it.

Mara had stopped swimming. She'd seen it at last, and was treading water, looking at it.

Now we'll see how good that amulet is, Miller thought.

He caught up with her, but she put an arm out, holding him back, and before he could protest, she had kicked forward to meet the thing.

"Oh, God, no," Miller moaned, waiting in an agony to hear the strangled gasp as the thing sank its enormous teeth into her and pulled her down, to see the vicious swirl of water, the bloody whirlpool surging up around the spot where she'd been, and then the fin coming up again, circling, and heading for him.

He watched Mara, knowing there was nothing he could do to prevent the huge creature from cutting her in half and dragging her under.

She held out a hand—not as if she were trying to stop the thing, Miller realized, but as if she was *welcoming* it.

Which she was.

The fin slowed, paused, circled her once. Directly under him Miller could see a huge shadow that seemed to go one forever. It bumped against him, but did him no harm.

Instead, the huge head broke water beside Mara, and it was worse than Miller had imagined. The head was the size and roughly the shape of a killer whale's, but the teeth were taken from a shark out of a nightmare. Three rows were visible, and in each row hundreds of large, sharp-looking teeth jutted out.

As Miller watched in horror, the jaw opened, leaned in toward Mara—

—and made a sound somewhere between a sigh and a giggle.

But then, while Miller was still trying to convince himself he had actually seen it, the thing leaned its head closer and nudged Mara affectionately. She laughed aloud and stroked its nose, and it absolutely cooed at her.

After a moment of mutual affection, Mara beckoned to Miller. Still expecting the creature to snap her up and gobble her down at any second, he approached. The monster looked at him warily out of one eye, but Mara spoke to it firmly and it left Miller alone.

Miller came close and, treading water, just looked at the two of them. "What the hell did you do?" he finally asked Mara.

She laughed again, and held up her amulet. She spoke, telling Miller the Celtic equivalent of "I told you so," and stroked the monster's nose again.

"All right," Miller said, shaking his head. "Chalk one up for primitive superstition."

He looked at the creature as carefully as he could without getting too close. Either it was some new mutant form of sea life that had arisen after his own time, or it was a deliberate genetic experiment. But it was clearly not a natural offshoot of anything he knew about.

Along its back it had a dorsal hole for breathing, but the teeth were unlike anything a true cetacean had ever had. And the behavior it displayed toward Mara was affectionate, intelligent; very similar to the way he knew dolphins and killer whales often behaved.

But the jaw, especially the teeth, and the dorsal fin,

were pure shark. The tail looked like it had been removed from a thresher shark and grafted on. It was a large, powerful, fierce-looking animal.

And whatever it was, Mara had it eating out of her hand.

They made the dock easily, the sea creature swimming beside Mara and demanding occasional pats on the snout. Miller pulled himself up out of the water and then held a hand down for Mara, who gave the monster a final petting and a kiss below the eye. It was so pleased that it tail-walked briefly before disappearing into the depths once again.

Miller pulled Mara up onto the docks. He turned around, still holding onto her hand, and stopped short.

Every guard on the dock was staring at them, standing in a half circle around them.

The slaves, too, had stopped their work to watch. There was a complete, motionless silence throughout the busy unloading area.

Miller realized this was going to call for a spectacular bluff. He cleared his throat and stepped forward. "Ahem," he said. "By the order of Osiris—"

He stopped speaking; it wasn't necessary.

As he stepped toward them, the guards had all stepped back.

He reached back for Mara's hand and led her toward the row of waiting subs. As they passed through the line of guards, the guards almost tripped over themselves in their effort to stay out of Miller's way—and more particularly, Miller realized, out of Mara's way.

Of course, he realized. *They saw her with the monster. They must think she's some kind of god, too, like Osiris.*

Miller had never been able to lie convincingly. He was, for example, a lousy poker player. He just couldn't bring himself to fib well enough to bluff convincingly.

But he was learning.

If nothing else, this trip was teaching him to see an advantage and do whatever it took to push it.

And so, holding Mara's hand firmly, he walked right up to the guard closest to the line of minisubs. "We need a sub," he said. "Which one is ready to go?"

The guard stared at him and blinked stupidly.

"Come on," Miller said, "I'm in a hurry. Which one?"

The guard licked his lips. Sweat was beading on his forehead. "Uh," he said, "I'm, like, you know. Not actually supposed to—"

"Can you swim?" Miller asked him.

"This one over here is good," the guard said, pointing toward a sub slightly larger than the others. "A new model, roomier, a little faster maybe."

"That'll be fine," Miller said, leading Mara toward the open hatch.

They were inside quickly. The hatch was easy enough to dog down; it worked with a large wheel, exactly the way hatches had always closed in every submarine movie Miller had ever seen. And there was no question about where the control room was, either. It sat on top, up front, in a glass dome that was streamlined into the body of the sub and wrapped around to give a 180-degree view.

Miller settled into the pilot's chair and breathed a sigh of relief. There were no surprises at the controls. There was a simple joystick planted in front of his seat, and three rows of toggle switches, each with a very clear picture-symbol underneath to indicate what they were for.

Miller got the engine running easily, and motioned Mara to another seat, in front of what seemed to be the navigation-communications panel. "Sit here," he told her. She was still looking around the room and out the window wide-eyed, but she sat gingerly, as if the chair might break under her.

Miller showed her the seat belt harness. "This strap goes across like this," he said, demonstrating. "It snaps in here." He secured her in place; she didn't object.

He snapped himself in then, rubbed his hands together, and pushed the throttle forward. The pitch of the engine moved up from rumble to roar. He eased back slightly and pushed the stick forward.

Nothing happened.

Frowning, he pulled the stick back toward his seat, trying to move in the other direction. The sub lurched slightly, but stayed in the same place.

Miller looked out the dome, craning his neck to see around the sub and determine why they weren't moving. It was clear in one quick glance.

"Oh," he said. "The ropes."

He unbuckled from his seat. "Stay here," he said to Mara. "I'll be right back."

Miller opened the hatch and looked out. The guards were still staring, perhaps wondering why a deity would forget something as basic as untying the mooring lines.

"You there!" he called, pointing to the guard who had shown them to this sub. The man lurched to attention. "You were supposed to untie us!" The guard opened his mouth, but nothing came out. He looked around for help, but all the others were moving away from him.

"Well?" Miller said.

"Uh—sorry!" the guard said. But he made no move to grab the mooring lines.

"Well, untie us," Miller commanded, pointing to the thick ropes.

"Right!" the guard said, falling forward onto the lines as if he'd been stung.

Miller watched to make sure the guard was actually untying them, and when he was reassured, he ducked back into the sub. But as he started to pull the hatch closed, he heard a commotion at the far end of the docks, down by the water-tunnel station, and looked back out.

The doors to the lift were open, and a line of twenty-some guards was double-timing out onto the dock, moving toward them. And behind them, striding out of the elevator and looking straight at Miller, came Osiris.

"Quickly, man," Miller called to the guard. He was bent over a cleat and unaware of his master's approach. And as he fumbled off the last line, Miller slammed and dogged the hatch and raced back to the controls.

Mara looked up at him questioningly as he dove for the joystick, not bothering to strap himself in.

"Osiris," he told her. "He's here."

She nodded and gripped the armrests, and Miller pushed the joystick forward. The sub began to move. He looked out the window. The nearest guards were about twenty feet away. Miller pushed the stick forward to move away faster, and cleared the dock as the first two guards arrived.

The man who had untied them was standing on the edge of the dock. He waved as he saw Miller look at him. Miller waved back—just as the arriving royal guards shoved the man into the water. There was a familiar swirl and splash in the water, and the helpful guard disappeared beneath the surface.

Miller looked away and accelerated slightly. The casual brutality of the guard's murder sickened him. It was tough to feel bad about the death of a man who was basically a death camp guard, but he had spoken with the man, and there was a human bond between them, however slight.

But there were other problems now, and they were more pressing. Now that they were away from the docks, where did they go next?

There was what looked like a viewing screen set into the control panel in front of Miller. Under it was a knot of four arrows, pointing at the four cardinal points of the compass. A toggle switch was set in the middle of the arrows, and another switch was beside the screen, with a blue dot at one end and a red dot at the other. Miller frowned, then flipped the switch beside the screen. "This has to be it," he muttered.

The screen came to life. It showed the water straight ahead of them. The picture was video, but computer-enhanced. It had no fuzziness of detail, as a plain camera shot would have. Instead, the farthest point in sight ahead of them was crystal clear, every line and shadow as cleanly visible as if it was on the panel in front of him.

"Wow," he said, impressed with the technology in spite of himself. "Now if it will only tell us how to get out of here."

Miller turned the sub slowly to the left. A small *ping* sounded and a red arrow flashed at a point on the screen.

"Bingo," he said. He aimed the boat at the arrow. "Home free."

"Millahr," Mara said.

He looked at her. She had been gazing out the dome, and now pointed back toward the dock. He craned his neck to see.

Behind them, Osiris stood in the middle of the dock, one arm on his hip and the other arm outstretched, pointing at them. His beak was open as if he was speaking.

And all around him, at the slips where the other submarines were moored, there was movement. Ten of the slips were now empty.

The subs had pulled out and begun to move.

Coming after them.

25

CHAPTER

Miller didn't know this ship, and he was in an unfamiliar place, a confined space that was actually too small for maneuvering to evade ten pursuers. But he moved the throttle lever forward as much as he dared and concentrated on making progress toward the blinking red arrow. He still assumed that it indicated the exit; he had no other choice now, no clues about any other options. If he was headed for a dead end—well, it would be a literal dead end as far as he and Mara were concerned.

So he concentrated on keeping the sub on course and, as he gained more confidence in his ability to operate it, he increased the speed slightly one more time. The little sub responded beautifully to the controls. It reminded him of an airplane in many ways; it responded so quickly and handled so smoothly.

"Millahr," Mara called, and he half turned to look at her.

She had apparently gotten over her fright and shock

at all that had happened, at least enough to experiment with her new surroundings. On the panel in front of her she had found a view screen like Miller's and turned it on.

But additionally, she had toggled a switch on the side that had turned her view screen into a kind of radar display, but with much better graphics than the ones Miller knew.

Mara was pointing at the screen, which showed a large blue blip in the center—obviously representing them—and ten smaller red blips around them. And one of the red blips was close, practically touching them.

In fact, as he watched, they heard a scraping sound, and their sub began to stagger slightly. Miller turned to his own view screen. One of the switches beside it showed a circle with four eyeballs in the middle, looking in four directions. He toggled to look behind.

The attacking minisub had its tentacles out and wrapped around the tail of the sub Miller was operating. The arms crawled along Miller's hull, searching for a grip, pulling them closer.

Miller grabbed the joystick and flung them hard over to one side. The attacker's tentacles slipped slightly, but caught and held.

Miller threw the joystick the other way. Again he gained a few feet, but could not break the other's grip. He felt their sub slowing as the other threw its engines into reverse and began to drag them slowly back to Osiris.

Then he remembered the guard saying that this sub was a little faster. That meant a more powerful engine, which should give him an advantage if he was willing to take a few risks. He could use his engine's stronger thrust to break the grip of the tentacles—if the strain didn't break up both ships.

It was chancy—but he had nothing to lose.

"Hang on," he said to Mara.

He pushed the throttle forward, quickly and hard, hoping to gain some room by the brutal surprise of his move. He felt the tentacles slip slightly, and for a moment his sub surged forward, dragging the other one along.

But then the attacker kicked his engines higher. The two subs were locked together, moving in neither direction, groaning and straining like two wrestlers in the middle of the mat.

Miller eased his throttle forward.

So did the attacker.

The engine noise climbed to a hysterical pitch and the whole submarine began to quiver and shake, everything on board rattling, including Miller's teeth.

The vibration climbed. A rivet popped out of the base of Miller's chair and pitched to one side.

"Millahr," Mara called.

She indicated a corner of the glass dome, where a thin stream of water had begun to trickle in.

It was no good. They were making no progress, and destroying their ship.

Worse, on Mara's screen the other subs were almost on them.

Miller had one slim chance remaining, and without pausing to consider the risks, he took it.

He pulled back hard on the joystick, slamming the sub into reverse and flinging it directly at their attacker. At the speed their engine was revving, the results were impressive.

The tail of their sub caught the other on one corner of its glass dome. There was a tremendous, jolting smash. It sounded like somebody had dumped thousands of auto parts into a bathtub filled with cement. The attacker's dome instantly shattered into shards. Water flooded in and the other sub began to settle toward the bottom, dragging Miller and Mara along with it.

Miller pushed at the controls, trying to slip out of the tentacles that still gripped them. He juked to the left and right, back and forth, up and down. The mechanical arms loosened their grip but would not let go. But after what seemed like ages, their was a muffled *wumpf-snapp!* from the other sub. The water had finally filled the engine room and all the circuits were shorted out. Miller managed to slip away as the tentacles went slack and the other sub sank out of sight.

They were free. But the screen showed the other subs coming up fast.

Miller wasted no time watching them. He aimed the sub at the blinking arrow on his screen and eased the throttle forward as fast as he dared to push the sub.

Fifty yards away, and it occurred to him that he had no idea yet how to make the machine go up and down. The attacking sub had pulled them under, and, according to the digital readout above the screen, they were still at a depth of 37.48. Feet or meters? he wondered. It must be meters.

But he could be reasonably sure that the gate out of the enclosure and into the open sea would be at a different depth. It might be deeper or shallower, but it would a colossal coincidence if it happened to be at the same depth as the sub.

He looked around and spotted foot pedals ahead of

his seat—that had to be elevation. He eased his feet into them and slowly, experimentally, pushed down.

The sub's nose went down. They began to go deeper.

"Gotcha," Miller said softly. Mara looked up at him inquiringly; he shook his head. "Nothing," he told her.

The red arrow began to beep. As he looked up at it, it swung downward, blinking more rapidly now, pointing down. Miller moved the foot pedals forward, easing the sub deeper. The arrow blinked and beeped slower, slower, then stopped altogether, and Miller leveled off.

"Not bad for a boat," he said out loud. He was a pilot by choice, but he was beginning to like this thing. It was built by a genius for a moron to use. All the controls were simple, effective, easy to use and understand, and elegant in design and response.

The red light held steady now, and in the visual display screen he could see a vast archway leading out into the open sea. It was a fine, wide opening and so he moved the throttle forward a bit.

He checked Mara's screen. The other boats were closing in fast. More used to their subs and to their home water, they didn't hold back at all. He did some rough guesswork, but it was no good—they were going to catch him.

Grimly, he moved the throttle farther forward. He had one chance that he could think of, a maneuver he'd picked up from a British pilot he met on a NATO exchange. The Brit claimed he had used it in a Harrier, but Miller was hoping it would translate to the subs. He tried to set his speed so he was only slightly slower than the pursuers, timing it so they would catch him at the gate out of the harbor enclosure.

It was working. The two lead attackers came in from the sides to flank him; the other seven dropped back to give the lead subs some room and seal off retreat at the same time.

Miller watched the flankers carefully with one eye and the screen with other. It was closer now, closer— three, two, one—

NOW!

He slammed the joystick into reverse. His sub came to a stop so suddenly the belt bruised his ribs. The two attack subs shot past him, completely surprised, and barreled ahead through the gate. Miller quickly followed into open water.

By the time the two lead attackers had turned around, he was headed away from them at full throttle. They continued to follow stubbornly but couldn't hope to catch up now. Far back, the other seven subs spread out and trailed after him, hoping for some miracle of stupidity on Miller's part. But he had no plans to give them any chance at all. At full throttle, he headed at a sharp angle away from his pursuers, and away from Duat, the City of the Dead.

The pursuers gradually dropped away and out of visual contact. Miller checked the radar screen and saw that only two of them remained on his tail, and they were dropping slowly back. He relaxed a little and turned to smile at Mara.

"I think we're safe," he told her. "We've gotten rid of them all."

But Mara frowned and gave her head a half shake.

"What? They're gone, Mara. Come on, cheer up for God's sake, we're going to make it."

For answer, Mara shook her head. And as she did, both the radar and the visual screen began to beep.

Miller whipped around to look at his screen, and his jaw dropped.

Ahead of them, fanned out in an attack formation, were seven of the minisubs.

"But that's impossible!" he blurted.

But it wasn't.

The subs ahead of him began to close the distance, moving in to block him from all sides. Bewildered, Miller reacted automatically. There was a small opening above him and he headed for it. The attackers responded quickly, but he was just ahead and slipped out above them.

But now what? He could only go up thirty or forty feet and then he'd be on the surface. Then he could only maneuver in two dimensions, and against seven attackers—no, damn it, *nine* of them; the other two were closing in fast. It didn't look good.

But he had no other choice. He headed straight up, pursued by an increasingly tight formation of pursuers. He took his eyes off the controls to check the radar, and in that half a moment his submarine broke the surface.

For a second he was afraid he'd cost them their lives. He waited for the sub to slap back onto the water, sure that the force of that landing at this speed would break the boat's back.

Instead, as the nose and then midsection emerged from the water, Miller heard a new sound, and felt a new vibration, as if completely different engines had automatically cut in.

And then he noticed that, even more astonishingly, the submarine was airborne, skipping away across the waves at an altitude of about twenty feet.

The submarine had become a hovercraft.

His jaw dropped. "*That*'s how they did it!" he exclaimed. "That's how they got in front of me! They *flew*!" And in the air, he was in *his* element. His odds had suddenly gotten a lot better.

Mara said something that sounded like a question beside him and he turned. She appeared alarmed at this new way to travel. It was a great deal faster, and being above the water gave a sense of speed that traveling under the waves did not.

"It's all right," he said. And then he felt his face move into an actual smile. "In fact, it's wonderful," he told her, and turned back to the controls, oddly exhilarated. But of course, it wasn't that odd. Miller the pilot was a much more dangerous opponent than Miller the submarine captain. Facing nine opponents was not nearly so scary in the air.

The first thing he did was to shove the throttle all the way down. The little craft took off like a shot. Miller banked at an oblique angle to the direction he'd been heading, and as the first of the pursuers broke water, he was far away and in the wrong direction. All nine came up, but they circled for a good minute before spotting him and giving chase, and in that minute Miller had gained such a commanding lead that he was confident they would never catch up.

It eventually occurred to the attackers, too, and one by one they dropped away. Soon he was skipping over the water's surface alone. He checked Mara's screen in all directions; there were no blips of any kind.

They were alone on the ocean.

26

CHAPTER

It took Miller about forty minutes to find the best speed—one fast enough for them to make their goal in plenty of time, and slow enough so the ride wouldn't kill them. Through cautious experimentation he had found an automatic pilot of sorts, one that would keep them on the same heading until he toggled it off or touched the joystick.

After that it got a little easier. It would have been a daunting trip in a conventional boat, and a long one in a plane, as he well knew. But they skimmed easily along at a rate that he estimated would get them to their goal with about ten hours to spare.

In fact, the little hovercraft was so speedy that he'd chosen an extremely conservative course, one that would guarantee they hit the coast somewhere in California or Baja, Mexico; without charts it was hard to be sure. But it would have been harder to miss a coast that size if you knew its general direction, and that part was easy.

Miller reasoned that when he hit the coast, he should find it easy enough to follow it northward—or south in the unlikely event that he'd gone too far up the coast—until he came to the familiar landmarks of the Channel Islands, and then San Francisco Bay. With or without modern landmarks like the Golden Gate Bridge, he was sure he would find his target. And thanks to this wonderful little ship, he should have time to spare.

"We'll make it, knock on wood," he said.

He looked around for a piece of wood to knock, found none, and instead gave three quick raps to the armrest of his chair. He had never really been superstitious—but then, he'd never flown a submarine to California to save the world, either, and the homey little gesture made him feel better.

Mara looked up at his rapping and smiled. She said something in her wonderful, lilting language, but Miller couldn't make out even a single word. "Sorry," he said, shaking his head and smiling ruefully.

Mara smiled back, and held out her amulet. She pointed to several of the beads, and he examined them. "Wood," he said. She nodded and gave the beads three miniature knocks, then held it out for him.

"Thank you," Miller said, and tapped softly on the wooden beads. As he did he realized that he hadn't been this close to Mara before, except when they were facing some kind of danger together. Now, with the ship running smoothly and his hopes rising, he had time to look at her.

She was wearing her woolen shift. It had been meant to be worn under her Druid robes, but with those long gone, it would have to do as an all-purpose garment. At least, until they got someplace where they could find new clothes.

He was again surprised to see how young she looked without the ponderous robes, and how attractive. He'd become used to her face, had always found it pleasant, well-formed. But now he found himself looking at her in a different light. Dressed in only the flimsy shift, she was quite clearly a very beautiful woman. And in spite of his recent time with Yuki, he found himself powerfully attracted to her.

But what were the rules about sleeping with Druids? He had no idea—were they celibate? Would she feel obligated to kill him if he made any move in that direction? There were so many things about her he didn't know—so many things no one would know, the world over, about interacting with all these other cultures.

And what would happen to Mara when he got to Bodhi headquarters and fixed things? Would she be instantly whisked back to her own time? Would she be trapped in the present, whatever it might be, with him? How would he feel about her if she became a permanent obligation?

He kicked himself mentally. He hadn't even kissed her yet, and he was already wondering how to end the relationship. What a jerk he was being. He gave her another smile, got one in return—

And whipped around to the control panel as he heard the alarm go off.

The red light over the view screen was flashing, and the alarm gave out a steady *bleep—bleep—bleep*. He turned the viewer to the spot where the arrow pointed. A three-masted ship was bearing away on roughly the same course they were taking. Its sails were reefed, in spite of the moderate weather, and a huge cloud of black, oily smoke came up from the deck.

"A whaler," Miller exclaimed. "It's a whaling ship!"

He grabbed the joystick and slowed the hovercraft. He was not terribly worried about an encounter with an old whaling ship, but caution dictated avoiding any chance of an accident. There was just too much at stake. So he slowed the sub further, brought it down to the surface, and put her nose into the waves.

Mara looked at him questioningly.

"Just until we're on the other side of that ship," he explained. "Just to be cautious. Aw, forget it," he said, seeing her blank look. "I wish we could communicate." But Mara, of course, had no answer.

Miller took the sub to a cruising depth of twenty feet, to provide plenty of room to get safely under the whaler and away on the other side. He calculated he would lose about twenty minutes, since traveling underwater was considerably slower than skimming above it, but he had enough time to spare that he wasn't worried.

He was fairly close to the whaler, his mind still on Mara, when he heard a dull *BOOM* and the hull rang like a gong. The little submarine quivered, jerked once or twice, and then water was pouring in across the floor from somewhere aft. Alarms began to beep, ring, and flash.

Mara cried out and they were both pitched from their seats as the sub's nose jerked upward. Then, with a whine of servomotors, it leveled off again and slowly moved back to speed.

"What the hell happened?!" he yelled. But at the moment it didn't really matter. He had to get to the surface before the sub was overwhelmed with water and sank.

Miller pulled the joystick and gave it all the throttle

he had, hoping to get out on the surface before his sub's neutral buoyancy was canceled by the weight of the water, which would sink the ship.

He had time for a quick glance at his view screen. It was showing a computer-generated picture of the sub with a bright red, flashing spot on the top, just behind the middle of the boat. It was here, obviously, that the water was coming in. Miller glanced again; under the red spot, the screen was flashing a message. *HULL PUNCTURE*, it said. They had somehow grown a hole in the hull.

He could feel the boat slow as he approached the surface. The water was sloshing around his ankles now, and the sub was no longer responding to the controls as easily as it had. It must be quite a good-sized hole, he thought, whatever had caused it. But he was going to beat it, to get them up in time. What happened after that was anybody's guess, but he would not let them sink and drown in this little boat.

The water around the dome grew brighter; and then suddenly they broke water and were on the surface. Immediately, as if somebody had turned off the valve, the water stopped pouring in.

A chime sounded; it was a different tone from the emergency alarms they had been hearing. Miller glanced again at the view screen. It showed a computer picture of the control panel. One small button at the top of the console in the picture was blinking bright blue.

He found the button on the actual panel and punched it.

"Your immediate emergency is now over," said a cool female voice with an Australian accent. "Please begin pumping out the water now."

"I'd love to," Miller replied. "How?"

"Locate the main emergency drain pump control," the woman said. "It looks like *this*."

Another segment of the control panel showing three small buttons began to pulse with a blue light on the screen. He found the correct corresponding buttons on the panel. "Got it," he said.

"Now begin this sequence," the recording said, "one, three, two, two, three." The lights on the screen blinked in sequence as the voice spoke.

"One . . . three . . . two-two-three," Miller said, finishing with a flurry.

He heard a slurp, then a steady whining sound, and the water quickly began to recede. "Bingo," he said.

"That's got it," the recorded woman said. "You may now inspect the damage on the hull. Please use control area exit three." The location again flashed on the screen.

"Thank you," Miller told the recording.

Mara was sitting in her chair, gripping the arms and looking out the window. So far she hadn't panicked, and she looked like she was in control of any fear she might be feeling.

"Are you all right?" Miller asked her.

She looked up at him quizzically and pointed out the window.

Miller looked.

They were still traveling at a good clip, better than thirty knots. And behind them, still pulled taut at the end of a thick cable, they were towing the whaling ship.

Miller saw three men struggling to undo the rope as the rigging crashed around them. The whaling ship clearly couldn't take the strain of being hauled at this speed; the battered old tub was never meant to go more than ten knots. And the submarine, built for salvage and piracy, designed to pull huge dead weights, was having no difficulty hauling the old sailing ship.

Even as Miller stared, the main mast snapped in two. The top half came crashing down and plunged straight through the deck, knocking over the two huge kettles where whale blubber was being rendered down to oil.

Miller jumped to the controls to stop his submarine. He jammed the throttle down to idle and put the engines into neutral. Then he ran for the hatch, undogged it and flung it open.

The first thing he saw as he stepped out onto the small observation deck of the submarine was the thick shaft of a harpoon sticking out of the hull, right beside the hatch in the center of the sub's deck. He grabbed the harpoon with both hands, wiggled it back and forth and braced his feet. It came out, and Miller flung it into the water and turned to look at the whaling ship.

It was breaking up. The mast had gone butt-end first through the hull, smashing a hole and letting the water gush in. But even worse, the boiling hot whale oil had spilled and was pouring across the deck. As it touched the fires under the kettles, it ignited. The ship was turning into an inferno.

There was a crushing sound and the ship creaked heavily over to one side. Burning whale oil poured through the scuppers and onto the ocean's surface. Large slabs of whale meat followed, splashing into the water. In only a few seconds the water around the ship began to boil, and Miller saw with horror that a large number of sharks had been following the whaler and were now whipping themselves into a feeding frenzy and ripping into the whale meat.

One of the hands on the ship, half ablaze with burning oil, slid over the rail and into the water. He sank under and then, almost immediately, seemed to fly straight out again. But he was not flying under his own power.

"Oh, my God," Miller whispered.

The sailor had been lifted up by a big shark. It had grabbed him by the back and taken him up, out of range of the other sharks as it bit down on him. Miller had one quick glimpse of the man's face, twisted into the most complete agony he had ever seen. Then the sailor and the shark vanished below the waves.

More crunching, grinding, and groaning noises were torn from the old ship. It was burning, settling, breaking up. Miller knew it would be only a minute or two before it slid under the water—or, he realized with a start, before it exploded. If there were even a few barrels of oil already in the hold, and a few barrels of gunpowder, the ship would go up like a roman candle when the flames reached the storage area. Anyone on board who wasn't blown to pieces would be ripped into small chunks by the sharks.

And it was his fault.

"God help me," Miller whispered.

He had to help. In spite of the terrible risk of maneuvering into the burning oil, falling debris, and the suction a sinking ship always created, he had to do something to try to save these men.

"Jump!" he bellowed. "Swim for my ship!"

And he ran below again to the controls, inching as close to the burning whaler as he could get. The sailors were jumping now, whether because they had heard him or because they had no choice, Miller didn't know. He counted eight men in the water, and a small series of explosions began to rip through the whaling ship. A large chunk of the rail, half on fire already, exploded into the water from a blast aft of the wheel.

One of the swimming sailors screamed; the sound was cut off as the man vanished, yanked below by an unseen predator. Mara made a noise that sounded like a cross between a moan and retching; she began to chant something desperately.

The remaining men in the water swam faster, stretching out for the sub with all they had. But one more man screamed and was literally pulled in half by two large sharks.

The last six reached the sub and clambered up onto the hull as quickly as they could. Miller moved the boat away from the burning, disintegrating hulk as fast as he dared with the sailors clinging to the sub's hull.

When he was well away, he set the autopilot and went back out on deck.

The sailors seemed to be in shock. One of them was moaning, repeating the same thing over and over.

"Gone," he said. "Sweet Jesus, gone, all gone, fourteen months and it's gone. All gone, sweet Jesus . . ."

"Shut the hell up, Keane," another man told him.

"Gone," Keane replied. "Sweet Jesus—"

"Is anybody injured?" Miller asked anxiously, unsure of what to do or what to say.

The sailors looked at him. Through their shock Miller saw that they were afraid of him, unsure of what he might be in this magical boat that came up from under the water.

"Gone," said Keane. He didn't even look up. "Sweet Jesus, fourteen months—"

Another of the men laughed bitterly. "It's his profits he's crying for," the man said. "His uncle Benjamin chewed into rags by the sharks, and he's counting his lost gold." The man stood up. He wasn't tall, but his shoulders were remarkably wide. His arms were long and powerful, and his face, battered and sunburned as it was and half covered by reddish beard, was open and friendly. He held a hand out to Miller. "We're obliged to you for the rescue, Captain. I'm John Grove, late of Nashua, harpooner."

Miller took Grove's hand. It was huge, immensely strong, and covered with a thick layer of callus. "I'm Tony Miller. Ah . . . my God, the—" He found it nearly impossible to say anything meaningful. "I'm sorry. Your ship—I'm terribly sorry."

Grove laughed again. "It's I who am sorry, Captain Miller, for it was I who harpooned your vessel. From the deck you looked to be the great whale himself." He nodded at the bowling-ball-sized hole in the center of the deck. "All said, it was a fine shot, at least." And then he looked embarrassed, coughed, and added, "If I've done any damage, I ask your pardon, sir."

Miller opened his mouth to speak—when the sub was slammed hard on the side and tipped far over. The sailors shouted and began to slide back into the water, screaming and calling out.

Miller and John Grove, because they were standing by the hatch, were able to grab on and avoid tumbling into the water. But all the other sailors poured helplessly back in, and in a heartbeat the sharks were among them.

"Bill!" John Grove called out. "Oh, Bill, I'm coming!" And he jumped for the side of the boat, holding out his arm for one of the sailors who had almost made it back out again.

But as John Grove watched, his friend was savaged by an entire pack of the sharks, and he sank gurgling under in a cloud of his own blood.

Miller ran to the other side of the deck, where one of the men hung on, a pale and shocked expression on his face. It was Keane, the man who had repeated the same phrase over and over.

"I've got you," Miller called to him, and took his hand. "Hang on now—*awwwgg!*" Miller stared in horror at what he'd pulled out.

He was holding less than half of Keane.

The rest was gone, cut cleanly away by the sharks.

Miller gagged and jumped back, dropping the half body back in. He was still teetering in horror when he heard Grove call out behind him, "Hang on, Captain! It's a great white, the biggest I ever—"

BAM! The shark rammed the sub hard enough to keel it over, and as it did, Miller lost his footing and fell to the tilted deck. He slid straight for the side.

"Captain!" Grove called out, and tried to reach him. But the distance was too great, the deck too slick and tilted too far over.

Miller slid into the ocean.

27

CHAPTER

As the icy waters of the Pacific closed over his head, Miller had time for only one quick thought: *Oops,* is what went through his head. And then he bent all his energy, all his thoughts, on getting back to the submarine as fast as he could. He flailed to the surface and struck out strongly, the image of what had happened to Keane still clear in his mind.

But the submarine still moved slowly away from him, rolling on the long Pacific swells, and Miller knew it would take a miracle for him to make it to the boat before the sharks made it to him.

"Captain!" John Grove called from the deck of the sub. "Behind you!"

Miller glanced back. The huge great white shark that had rammed them was headed straight for him. It was on the surface, dorsal fin out of the water, its great jaws with their thousands of razor-sharp teeth parted, and it was coming for him; closer, closer—

There was a blinding flash of light, an incredibly

powerful explosion, and Miller no longer knew where he was, or even who he was. But it was cool here, very nice. Perhaps a nap would be a good idea, nothing pressing to do right now, so—

He coughed explosively.

"He's coming 'round, miss!" John Grove said.

Miller found himself on the deck of the sub's control room, lying on his back and spewing out seawater. John Grove kneeled beside him, and Mara was closing the hatch to the outside deck.

As Grove spoke, Mara whirled and came to Miller's side. She placed a hand on his forehead, the other on his wrist, and closed her eyes for a moment. Miller felt better at the soothing touch of her hands. He closed his eyes, too.

"What happened, John?" he asked. The words made him cough, and he turned his head as a small pool of ocean came up out of him.

"Damnedest thing I ever did see," John Grove answered. "The shark fair had you, Captain. Were no more than ten feet away, when by God, a bolt of lightning came from the clear blue sky and blasted that shark into soup." He laughed, a quick, explosive sound, and shook his head. "Must be like Keane used to moan all the time: 'The Hand of the Almighty reaches into the remotest spots of the earth, and where it touches there is miracle.'" He spat over his shoulder, relatively near the hatchway. "Never did pay that sort of talk any heed before now, Captain, but for lightning to come from the clear blue sky like that ..." Grove shook his head. "I just never seen anything like it."

But Miller had.

He had seen something very much like it before. Twice before.

He knew whose hand it was—and it wasn't the Almighty's.

Still weak, he rolled his hand over and grasped Mara's wrist. He gave a little squeeze, but let her know that he was not going to let go, either. "Thank you, Mara," he said.

She looked at him, flashed her teeth and shook her head.

"Thank you for saving me from the shark," he said. "That's a very bad way to go."

Mara shook her head again and said a few words in Gaelic. Miller closed his eyes with a half smile and shook his head. "I'm sure they had time to teach you English, whatever your original language is," he said to her. She began to speak again, but Miller reached a finger up and placed it on her lips.

"It's a wonderful act," he said. "You could have gotten away with it indefinitely if you hadn't had to save my life. It's terrific, really; completely convincing." He grabbed her other wrist now, with the hand that had been at her lips. "But I know who you are."

She frowned and tried to free herself, protesting in her lilting speech, clearly demanding that he let her go.

"I can't let you go just yet," Miller said. "I need to know what's going on. I need to know what you're planning, why you're here." He sat up and faced her, still holding her wrists. "I need the truth, Mara. And I need it now. Because I know who you are.

"You're a Bodhi," Miller said.

Mara was silent.

"It's a bit of a problem," Miller said, and he tightened his grip on her wrists. "Because I really do appreciate what you did, risking your cover like that to save me. But on the other hand, I know damned well that you didn't do it to save *me*—but to preserve some plan your people have."

Mara tried to pull free again. Miller clamped down hard.

"I have to stop that plan," Miller said, an edge in his voice that seemed to surprise her. "I have to stop *you*. But I need your help to do it, too.

"So I'd like to help you for what you did, but I'd also like to kill you for what you are—because I am sick to death of being *used*!

"So it's troublesome, isn't it, Mara? Or whatever your name really is."

She looked at her wrists where he was holding them, bit her lip and looked away.

"Say, Captain . . ." John Grove said uneasily.

"Stay out of this," Miller said. "I'll explain it to you later. Which is more than she would have done," he added, nodding at Mara. "Isn't that right, Mara?"

"But she doesn't even speak our language, sir," Grove said.

"She speaks it as well as you or I," Miller said.

Grove looked uncomfortable. He cleared his throat and looked away. But Mara still would not look him in the eye.

"I need your help," Miller said to her. "No more games or pretending or trying to make me jump through whatever hoops you have lined up for me. I don't know how to make you help, and I don't want to hurt you—"

"You can't hurt me," Mara said. "I can protect myself."

"Good Lord," Grove said.

She spoke clearly, perfectly, with a very slight accent that in his own time Miller would have thought might be Israeli.

"Pretty good English for a Druid," Miller said dryly.

She shrugged—still a pretty gesture, no matter who she was. "You had guessed it any road," she said. "When I blasted the shark. But I had to save you."

"To protect your plan," Miller accused her.

"You are just as alive as if I had saved you for love," Mara said. "Is motive more important than ultimate result?"

"I think it might be," Miller replied. "But the important thing now is, what happens next? Now that it's all out in the open."

"That's up to you."

"Bullshit," Miller said, surprising even himself. He never used words like that. But he was learning just how mad all this playing around with his life had made him.

"You've been on to me from the beginning, haven't you?" he asked her. "You've been moving me back and forth like a chess piece. Why?"

"We need you," she said simply.

"So do I," Miller replied.

"History says we can use you."

"It's not up to history," Miller said. "It's supposed to be up to me."

"Miller—" she started, and then shook her head. She tried to pull a hand away from him, and this time he let her. "You are more important than you know, and if you did know it—that would change how you might react. Alter your chances. Degrade your performance. And you're the only one who can do . . . certain things."

"Cook said pretty much the same thing. But nobody has really told me what those things are. And you haven't asked me if I wanted to do them, either."

She shook her head, then took his hand back. "You think we are the bad guys," she said, as though using a foreign phrase. "But that's only because the GECOs got to you first. We can show you things that might change your mind."

"I don't have time," Miller said. "I have—" he glanced at his watch. "—eight hours to stop this, or it's all over, as far as I can tell."

She didn't say anything.

"Is that much of it true? Or do you want to tell me something different?"

"It is true," Mara said slowly, almost reluctantly, "that you have seven hours and fifty-eight minutes in which to act, if—" She paused on the word. "—*if* you are going to reverse the effects of the Artifact's destruction."

"And your people, the Bodhis—they don't want those effects reversed?" he asked.

"That is correct."

"Why not, for God's sake?" he asked, genuinely puzzled.

She looked away. "I don't—I can't really tell you. And it is rather complicated, as well."

"But the GECOs want it reversed."

"Yes."

Miller shook his head. "This is something I haven't been able to understand from the beginning. Why would anyone want things to stay like this? Totally fragmented, everything ripped to shreds and poured out across all time and space like it had been run through a blender.

Wouldn't a normal, rational person want that stopped, Mara? Shouldn't a human being do everything in her power to make things *real* again?"

"Perhaps . . . 'real' is not as absolute an idea as you would like to believe."

"That's very nice," he said, almost snarling at her. "And sometime we should sit down together and figure out how many angels can dance on the head of a pin. But right now I need some answers, or I'm going to take my ball and go home."

She shook her head. "I've already said too much," she told him. "There is so much at stake—I don't dare say anything else."

"Then what am I supposed to do with you?" Miller demanded.

"Take me home," she said. "I'll get you to our Sanctuary. They can decide there how much to tell you. And then—" She took a deep, ragged breath and looked him in the eyes. "—then you must decide what you will do," she said quietly.

"That's not good enough," Miller replied, and his voice grated even on his own ears. She looked surprised, and he felt a small flush of triumph. *I'm supposed to accept gratefully*, he thought. *Well, the hell with that.*

"I need to know what I'm walking into," he said. "Because what I know about you Bodhis is not exactly reassuring."

"That's because you heard it from a GECO," Mara said with some heat.

"All right," Miller said. "Here's your chance to set the record straight." He stood up—a little wobbly, but he would make it all right. He moved to the controls and put the little sub in hovercraft mode, heading for the San

Francisco Bay. He checked the speed, did some rough figuring in his head. "We have about four and a half hours," he said. "Talk."

"I don't—" she began, looked over at John Grove and shook her head. "I'm afraid—"

"You get used to fear," Miller told her. "Trust me."

She looked down at her hands and finally nodded. "All right," she said.

She spoke quite simply at first, her voice staying relatively neutral, as if to assure Miller that what she was telling him was the real, objective truth.

Four thousand years into the future, from Miller's perspective, the world had settled into two completely separate cultures; effectively speaking, two different races. The Bodhis lived in harmony with Nature. They had no cities; just clusters where a small or large group might live for a while. Together they would ask Nature to "cooperate" in forming shelter from Megacrystal. Food and water followed in a natural, organic way; Miller didn't quite get it, but the details were not important right now. He let her continue to explain that the Bodhis worked to clean and maintain Nature and to live with it in harmony with its wishes. They nurtured, protected, and preserved.

The GECOs, on the other hand, were no longer even truly human.

Miller cleared his throat at this statement. But Mara met his eye and nodded. "It is true, Miller. This is not an exaggerated emotional statement. They truly are no longer human. They *boast* of it. But what they have done to themselves—" She shuddered.

"What?" he asked.

"In your time you have some limited genetic engineering, don't you?"

"We have it," Miller said. "We don't really use it."

"The GECOs use it," she said with a small, unpleasant laugh. "Oh, yes, they use it. GECO is an acronym, you know. It stands for Genetically Engineered Computer Operators. And they have coldly, deliberately, used their advanced techniques to turn themselves into something they think of as beyond human."

When the environment began to rot and fester to the point that the planet was becoming uninhabitable, some technical genius had stood the whole problem on its head by announcing a new solution: Looking at the dilemma backward, it made much more sense to adapt humans to the environment, instead of trying to force the nearly dead environment to adapt back to human standards.

This they had done. A huge section of the population, filled with the self-hatred that had been nurtured through the last miserable decades of cooperative planeticide, had agreed to attempt the experiment. They went underground, and within two generations emerged as a new race. They had changed the way they looked—better, they claimed. They had altered their body chemistry to thrive on pollution.

But those remaining aboveground were fully committed to an ecological solution. They had spent the time restoring their planet. And when the GECOs came up from underground looking for air loaded with lead, carbon monoxide, and polymers, they found clean, rich, *pure* air instead.

"And that's why you're at war," Miller said.

Mara blinked. "Did he say that? That we're at *war*? What an . . . *interesting* perspective." She smiled and shook her head. "There are no wars in my time, Miller.

We do not agree—we don't even interact with them. But war—what an odd idea.

"No, the GECOs live underground and we live above. Their bodies need the controlled foul air they generate below. We could never survive down there."

"Cook said it was war," Miller insisted. "A thousand-year war."

"War against the Earth, perhaps," she said. "War against the atmosphere, war against all plant and animal life. Genocide, animal extinction, water pollution, ozone depletion. These are their victims, and their enemy is life itself."

"And you, on the other hand, are fighting for the sanctity of all living things, and returning humanity to the Garden of Eden?"

"Ah, Miller, sarcasm is easy when you have no conviction," she said. "We have worked to turn the world back into what it was meant to be. Restored a balance of life. Water cleaned, air pure. Brought species back from extinction. Achieved for ourselves a nonintrusive lifestyle. We had *succeeded*. Attained the balance we had struggled to reach for so long. And then, the bad things began to happen. Whole ecosystems destroyed. Entire tiers of species wiped out again.

"And so we knew the GECOs were traveling."

"I thought you said they couldn't breathe your air," Miller objected.

She shook her head impatiently. "They can't. Did you think the thing you keep calling 'Cook' had physically traveled from the future?"

"They travel by possession?" Miller said. "By taking over a person already at the spot where they want to go?"

"Yes," she said with venom, "they are horrible."

"But don't you people do the same thing?" Miller asked her.

She bit her lip. "There is a very great difference, but it is difficult to explain. It is— We create a positive spiritual nexus and allow an interchange to grow organically. The GECOs do it with neural stimulants, computers and machinery. It's ... *invasive*. It's like rape."

"But you still take possession of someone else, don't you?"

"Oh, no. That would be unthinkable for us. We don't—the whole idea of possession, even on the material level of ownership—it's so, so—" She shuddered. "No, Miller. What we do is very different. We join the spirit. A Bodhi will not, *can* not, make a host do anything he or she would not normally want to do. Never. The GECOs—they overpower, brutalize, take complete control. It's evil."

"But the result is the same, isn't it?"

She cocked her head at him and for a moment allowed a very small smile to play across her face. "Aren't you the one who told me that the motive was as important as the result?"

"You're avoiding the real question," he said, annoyed at the smile—more so because it almost worked, almost made him soften toward her.

She looked down, contrite. "I suppose I am, Tony," she said softly, and Miller realized with a small thrill that he tried hard to suppress, *That's the first time she's used my first name.*

Mara looked up at him again and took his hand. "But you have to know how much this means—not just to me, or just to the Bodhis. To everyone, for all time. Past, present, and future. This may be the most important decision any individual has ever made, Tony. Please—can't you see what's at stake here?"

"I can," he replied, "and I don't like it."

"Captain," John Grove called from the control panel. "Land ho."

Miller looked hard at Mara; she looked back with a soft, pleading expression. He shook his head, exasperated, and went forward to stand beside John Grove.

Grove was right; the California coast was in sight ahead. Miller could see the tall headlands of San Francisco Bay. They were here—and one way or another, he had to decide, soon.

"Home," breathed Mara, coming up beside him to look. "I thought I'd never see it again."

"Really?" Miller asked. "Why not?"

"The chance of your success was rated very low, Tony. That meant I probably wouldn't survive, either."

"But you went anyway, knowing you were probably going to die?"

She nodded. "I told you it was important. I meant that. It's the most important thing in the world. In a way, it *is* the world. I would die willingly to achieve our goals. But it is truly your decision, and I will not try to persuade you. What will you do, Tony?"

Miller looked out the window at the approaching coastline. "I don't know," he said.

28

CHAPTER

The Bodhi headquarters—*Sanctuary*, it was called—sat on a high cliff overlooking the Pacific Ocean. Seals barked and played on the rocks below, and hundreds of birds, butterflies, and small animals chirped, hummed, and chittered in the tree-lined meadow around Sanctuary.

Miller thought the air was the best he had ever breathed, and he'd never seen so many animals and insects in one place before. They were not bothersome; they appeared almost to be from some Disney movie, the way they frolicked and sang without trouble, without bothering each other or the humans moving among them.

They saw a few people as they walked through the ankle-high grass, and Miller assumed they were all Bodhis. But they wore no uniform style of clothing. In fact, some wore no clothing at all, and John Grove looked quickly away, blushing furiously.

Other people they passed wore sarongs, or bikinis, or a garment that looked a lot like a leotard. Some wore what were obviously period costumes, ranging from a man in pumpkin hose and a slashed jersey to the young boy playing tag with him, who wore something that seemed to have evolved from the suits worn by Osiris's guards. A group wearing kilts walked in from the other side of the meadow as Mara led them up a path toward Sanctuary itself.

Miller had been expecting something striking for the Bodhi's central headquarters; perhaps a building with a lot of clean white pillars in front, or great marble facades that gleamed with artificial purity. Sanctuary itself was far beyond what he could possibly have imagined.

As they came up the last hill and around a stand of redwood trees, Miller was face-to-face with something unlike any building he had seen or heard of before.

It was a large crystalline structure that was without definite shape, and yet, somehow, it was symmetrical, pleasing to the eye—much the way a large tree or mountain range might be. The sun hit the thousands of facets of the gigantic structure and shattered into all the blinding colors in the universe, making Sanctuary almost impossible to look at directly.

Miller stopped and simply stared. "Great God Almighty," he said. John Grove actually wobbled as he looked up to see the enormous sprawling building, gasping out a salty oath and pulling hard at his beard with one gnarled hand.

Mara stood and watched them react to Sanctuary with a small, proud smile. After a moment she stepped to Miller and took him by the arm. "Come," she said, and led them up the path to the entrance.

"Sanctuary is what you might think of as an organic building," she said as they approached, "but it's more than that. It's actually the realized psychic agreement between the specific biosphere of this location and a group of our, ah—not leaders in the sense that you would use the word, but that's more or less the idea."

"What is it made of?" Miller asked.

"Megacrystal," she said. "It's a silicate of materials from the site. We brought nothing in from outside. That would be Invasive."

"Miss, excuse me," John Grove said. He'd stopped in his tracks and planted his feet wide, as if standing on the deck of a ship that was pitching in great swells.

"Yes, John Grove," Mara said pleasantly.

He cleared his throat and blushed. "I am an ignorant man, I know," he said. "Even by the standards of my, uh . . . my time." He looked uncomfortable, as he had when they tried to explain to him the concept of travel through time. "I mean no disrespect, miss. But I'll do nothing ungodly, nor have ought to do with any work of the Devil. Ahem. Excuse me, miss. I don't mean to say that— That is, I'm no holy Joe, but—" John Grove stumbled over his words and came clattering to a halt, blushing furiously and knotting his huge hands. "This place, if it be not Paradise, then, ah—ah—" He stammered for a moment, and then clamped his jaw shut. Miller could see the knotted muscles of his face and neck stand out.

Mara smiled and took his hand. "John Grove," she said. "I give you my word of honor that nothing in this place is ungodly, nor will I or any of the people here knowingly submit you to anything to which you might object. That is our most sacred belief, and we will not violate it. Do you believe me?"

At the touch of her hand, Grove had grown even redder. He now looked as if a blood vessel would have to burst, but he nodded. "Yes, miss. I believe you. Thank you, miss."

Mara squeezed his hand, then dropped it and led them both into Sanctuary.

There was no receiving area, no waiting room; there were no secretaries, nor offices, bulletin boards, coffee machines, copiers, computers, storerooms—nothing one might expect from a so-called headquarters. Instead, they walked in the entrance and into a large, airy, lofty room that was open to the breeze and the light.

Four people were waiting to meet them. It was impossible to tell their age. Two were male, two were female. They were dressed in plain, off-white jumpsuits, although one of the men also displayed a plain but elegant gold bracelet.

"Mara," one of the women said with obvious delight. She stepped forward, and so did Mara; the two embraced. Then the woman looked up to Miller and John Grove. "Welcome to Sanctuary. I am Yeshiva. This is Arno, Frank, and Isolte."

Miller gave them a stiff half bow, and John Grove followed his lead, and knuckled his forehead, as well. "Are you the Bodhi leaders?" Miller asked.

Arno, the man with the bracelet, gave a silvery laugh. "We don't have leaders," he said. "That would be Invasive. We are the Partners in Concern for this matter, if that answers your question."

"It doesn't," Miller said. "I have—" He glanced at his watch. "— two and a half hours to make a decision. That's not enough time for semantic niceties. Are you four able to make decisions for your people?"

"In this matter, yes," Yeshiva said. "We five can do so," she said with a slight nod toward Mara. "Would you come with us to a place where we can speak?"

Miller looked at Mara. "So you're not merely a foot soldier in this, is that it?" He couldn't quite say why that made him angrier, but it did. It somehow made Mara seem even more manipulative. "You're not just a flunky doing a job, you're one of the—what do you call it? Noninvasive shareholders of ubiquity?"

Mara looked hurt. "Tony—I understand your anger. But I regret it, too. Please believe me—it was necessary that you did not know, that you made your decisions on your own."

"I haven't been on my own since the tsunami wiped out my research," Miller said.

Arno smiled. Yeshiva stepped in front of him and placed a hand on Miller's arm. "We have an area prepared to talk about this matter," she said. "We find that it helps us focus if we share our thoughts and concerns in areas like this."

"A conference room?" Miller said.

Isolte spoke up. "We call it an Area of Concern. Serious matters are better discussed there. It's designed to remove the tension from your thoughts."

"Then for God's sake, let's hurry," Miller said.

The Area of Concern was in what seemed to be the center of Sanctuary. Isolte led them along a rambling corridor that didn't move in a straight line for longer than six feet at a stretch until it gradually opened up into a pyramid-shaped chamber. There were no doors or walls, but even though there was no outside view, Miller could somehow still feel the tang of the fresh breeze.

Several amorphous blobs were scattered in the center

of the area; Yeshiva waved at them. "Would you like to sit down?" she asked him. "It will help you focus."

"Bean bags?" Miller blurted. "You want me to sit in a bean bag?"

Frank walked to one of the blobs and pointed. "These are ergonomic support chairs. They are sensitive to your feelings and will adjust to what you need. They anticipate your comfort without forcing it on you."

Miller moved to sit in one of the things. "They still look like bean bags," he grumbled. But when he sank into one, he was amazed at how much solid and comfortable support they gave him. And as he leaned back experimentally, he felt small fingers kneading gently at his back and neck.

"Isn't that better?" Yeshiva asked him.

John Grove stood beside his chair, staring at it dubiously. Finally, when everyone else was seated, he eased gingerly into it. The look on his face as he leaned back was so shocked and then pleased that Miller had to laugh.

"There, you see?" Arno said with a wave of his bracelet. "We're already loosening up a bit."

Miller had to admit that it was true. Whether it was the gentle massage provided by the chair, or there actually was something about the room—that is, the *area*—that was affective, he was relaxed, alert, ready to reason his way through the problem. He felt as if he'd just about finished the first cup of coffee for the day; he was ready to go without being jittery yet.

"All right," he began. "Mara said you can tell me why I should allow the universe to end."

Yeshiva smiled. "That may be overstating things just a little, Dr. Miller. We would simply like you to consider our viewpoint, as well as the GECOs', which you have already heard."

"Which you share," Isolte said with some heat.

"Isolte," Mara said warningly, and Isolte settled back into her chair, looking grumpy.

"You want to influence me to decide your way," Miller said. "That may be the only part of your plot I can understand."

"It's not a plot," Yeshiva said. "And we will not force a decision on you."

"If I were in your position, I would," Miller replied. "Why won't you?"

"That would be Invasive," Frank said. He sounded like he was scolding a child.

"We will supply you with whatever information you feel you might need to decide," Yeshiva explained. "But we will not try to coerce you."

"Maybe not," Miller said. "But you'll manipulate the hell out of me, won't you? Like you already have."

The Partners in Concern glanced at each other. The other three finally looked down, leaving Mara and Yeshiva locked in an intense but nonhostile stare.

"I told you it was wrong," Mara said at last.

"Yes," Yeshiva replied. "You were right. But with so much at stake—"

"Wrong is wrong," Frank said.

"Oh, please," Arno muttered.

"Wrong is wrong," Frank repeated.

"Yes, all right," Arno said. He looked at Frank and nodded, and they looked at the three women. There was a sense of agreement in the room that Miller could almost feel.

Yeshiva turned to Miller. "We are very sorry, Dr.

Miller," she said. "But this decision has fallen on you. It is the only thing the Bodhis and GECOs have agreed on in 874 years. *They* have loaded you with their ideas. We simply want equal time."

"We don't have equal time," Miller said. "We have about an hour and three-quarters. And I still don't know how I'm supposed to stop the change from becoming permanent." He saw the dismay on their faces and reluctantly added, "If that's what I decide to do."

"You can decide whatever you will," Mara said gently, for a moment sounding again like the Druid healer from what seemed so long ago. "We will help you, as we said."

"And if you decide for the GECOs," Frank said, "we will show you what to do."

The other Partners nodded reluctantly, and Arno added, "You have to be so *stubborn*."

"Very well, then," Yeshiva said. She stood up.

"I'll come, too," Mara said.

"Yes," Yeshiva agreed. The two of them stood in front of Miller.

"Come, Tony," Mara said.

"Come where?" Miller asked her.

"We're going to the Gate," Mara said. "There, you can learn all you need to know."

"And then," Yeshiva added, "you must decide."

29

CHAPTER

The Bodhis had already shown a habit of defeating Miller's expectations—the look of Sanctuary, their unwillingness to coerce him—and now they did it again. They had told him that the Gate was a window and doorway into time-space, that one could look anywhere/when and, with a little extra work, travel there. And so he'd expected something impressive. Maybe a larger area, with architecturally focused megacrystal arches and a nexus of concentrated light and . . . Well, something.

But the Gate wasn't much to look at. In fact, it was no more than another of the bean-bag-type chairs mounted on a slighty raised platform.

Mara and Yeshiva ushered him to the chair, and when Miller stood before it, he stopped and looked around. "This is it?" he asked.

"Of course," Yeshiva said very seriously.

But Mara smiled, perhaps understanding. "Nothing more is necessary, Tony," she said. "We have . . . reached an understanding with time-space here."

"Uh-huh," Miller said.

"The concepts don't translate to English very well," she admitted. "But we don't need machinery or computers to move through time-space."

"That would be Invasive," Yeshiva added. "The GECO way."

"The GECOs burn tremendous amounts of energy," Mara said, "with a great deal of poisonous by-product and waste, to essentially force open an unwilling time-space and shove something into it. Our way does not violate anything, and actually creates a small energy surplus."

"It sounds too good to be true," Miller said. "What are the drawbacks?"

"From the GECO point of view, those *are* drawbacks," Mara said. "Sit down, Tony."

Miller sat. He looked back up at Mara with raised eyebrows.

"It's all done mentally," Mara said. "You form a picture in your mind and concentrate lightly. The focused energy in this area amplifies the thought and moves through time-space to the appropriate point. You will observe whatever you think about."

And while he was still thinking about that, Mara leaned forward and kissed him on the cheek.

"Mara!" Yeshiva said, and Mara blushed.

"I'm sorry," she said. "Just— Good luck, Tony. Please, do what you know is right. Wherever it takes you."

Mara stepped off the platform and she and Yeshiva walked away. Miller watched them go, looking for Mara to turn around to meet his eyes one last time. But she didn't. *Of course not,* he thought. *That would be Invasive.* In half a minute they were gone.

He was alone.

Except, of course, for the entire human race, past, present, and future, looking over his shoulder.

He took a ragged breath, still uncertain what he was supposed to do. How did you concentrate lightly, anyhow? And what should he look at—or what-when?

He could review his life, try to figure out where to go from there. But was that the best way to . . .

To *what*? Nobody had instructed him, nobody was going to make him look at or do anything. Why not take a quick glimpse at Berkeley while he figured out what else to do?

As he thought it, the air in front of him bubbled slightly, as though a thick syrup were boiling over a low heat. And then he saw himself standing before a large lecture class—the students' faces, he had never before noticed how *young* they were. And then he was nursing a cup of coffee in his seminar as one of his favorite grad students presented her research. She was so bright, worked so hard.

And there was the kid he'd had to fail last semester. It tore a piece out of Miller, but he had no choice.

Campus life, the stacks in the library, all filled with so many energetic kids.

Miller sensed the pattern—was it something he was unconsciously doing?—as the images continued to move. It all focused on the kids.

And he realized that it was showing him a hole in his life. He loved to teach, loved seeing a face light up when he finally hit a point that resonated with one of them. And that was because he loved kids.

Miller realized he didn't miss his life at Berkeley. He missed the kids. Missed what his life might have been if he'd only had his own family. It could have been so perfect, coming home to a house that didn't echo with emptiness.

Was that dream gone forever, things being what they were? If he stopped the destruction of the Artifact, could he go back to an improved version of his former life—a version with a wife, children?

God, why hadn't he thought about all this when he could have done something about it? Why hadn't he realized how important a family was? A dull ache welled up inside him. It was too late. He'd put it off—to finish his schooling, his thesis, to secure tenure; always some excuse. And now it was too late.

Unhappy, and irritated with himself for being so, Miller pushed the thoughts away. *So what?* he thought. *Look at all I've done that I couldn't have done with a family.*

And he made images of himself appear in the Gate; flying across a gorgeous sunset; traveling with Professor Meyer to study the last of the Bedouin culture; and of course, the trip with Cook to Runa Puake.

Cook; Jesus. Dead on Artifact Island. Yuki's island. The thought of Yuki made her image appear, and more regrets. Such a short time with her, barely enough to get to know her. Yet they'd shared so much, and she was—

—was growing bigger in the images he watched. He flipped ahead, and there was no doubt. Yuki was pregnant. With his child?

His child?

It had to be. He moved forward through time and she gave birth to a daughter, a beautiful child, like her mother. And as he watched the child grow . . . Was it possible? Was he reading into it, or did the girl look like *him*, too? Like her *father* . . .

It was true. She had Yuki's beauty, but something about her definitely looked like him. She was his daughter, his child. He was a father after all. *Oh, my God*, Miller thought with a melting sense of sweetness and weight at the same time. *Oh, my God . . .*

"It is time, Tony," Mara's said in his ear, softly but insistently. He looked up. "Time to decide." She searched his face, her eyes moving over his features as if they might reflect some road map of his intentions. "Choose now," she said, and dropped a hand lightly onto his shoulder.

Miller looked back at the Gate. Already the images were fading from Mara's interruption. He saw one last glimpse, the face of his daughter as she danced around her mother, excited about something she'd seen—or was she? Was she excited—or was it terror, fear of something he couldn't see?

The image was gone, and Miller couldn't bring it back, not with Mara's hand on his shoulder and her presence gently insisting that he choose.

"I need more time," he said.

Mara hesitated. "Quickly, then," she replied, and stepped behind him.

Miller tried to clear his mind, tried to get back to the image of his daughter and Yuki. Had she been afraid? Of what? What turmoil could reach them there on the island that—

The images swirled. Roman chariots charged. Chinese rockets flashed across a sienna sky. Hunters shot seals, whooping with red glee. Jews died in Nazi showers. Black smoke billowed from endless rows of stacks. Mustard gas floated over a panoramic battlefield of choking, gasping men. Refugees gunned down. Rain forests burning. Animals, children, old people, slaughtered, falling like leaves, endlessly, over and over, through all time and all the world . . .

Miller took a deep breath. *Let the breath find the center . . . Let the worry drop away.*

He felt the clarity return and tried again.

The images changed to current time; Cook leaning over his desk asking him to go on the trip to Runa Puake. His first response was to refuse, but then with a little more discussion, he agreed. The image flashed ahead.

He saw Yuki holding his daughter. If he stepped through now, he could be with them forever. He was filled with desire to move, but stopped himself. And before he could change his mind, the image flashed again.

He saw the Artifact teetering in his seaplane. Could he stop it if he stepped into this moment? Probably not. He watched the Artifact fall. It hit the ground, the first lightning struck it. *Flash!* The image shifted again.

He saw thousands of small humans with large heads and huge, pale eyes. They lived in a vast underground chamber filled with poisonous yellow air. The GECOs—should he travel to them? But the images were changing faster now.

Flash: satellites orbiting the earth. Then missiles launched by sub, jet, silo. Countless nuclear explosions, a fallen Statue of Liberty covered in a snowdrift. The ruins of New York City peeking out of a new ice age, the result of a nuclear winter.

Flash: people entering caves. Doctors performing strange surgeries, producing a new human race, part bio-computer, part human.

Why am I seeing this? Where is my daughter?

And then he saw her—at the same age as before, dancing around her mother, her face alive with emotion. But still he could not tell—was it fear, or excitement?

Flash. The picture was gone again, and Miller couldn't focus enough to get it back.

Why can't I see her any older? he thought.

The Gate showed him another chaotic soup of images: destruction, death, filth spewing into air and water—

Why can't I see my daughter with me?

But he knew. Without seeing it, he was sure.

Something happened to her.

Something related to the chaos of a GECO victory. That's why the Gate was showing him these things.

And that's why the Bodhis were certain of his decision. They knew. They didn't *need* to coerce him.

But were the Bodhis influencing what he saw, in spite of their claims that they were totally noninvasive? Or was he just seeing what was/would be if he failed to act correctly?

And what *was* correctly, damn it? If it was Invasive to tell him what to do, couldn't they at least give him a hint?

But he knew he had his hint. His daughter. He had to stop this from happening. He had to see his child grow up and meet her father, had to see the wonder in her face as he showed her the world—a world that made sense again, a world where neither GECO nor Bodhi could twist time-space into a vicious playground.

He had to stop it all before it even began to happen.

But how?

The Gate flashed: A space probe hovered over an

asteroid. The surface of the asteroid rippled with color, sound, light, pools of time and gravity moving out in waves from a strange object about twice the size of a basketball. It looked like a giant ball bearing, as if it had been machined. Its color was shifty, uncertain, but nearly always dull and pulsing with a strange light . . .

The Artifact.

He was watching the discovery of the Artifact.

"That's it," he said, glancing at Mara. "I'll stop it here." He watched her for any sign of emotion, negative or positive, but she showed nothing. Was this the right choice? Was it what they wanted him to do, or, as he hoped, something unexpected?

"If that is your choice," she said.

"Yes," he told her. "I can make it never happen. Avoid the whole thing. I'll stop it here."

"Step through," she said, holding out a hand to help him up from the seat. "You'll feel a few moments of disorientation, a slight discomfort, perhaps. You won't know where you are at first, nor why. But that will pass."

Miller stood in front of the image of the asteroid and looked at it long and hard. He became aware that he was still holding Mara's hand, and he looked at her.

She gave his hand a squeeze. "I wish you well, Tony Miller," she said. "Truly."

Still there was no clue in her face. Miller nodded and turned away from her, back to the Gate.

Back to the asteroid, and time-space and the Artifact and . . .

And what?

There was no way to know, not from here.

Only from inside the moment. Through the gate.

Miller breathed, a deep centering breath again, and took a moment to feel its calmness move through him.

He looked back at Mara one last time.

"Preserve," she said. But it was not her voice. "Defend," she added. It was The Voice—the Voice that had come at him three times before, with the bangers in Osiris's world, and out of the radio on his way to Tahiti. And now, it was coming out of Mara.

What did it mean? What was the Voice telling him? Where was it coming from, and why?

But before he could think of any more than the questions, the Gate whirled in front of him and a slow but powerful vortex pulled him in.

"Go now," It said.

And then, he was falling through the Gate.

Here ends Book One of TIME BLENDER